Praise for Melinda Viergever Inman and *Fallen*

"After reading *Refuge* last year I was anxiously awaiting Melinda's next fiction release. *Fallen* did not disappoint. Melinda has a fabulous ability to take you "on location" with her writing, even with this story that most know well. Clearly she spends time researching and studying before just tossing words on paper. *Fallen* became reality. The epiphanies, the struggle, the communication trials between the characters were perfectly on point. *Fallen* is not another 'old story' retold, it's a new way of viewing details we now pass over in haste."

—KARINA HERRING

"*Fallen* is a poignant love story of the first two humans, woven alongside the glorious story of love and hope that is offered to all humans by their Creator. The perfection of creation in the Garden of Eden is starkly contrasted with the world outside the Garden after the fall. The author took a story that was very familiar to me, and added new depth and meaning, allowing me to understand my own fallen and sinful nature more clearly. Also highlighted is the immense love God has for us, and the lengths to which He is ⸏⸏⸏⸏⸏⸏⸏⸏⸏⸏⸏⸏⸏⸏⸏⸏⸏⸏⸏ His love."

—LIZ MULLER

D0875107

"After reading Melinda Inn⸏ ⸏⸏⸏⸏⸏⸏ ⸏ously awaited the release of *Fallen*. I was anxious as ⸏⸏ ⸏⸏⸏⸏⸏⸏, ⸏ and anxious as in fearful. I'd enjoyed *Refuge* so much I was afraid I'd be disappointed with *Fallen*. I need not have worried. Though a 'prequel' of sorts, *Fallen* continues what *Refuge* began—encouraging readers in their relationship with God by displaying historical characters in their personal cycle of sin, repentance and reconciliation with their faithful and loving God. I approach speculative Christian fiction with caution; concerned readers might mix fact and fiction, leading them on an unbiblical tangent. Inman's plot carefully navigates this. She keeps her storyline close to the biblical account, generally limiting speculation to characters' thoughts and feelings about events rather than adding, subtracting or embellishing biblical history. At times I found the dialogue stilted and overly formal. However, considering the characters are the first to ever engage in conversation, the newness of speaking would be awkward. I don't know if this was deliberate on the author's part or if it is a weakness in her writing, but it did not affect my enjoyment of her work. Her descriptions of Eden are lush and sensual, deftly capturing the newness and wonder of experiencing all of creation through the eyes of the first human beings. And from personal experience, I can attest Inman accurately describes the dark, raw emptiness of separation from our Creator. As was the case with *Fallen*, *Refuge* is more than entertainment; this novel will stimulate readers spiritually, giving them insight in to the character of God, His justice and love for His people."

—BARB BEST

"Captivating! *Fallen* is the epic and tragic tale of two young lovers who literally have everything they could ever want or imagine but yearn for more and lose it all. Melinda's masterful story-telling weaves a fluid narrative of the first man and woman that provides creative insight about what it means to be broken and brought back to peace with themselves, one another and God. The characters are portrayed with vivid detail striking at the core of who we are as human beings and the image bearers of God. It's a powerful and heart-warming glimpse of two individuals who enjoy intimacy with the Creator, yet must confront the driving force behind their struggles to overcome anger, pride and hard-hearted selfishness. And the battle still rages!

"*Fallen* compels the reader to explore the creativity of God and the wonderful depths of His love and compassion. Thought-provoking discussion questions at the back of the book provide inspiration for group interaction. *Fallen* offers a fascinating peak at the corruption in the Garden. Familiar characters are crafted from a fresh and insightful perspective. Page by page, the portrayal invites you in - with incredible spiritual impact."

—DIANE PRIEUR, WRITER

"*Fallen* is a stunning depiction of the enduring story of Earth's first inhabitants. Powerfully evocative, it stirs the emotions and captivates the mind while filling in the details of what Adam and Eve may have experienced from Creation through the Fall and beyond. Fact and carefully woven fiction intermingle in this story of God's redemptive plan for mankind that has been at work since the beginning."

—ELLEN EVANS

What in the world is wrong with people? Why do we act the way we do? *Fallen* is an unusual book because it answers so many questions about human behavior. Melinda Inman's book is a beautiful story based upon the Bible, the most authenticated book in existence. It brings to life and fleshes out those few verses in Genesis and gives us such an amazing glimpse of Eden that we long for the New Heaven and the New Earth when God restores what was lost. What an enjoyable read about those two people who are the ancestors of everyone on the face of the earth!"

—ELAINE VIERGEVER

"*Fallen* is a well-researched fictional account based on the scriptures, and it includes an in-depth Bible study. Just like its sequel, *Refuge*, this novel presents many foundational truths regarding salvation and redemption. It contains descriptive storytelling, with great character development. *Fallen*, just like *Refuge*, will challenge the reader to think authentically about their faith."

—STACEY THUREEN, PUBLISHED WRITER AND SPEAKER

"I love the author's fresh perspective on humanity's first family and how she kept weaving in the truth of God's unconditional love for all of us, even in our fallen state. Her sparkling description gives us insight into the beauty of our unsullied world at the dawn of Creation.

"In the Garden of Eden, Adam and Eve destroyed their perfect harmony with God when they believed the lie that God's goodness couldn't possibly be true. We still believe the same lie today and quickly discard, or at the very least, don't pursue God's unconditional love for us.

"The author showed that God's love is a force that is larger than we could ever understand, and she drives home the point that God's 'love would cover the mistakes they (Adam and Eve and all mankind) would make in the future as well.'"

—KIM FISCH, WRITER

"Many of us have read or heard the story about creation told in the Bible. We know that God created Adam and Eve, that they lived in the Garden of Eden, and that they fell to Satan's temptation to go against God's command to not eat from the Tree of Knowledge of Good and Evil.

"But have you ever thought about what it would actually be like to live as Adam and Eve? What would it feel like to awaken as the first human created? To be told to be fruitful and multiply without any knowledge of how to accomplish that?

"Through story and thoughtful descriptions, Melinda V. Inman takes us into Adam's and Eve's minds, hearts, and bodies as they explore the garden, their relationship to God's creations, their relationship to each other, and even how their bodies function. With beauty and sensitivity, we experience them discovering how wonderful it is to have physical intimacy as God intended.

"We also get a glimpse of how Lucifer's (Satan's) ego could have contributed to his rebellion against God, his jealousy of the humans, and his consuming desire to take revenge by enticing man and woman to fall from God's grace.

"I love it when a book gives me new insight into stories I've heard countless times before, and *Fallen* has done just that. Melinda Inman has brought this story to life for me and made it more real than anything I've encountered before. I'm now able to look at Adam and Eve with a different perspective.

"If you enjoy reading biblical fiction, I highly recommend this book."

—DAWN KINZER, PUBLISHED AUTHOR

"I loved this book. There were so many things about it that made me go, 'Of course! That makes sense with everything being brand new,' or, 'Wow! I never thought of it like that before!' It challenged my own responses to God's care of me and to the guidelines He gives to protect me and make me more like Him. Do I run to Him alone or do I seek to solve things in my own wisdom or out of a heart of fear and distrust? It also reassured me of His perfect plan in light of my broken nature. I cannot surprise Him or screw up too much for Him to withhold His grace, mercy, and love from me. Adam and Eve looked forward in hope for the promise as I look back on God's promise kept. Your perspective will be blown, your heart will be challenged, and your hope in God's faithfulness to pursue relationship with lost sinners will grow immensely. I cannot wait to share it with friends and family!"

—KRISTIN ROBINSON, LIFE COACH

"It seemed slow until...I realized that Creation itself was one of the five main characters. In fact, Melinda Inman writes more words, collectively, about Creation than any of the other four characters: God, Lucifer, Adam and Eve. Her imaginative word-pictures illustrate God's creativity in action, as she describes what the Garden of Eden might have looked like in exquisite detail.

"Don't be confused; this is not a first-person account. The author never implies she received special knowledge from God to write this book. It's drawn from her imagination—a gift God bestows to each of us. Melinda has allowed Him to refine hers, and we are the beneficiaries.

"Neither is it a theological textbook, written as the definitive answer to questions no human can answer. It's a fictional tale that we know the ending to before we begin; yet it draws us in, anyway. The author takes us further back than time itself, to when Lucifer was a beautiful angel, and before God created this sphere called earth.

"She reveals God's passionate love for humanity (meaning you and me). His warmth wafts up from the pages. His ability to see into the future and plan ahead of time for our provision—no matter our circumstances, no matter our needs—thrills.

"She exposes Lucifer's motives for humanity. He is not a poor imitation of God; instead, he seeks to annihilate us, one by one or in a group. We must be ever watchful.

"Her interpretation of marriage between two perfect people makes me yearn for what could have been—and I have a solid, wonderful marriage. If you've never experienced healthy love, you'll gain valuable insights into what such a relationship can look like.

"You will appreciate God more, and be more cognizant of your spiritual enemy, after reading this book. It's much more than a work of fiction.

"You can't skim this one!"

— PATRICIA DURGIN, THE CHRISTIAN MESSAGE COACH

Fallen

by Melinda Viergever Inman

© Copyright 2016 Melinda Viergever Inman

ISBN 978-1-63393-189-3

Published by

ShowKnowGrow
PUBLISHING

Ypsilanti, Michigan

FALLEN

A NOVEL BY MELINDA VIERGEVER INMAN

ShowKnowGrow

PUBLISHING

DEDICATION

Dedicated to generous friends and family members who supported, encouraged, and/or donated (some anonymously) to the successful Kickstarter campaign for Fallen:
My amazing, supportive husband, Tim.
My loving and encouraging children by birth and by marriage.

Alanna Wengrow Inman

Grant Inman

Dan and Elaine Viergever

Danielle Bancroft

P.J. Pinkerton

Dottie and Roger Koeppen

Michael Conrady

Holly Spencer

Kristin Lewis Robinson

Suzanne Jones

Edina Mann

Yvonne Cummins

Stacey Thureen

Katie Andraski

Jen Sloniger

Diane Prieur

Dan McAnarney

Elizabeth Greene

CHAPTER ONE

"LET THERE BE LIGHT!"

Radiant light blazed forth, bursting from God. His incandescence blasted into the abyss, exploding from His very Person. Breathless wonder seized Lucifer. *Astonishing!*

As God's light shaft beamed forth, a solo gushed from Lucifer's angelic throat, welling up, soaring higher and higher. His notes hovered pure and clear, his crescendo filling the vault of heaven. He was made to sing.

When Lucifer was created, his first act had been a song. It had seemed the only appropriate response. He had beheld Yahweh—God the Father, God the Son, God the Holy Spirit—the Three in One. At first sight of the One God, a song of adoration had welled up within him.

"Holy! Holy! Holy!" Lucifer had intoned, serenading each, emotions overflowing.

Brilliant Creator! How Lucifer adored Him!

The Lord God had made them all—myriads of angelic beings, thousands upon thousands, each exquisitely unique. From his superior position above God's throne, Lucifer led the rejoicing of all the angels in the heavenly abode. It was marvelous! Continuously, he sang to his God.

Lucifer was the best and the brightest, designed to praise Yahweh.

Looking down upon the Son, Lucifer floated above Him. As the Son spoke, His light transformed the chaos. Order began. Arms and wings unfurled as Lucifer spread himself wide, his soaring music accompanying the Son's creative acts.

As energy emanated from the Son, music emanated from Lucifer.

Mirth at God's wonder bubbled out of him. Lucifer laughed with delight as he sang. The other angels joined now in his Creation Song. Following his lead—their minds synchronizing with his—they filled in the harmony and layered the melody. As the Son worked, He smiled up at Lucifer, enjoying his symphony of musical accompaniment.

Each time the Son spoke, miracles formed before their eyes. As God spoke it was done. Through the inherent power of His deity, He held everything together. Erecting parameters within the void, He separated light from darkness, day from night, evening from morning.

Lucifer adjusted his song accordingly.

God was making this for him—the favored one, the pinnacle of all God had made. Lucifer was above all—the highest, the most beautiful, and the wisest.

The Son now constructed an atmosphere with His words. A sky arched over dry land, separate from the water, which He gathered into seas. Lucifer detected the microscopic, supportive framework built into each.

"Seeds," God spoke, scattering them across the rich and fertile soil.

Fruit-bearing trees—verdant, vibrant with life—burst forth from the loam.

The cosmos appeared at the sound of His voice. The order of the universe was established by His words. The constitution of space spread out before them all, upheld by God's power—an incomparable genius at work. Across the void, the Son spoke the stars—a dazzling array.

Lucifer heralded each one with bright, staccato tones.

Around one star a tiny blue globe now circled. This planet was perfectly positioned for the nearby yellow star to provide light and warmth. Its beams contained a life-giving substance. Lucifer detected that the earth's elliptical path and axial rotation established time. The Son had created the planet's time-path to fulfill His intentions. *Genius!*

A moon now revolved around the gravitational pull of the earth. It would purify the waters and provide reflected light to the planet's dark side, illuminating the evening. The moon's size and shape were precise. It would periodically block the star from the view of any being that stood on the earth's surface, providing a window of discovery into the heavens.

Brilliant! A mathematical wonder! Lucifer thought.

This small planet intrigued Lucifer. Beings upon its surface could learn of God from this platform He had erected for them in the heavens. His artistic evidence was everywhere. By studying His work, they could come to know God's person and character.

All was configured in love. It was all good!

God the Son had spoken all into existence according to the Father's purpose. The Son was the architect. He had created the blueprint—the Godhead's unified plan. *A miracle!*

In perfect unity the One God rejoiced in the glorious creation. Their laughter pealed and reverberated across the heavens.

"What will He do next?" Lucifer thought his question toward Michael, who hovered nearby with beaming countenance.

Shaking his head in wonderment, Michael shot back his thought, *The Lord God has prepared a habitat.*

"Yes, a living microcosm of the whole. But why? For whom?"

"He readies His world for *someone*. It's intriguing. He does all things well."

"He's creating this for me," Lucifer said. "I will reign over it."

With solemn face, Michael turned toward him. "Why would you assume that?"

"Because, it's obvious."

Lucifer skewered Michael with a hard stare then turned away. Fastening his eyes upon God's work, his oratorio soared. Self-assured, he sang the story of creation, basking in the fact that God formed this all for him. He would rule over earth, God's creation.

The Son now spoke living creatures, male and female, into His world. Exotic creatures of the sea swam into existence;

winged creatures took flight as He created them from the dust. Simultaneously, they all burst into life and sprang into action.

To these, God spoke a command: "Be fruitful; increase in number; fill the water and the earth." Immediately, these new life forms carried out His instructions.

Lucifer loved what the Son created. He appreciated God's craftsmanship. *God made it for me! Over all of these creatures and all of this creation, I will rule.*

Passion now rushed forth from the Son. Some mysterious purpose propelled His actions, but none knew the mind of God—not even Lucifer. The Godhead counseled only with One another, always One, always in unity.

All along, the Son had been building toward a finale. Lucifer felt its climax coming in God's tempo and adjusted the melody, his singing ever more triumphant. All the angels sang with gusto, their volume soaring. The Lord God reached the pinnacle, the culmination.

This would be the point of Lucifer's gifting. God would give this all to him.

Swelling with importance, Lucifer cut off the symphonic melody of the others with a flourish, leaving his own high and sustained note the only sound in the heavens. The moment had arrived! He prepared himself to be honored. All the others would see him.

Yahweh spoke. "Let us create human beings in our own image. Let them rule and have dominion over all the living creatures we have made, and over all the earth."

What! Abruptly, Lucifer fell silent. *Am I not made in God's image? Am I not to rule?*

Shaken, he watched as God the Son compressed Himself into angelic form, the Father and the Spirit entwined with Him. Then the infinite God rocketed toward the earth. Glowing fervor radiated from Him. Lucifer didn't understand! What was God doing?

Breathless now, all the angelic hosts beheld God, all of them bewildered.

The Son squatted down, raking His fingers through the brown earth to scrape a mound of dirt. With His own hands, He pressed the clumping mass together. Unheard by the angels, the Godhead communicated. Smiling, the Son nodded. With dirt-covered hands, He designed their intentions. A shape took form. It was similar to some of the angelic host, but it was small.

Inwardly intricate. Smooth and beautiful of form. Male.

The pure joy of the One God as He created this creature staggered Lucifer. A cold, hard knot grew and twisted within him. *God prefers this pathetic being of dirt. This thing!*

The being seemed complete, yet it lay there lifeless upon the dust. Sickened to the core, Lucifer seethed. *How can God do this to me? To me, the most glorious one He made!*

How could He prefer this drab creature?

Embittered and envious, Lucifer glared down at its form.

Gently, the Son cupped the face of the being, cradling it. God gazed upon the dirt-made form, scrutinizing every detail. A tender pause, a bittersweet expression flitted across the Son's face, a flicker of pain. The Spirit and the Father embraced Him, all Three entwined in fierce and vehement affection.

Why? Why this tenderness? Why this hint of pain? Lucifer needed to know!

The passion of Father, Son, and Spirit swirled like tributaries into one life-giving torrent, all of God's power funneled into a thin stream of flowing life. God now took action.

He breathed.

CHAPTER TWO

PERCEPTION. SWEET BREATH blew softly. Gasping for the life-giving air, he sucked it in. Self-awareness. A warm and vibrant aroma tickled the arch of his palate and swirled down his throat. His chest rose and expanded.

Light. Bleary void above. Soft dampness beneath. Moisture clouded his vision. A sob bubbled up. Love overwhelmed him, invigorating, bestowing life and strength.

Joy overflowed. *Euphoria!*

Enfolded in his Creator's embrace, he drew in God's warm breath. Vitality pervaded him. An ardent affection overpowered him—his chest felt expansive, his senses and awareness heightened. He was alive! A fervent attachment swelled within.

A cognizant thought. *I love my Creator!*

As the holy breath left him, his chest fell.

Satisfaction in his Creator's presence filled him. His vision cleared, and he beheld the Beloved Face leaning near, beaming at him with radiant brilliance. His next breath came of its own accord as the Creator gazed at him with passionate eyes. He inhaled the fragrance of God and of something dark and moist.

"You are mine," the Creator said. "I made you in my own image."

Staring into God's eyes, his mind surged into action.

The Creator smiled.

His thoughts ordered themselves. Reflexively, he categorized and labeled himself, his body, and his surroundings. Intently aware, he had classified everything from his first moments. Clearly pleased with him, God observed his mental designations. With warm and affectionate eyes, the Creator's joy and pleasure shone upon him.

A grainy, damp substance cooled his palm. Curiosity. Turning to look, his cheek sank into the softness. He reclined on a dark and vibrant reddish-brown surface.

Scattered across this brown expanse, tall structures with full green tops towered over him. These emitted a subtle, inviting radiance. Glimpses of small globes of glowing color peeked from within the green. Everything pulsated with sharp vitality.

Pleased, he looked into God's eyes and smiled.

The Creator beamed.

Again, he turned his attention to the soft brown surface.

What is this?

Bits of the reddish-brown matter clung to his hand. He lifted it to his nose, inhaling and touching his tongue to it. It was richly gritty. Yes, that was the smell—dust, dirt, soil.

He sat up. With an expression of satisfaction, the Creator watched him.

Now he caught sight of the rest of his body—his own flesh—for the first time. It was glorious! Like the Creator, his skin glowed warm and reflective. Inhaling, he pressed his nose to his arm. He savored the aroma, the smell of himself. Stroking the dark hair on his body, he considered its softness and fine texture.

Separate from the dirt, the properties of his body were distinctive.

Observing his body carefully, he attached labels—names—to each part. He held out his hands to examine them, splaying his fingers then clenching them, studying how they worked. The mechanics of his body intrigued him. He experimented with each part.

Filled with joy, he laughed out loud, relishing the hearty echoing sound.

God chuckled softly, delighted with him.

Swiveling his head, he gazed about, analyzing the sensation of his head's rotation as he investigated the expanse of brown spreading in all directions. More dirt. Noticing that his chest continued to fill and empty, he breathed deeply several times, sucking in the dark moist flavor of the dirt and savoring the sweet fragrance of Him, the Creator.

Conscious of Him at every moment, he felt full of the One who had given him life, as if observed both inside and out. God encompassed him in energy and light, wrapping him in His essence. Absorbing the intense affection of the One who had made him, he spread his arms wide, exhilarated by His presence.

Radiating love, his Creator drew him near.

His chest expanded with joy. He closed his eyes, basking in God's passion.

"You are the man," the Creator whispered into his ear. "I made you from the dust. This is the earth I created for you. Cultivate it. It is yours to care for, to tend, and to guard."

Excited by the possibilities, the man opened his eyes and stared at God. Adoration welled up in him. He had work to do, responsibilities to fulfill. Not comprehending all the implications, yet excited by the challenge, the man gazed at his Maker.

"Go!" God said. "Discover the world I created for you."

Inquisitive and filled with anticipation, the man rose onto the balls of his feet, squatting over his heels. Now he could see farther over the brown earth. Excitement rushed inside him; a pounding raced within him. He had to investigate.

Rising slowly, he stood at his full height. Swaying, his arms askew, he flailed, grasping for balance. Recurring spasms in his abdomen and back tightened and relaxed. Fighting to hold his body upright, his largest toes gripped the soft earth.

The effort was worth it. Smiling broadly, he observed it all, amazed.

Vivid globe-bearing structures garlanded the hills. The brown expanse anchored the horizon, which was tinged luminous orange and rosy pink. Just above the surface, an intense brilliant ball blazed. Captivated by the display of color, the man stood motionless. Moment by moment the exquisite loveliness of the atmosphere transformed.

The enormous dazzling inferno on the horizon was the sun. Peering at it caused the man's eyes to sting—he squinted. The sun shed bright warmth on everything, radiating like the Creator. The man watched it rise. The sun grew smaller as it gradually faded to glowing yellow.

"That is the sky." God swept His arm in an arc.

Throwing back his head, the man gaped at the expanse, nearly losing his balance. Motionless, he observed the sun traveling across the sky, altering the hues with its brilliance. His eyes followed the effect of the changing light, landing on two tall green-topped structures.

These towered larger and statelier than the others. The one to his right was filled with golden globes shimmering in the sun's illumination.

"That is the Tree of Life," God said.

The man considered these trees carefully.

The two trees differed. On his left, the other tall tree radiated dark green, seeming to block the sunlight completely. Deep crimson globes appeared dotted throughout its shadowed top. Curiosity about the colored globes stirred within the man.

What are they?

Eager to find out, he aimed for the dark tree, placing one foot before the other, steadying himself with his arms—walking. This seemed to be instinctive. Keeping his balance carefully, he moved toward the tree. As it loomed nearer, his eyes widened.

"You may eat freely from any of the trees in the Garden of Eden," the Creator said, his voice soft and low. "But you must not eat from *that* tree. It is the Tree of the Knowledge of Good and Evil. When you eat from it you will surely die."

The man halted in mid-step. Studying the tree, he stood motionless. He stared back at God. The Creator's face appeared solemn. His eyes glimmered, filled with pain.

This was significant.

"Die"? What does that mean?

"Your spirit—the very essence of yourself—will no longer have union with my Spirit. And then your spirit will be separated from your body."

This mystified the man. His eyes moistened, and his chest constricted. Internal agony swelled and enlarged. How could he live and move and breathe if he had no union with the Creator? How could he exist if his own spirit no longer inhabited his body?

I must avoid this!

When the man inhaled, his next breath drew ragged and uneven. He turned back to scrutinize the dark tree. He would heed this warning.

What else had God said? Contemplating God's words, the man comprehended that he was in a garden and the colored globes could be eaten. He didn't know what *eat* meant, but he could eat freely from any of the other trees. He must avoid only the one.

Immediately, he veered away from The Forbidden Tree. Looking back over his shoulder, the man narrowed his eyes to study it. He turned away and stumbled toward a smaller tree nearby, falling against its rough, brown...*What is it?* Bark.

Hugging the tree for balance, he peered at its stem, the trunk. Above him it spread into branches, which divided repeatedly, becoming thinner and more delicate. These were covered with brilliant green leaves. The tops of the trees appeared rounded and dazzling, because of the multitude of these vibrant leaves.

The tree was alive! It pulsated with some type of living energy. *Incredible!*

The man touched his tongue to the bark; then he licked his own arm to compare the two. Hmm. This wasn't like the dirt, and it wasn't like his flesh. A tree. Mentally, he organized this information. He fingered the leaves. They felt smooth and cool, living and growing. Grasping one of the colored globes—a piece of fruit—he yanked. It rolled into his hand.

Examining its radiant hues, he brought it near his face. An aroma wafted toward the man, arousing something inside. Wetness lubricated his mouth—saliva, spittle. He touched his tongue to the moisture leaking from the fruit.

The flavor spread and filled his mind. *Desire. Hunger.* He yearned for more of this! Sucking up the liquid—juice—he sank his teeth in, taking a bite.

Closing his eyes, he chewed.

The taste flowed through his thoughts as it spread across his tongue and palate. Delicious! Instinctively, he swallowed. His stomach groaned. *Eat*, it demanded. Gladly. The man devoured the moist, delicious parts of the fruit. Juice trickled down his chin.

Thank you, my God!

Inside he discovered a brown hard piece of something that looked like the bark. Curious, he used his fingernails to attempt to pry it open.

"That is the seed," God said from nearby.

The man met God's eyes.

His Creator had instructed him to work the soil and to tend it, so he squatted down and pushed the seed into the earth, shoving more dirt over it. The action gave him pleasure.

With a sense of satisfaction, he stood, thrusting out his chest.

The Creator nodded, His eyes upon him.

The man grinned at God, who returned his wide smile.

Propelling him to seek more fruit, the man's insides lurched. Hunger!

He surveyed the Garden. *So much fruit to try*. He laughed for joy.

In his excitement to sample them, he moved rapidly, eventually running. Enjoying the sensation, he dashed off, racing and leaping across the soft brown earth on his somewhat wobbly legs. His shouts and joyful laughter echoed across the Garden.

Ha! Ha! Ha! Whooo! Hoo!

Elated, he pounded over the earth, circling through the Garden. Then, still hungry, he sought more varieties of fruit, darting from one tree to another, eating until his stomach felt full. Wiping the juice off his chin, he sank to the ground, resting against a tree.

Slightly breathless, he studied his surroundings.

Now the ominous tree stood far in the distance. Tilting his head, the man examined it carefully so he could recognize it and its forbidden fruit. He would avoid it completely, never touching any part of it. He wanted to obey his beloved Creator.

He didn't want to die. He wouldn't eat from that tree.

As he surveyed the rest of the Garden, all was quiet and peaceful. Though he couldn't see Him any longer, God's presence filled him. His God was near. The sun was warm. The man felt full of the delicious food the Creator had made. He went still inside, tranquil and calm.

In the air, he smelled and tasted the breath of his Creator.

"It is not good for the man I have made to be alone," God said. "Now I will make for him his strong helper, his perfect match."

What is that? Why do I need it?

The Creator stepped from behind a nearby tree.

"You need a warrior ally, one to fight alongside you in the battle, a counterpart. She will complement you, supplying the strength you lack as you both rule and reign. You cannot do everything I mean for you to do until you have her. You are alone. This isn't good."

The man didn't understand. What was a battle? What did he lack? Why did he need a warrior ally, whatever that was? What was wrong with sitting here with his Creator, full of fruit, enjoying this garden?

"You will see." His Creator answered his thoughts, softly chuckling.

CHAPTER THREE

HIS HUNGER SATIATED, the man lounged against the tree. *Why isn't it good to be alone?* Facing him, his Creator now sat under a neighboring tree. God's presence was enough. Every need was fulfilled. But God watched his reactions with a gentle smile.

Detecting a buzzing noise nearby, the man sought the source. Tiny creatures zipped across the sky and crawled up the tree bark. Minute flitting creatures—*insects,* he labeled them—surrounded him. Such a variety!

A clamor of noise moved nearer—calls, roars, and screeches. Heavy vibrations shook the ground. Dust rose from the earth. The man peered into the distance.

Two powerful, tawny creatures on four feet rushed toward him. These were not insects or birds! The creatures didn't stand upright as he did. Instead, they ran on what would be their feet and hands—large, padded paws. One was larger with long golden hair around its face; the other had no mane. Other than that, the two looked alike, as far as the man could tell.

They raced up and rubbed their sizeable heads against his, sliding their furry bodies along his shoulders and head, rumbling inside their chests as they flopped down into the dirt.

Laughing, he embraced them. Together they rolled in the dirt. After disentangling himself from their large sinuous bodies, he rose. They jumped up, circling him, leaning into him with each pass.

He extended his arms, and their backs slid under his outstretched palms. As they glided by, one on each side, he felt the rumbling within their barreled chests. Their hair covered their entire bodies and felt coarser than his. They had long tails that extended from their backsides.

Did he have that? Had he missed something? He twisted to peek at his buttocks. No tail. These two creatures differed from the insects. He categorized these as *lions*, big *cats*. Naming creatures engrossed the man.

Now, noisy animals crowded in from all sides—purring, growling, squawking, bleating—different sounds emitting from each pair as they stepped toward him. He had been alone before they arrived. That must be what the Creator meant. It wasn't good to be alone. The Creator had brought him helpers. Though he couldn't discern their thoughts and neither did they speak words as the Creator did, still these were part of the creation over which he was to rule.

The fastest runners arrived first. There were more cats like the lions, and again, they traveled in pairs but arrived in a variety of colors. What creativity he detected in their design. The Creator enjoyed diversity and color, equipping each one with different skills.

This was fascinating!

The man examined each type, running his hands over their backs, assigning them names, and watching each pair dash away over the brown earth. The cheetahs ran fast, and he longed to race with them.

He took a stride but nearly stepped on a small creature—a bird, oblivious to his foot poised above its diminutive body. Birds covered the ground, pecking at the flecks that lay scattered throughout the brown soil. He squatted to investigate. These were tiny seeds.

Scanning the surrounding trees, he discovered birds perched on all their branches. *What a multitude!* Songs rang out, a tumult of sound. A smile spread wide across his face. They sang in praise to the Creator. He attempted to mimic their cheery singing. Their songs, feathers, eye placement, wings, feet, and legs varied. But there were two of each kind.

Two ostriches stood as tall as he. Fine white feathers covered their long necks and powerful legs, yet black plumes clothed their torsos. Once named, they raced away with the speed of the big cats. Beautiful azure peacocks strutted by, one with astounding bejeweled feathers fanned wide as it paraded before the other.

Pairs of birds waddled on webbed feet. The coloring of the feathers differed between the two of each pair, like the peacocks. But they were clearly of like kind. Solemn birds with enormous eyes seemed to turn their heads completely around, looking behind them. The man turned his head far over his shoulder, but couldn't do that.

On long stilt legs, stately birds minced by with steps slow and deliberate. Smaller flitting birds in varieties of colors hopped around, pecking at the seeds. The bird types seemed never-ending. *So many kinds. So much variety.* When he labeled each pair, they flew or ran away, their happy calls, whistles, and trills wafting after them.

Absorbed in his task, he studied each type of bird and its unique characteristics.

The Creator supervised the arrival of animals, so he was always surrounded. Each group departed in an orderly fashion. The man spread his arms wide, laughing for joy. This was what he was made to do! Warmth filled his chest. He felt light, as if he himself might fly away!

But he noticed something that disquieted his mind.

As each animal and bird came to be examined and categorized, they all arrived in pairs, two of each kind. None came alone. Yet he hadn't discovered another of his own kind.

Is there no one else like me?

His Creator didn't answer this thought. He remained silent, His kind eyes fixed upon him, and the corners of His mouth gently curved upward.

Nudging their heads together, the animals leaned against the other of their kind, some frolicking together and rolling on the brown earth as they awaited the man's labels, some playfully nipping at each other after they received their names. They all seemed to be filled with joy and a kind of frenetic energy simply from being in the presence of the other.

When the man pondered this he felt hollow, and wasn't sure what the sensation meant. He became self-absorbed and introspective. Smiling tenderly, his Creator observed his reactions and appeared before the man. He stared into God's eyes and drew a deep breath. All was as it should be. Tranquil now, he absorbed the peace of God's presence, but still, the man didn't understand what his emotions signified.

Feeling a nudge against his shoulder, he turned to look into the large, placid eyes of a sizeable creature. Back to work. The animals surrounding the man now possessed strange feet. Squatting, he stooped for a closer look. They had hooves. Some had a similar hoof-like substance protruding from their heads. He called these *horns*.

The group held numerous animals, including small goats and sheep. The coarse, thick hair of the sheep surprised him. Squeezing it, his fingers sank in, warmed by the coarse thickness. Intuitively, he knew these animals would help him. They didn't run away as the others had. Rather, they spread out in their matched pairs, as if patiently awaiting him.

Behind them stood similar animals, but more exotic with twisted horns and multi-colored coats. Some raced up at great speed; others dashed away with startlingly quick reflexes. Two long-necked giraffes galloped away with an undulant gracefulness.

While the man named the pairs, he contemplated the creativity of God's design. *So much diversity.* He exercised his own creativity in naming them. He was made in God's image, a thinker and creator. His Creator was an artist, His work magnificent. The man was filled with wonder. He was an artist as well. *What will I create?*

But, even though all the creatures had come to him in matching pairs, he still hadn't seen any creature like himself. Was he not part of a pair? Did no one match him?

Feeling incomplete, he surveyed the Garden, scanning far into the distance.

He detected no one.

The light had changed. Shielding his eyes, he peered at the sun. It was now directly overhead, beating down upon his head and shoulders. Heat shimmered in the brilliant and glaring light. His body had become damp. Moisture—sweat, perspiration—trickled from his hair, his armpits, and his groin, beading on his skin.

He hadn't realized the sun's movement would take it across the sky's arch or cause the day to grow warm. He would observe the sun's motion more carefully. Stepping into the shade of the nearest tree to escape the glare, the man discovered coolness in the tree's shadow.

He labeled the creatures that had found respite there. With wagging tails, wolves barked and jumped on him. They panted, their tongues lolling out of their wide mouths. Slobbering on him, they licked his face. He laughed and rubbed behind their ears. Flopping down in the dirt, they bared their bellies to him, which he squatted to rub as well.

A chattering sound distracted him. He peered up into dark faces with ample mouths, barking out screeching noises as they swung from branch to branch—numerous kinds of monkeys and apes. They showed him their teeth and then pursed their lips at him. He repeated the gesture. They amused him, and he enjoyed their antics.

Enormous creatures now lumbered near. Astounded by their appearance, the man stood to face them. The earth trembled under his soles. These were the largest animals he'd seen. Their skin was different, too. Some had hard, scaly skin; some...tough, wrinkly gray skin.

Gigantic creatures towered above him, upright, treading heavily on their back legs. Gazing upward, he gaped at their massive jaws and jagged teeth. Their arms were disproportionately small compared to their bodies. These were leviathans. The earth trembled as they lumbered away. The man stood amazed by what the Creator had made. *Stupendous!*

With heavy steps, two massive creatures with long curving necks approached. Their equally long tails—the size of tree trunks—swept the brown earth. Eating from the leafy treetops, they advanced with ponderous strides. One lowered its head, dwarfing him. These were behemoths.

He examined and labeled many varieties of these. Some had sharp horns protruding from their foreheads; some had mouths so large he could place his head inside. Others had long noses constantly in motion. Their noses could even reach into the trees to grab leaves. After he named them, they strode away, stirring up the dust and trumpeting joyfully.

The man's work occupied his mind, giving him joy.

But now, he detected that the sun had crossed the sky and dipped toward the opposite horizon. Most of the animals headed in the same direction, toward the sun and over the nearest hill. He followed them, grabbing a piece of fruit to eat.

The juice flowed down his parched throat and eased the dryness. Yet he needed something more and wasn't sure what. As he strolled along, he continued to examine and name the creatures surrounding him, keeping an arm around one or the other as he ate.

When the man crested the hill, all the animals had clustered around something that wasn't brown earth. The substance glittered in the sunlight, splashed into the air, and gurgled a liquid, soothing sound. Some of the animals stood in it with only the top half of their bodies showing.

What is this? A scent drifted toward the man, different than the dirt and the trees. Instinctively, his nostrils widened. The aroma tugged at him. He loped down the hill.

Inspecting this peculiar substance, the man shaded his eyes from the glare. In the middle, the stuff seemed to move rapidly. None of the animals had ventured out that far. They stood along the sides, where it moved slowly and reflected the sky in undisturbed places. Each animal had its head down, lapping up the stuff, though a few sat upright, dipping in their forefeet.

The man tried to find a calm area where the earth seemed to end as it met this mysterious matter. When he discovered a flat piece of ground, he lay down, edging forward so his head was over the substance. He saw a face!

Who is that?

Startled, he jerked back and the face below him did the same. Curious, he leaned forward. The face reappeared. His Creator had said He would make him a perfect match. *Is this my strong helper?* Cautiously, he reached toward the face, and his own hand was reflected in the water.

As his hand broke the surface, concentric rings distorted the face. *This is my reflection. This is my face,* he resolved. Disappointed that it wasn't the helper, he handled the liquid matter, playing with its texture. The fluid ran down his arm and dripped off his fingers. He smelled the liquid then touched his tongue to it, sampling the moisture. *Wonderful!* He wanted more. This was what his body had been craving—water. This was a river.

Drink, his body demanded. Frantically, the man lapped up the water as most of the animals were doing. Discovering this wasn't effective, he pressed his hands together. *Ah! Better!*

After taking repeated drinks until he no longer felt the dryness and thirst, he let the surface resettle. When the ripples stilled, his face came into view. The man studied himself.

His face didn't look like any of the animals he had catalogued and befriended today—it was flatter, with a triangular nose and smaller nostrils. Out of his softly glowing countenance, dark eyes stared back at him. Above this, a shock of black hair.

Grimacing, he studied two rows of white teeth and a pink tongue. His mouth was wide, his shoulders broad, his head upright, compared to most of the animals. He had more skin showing than hair. *Hmm. Similar to the animals, but different— all made by the same artistic Creator.*

The animals strolled away in pairs, and he turned to watch. They seemed to communicate, as if they had some type of connection. He observed the games and frolicking of some pairs. Others lay down together. Their bodies intertwined as their eyes closed and their heads drooped.

The Creator had actually made them to connect in some essential way. Their bodies were designed to do this. Some pairs engaged in an action that joined their bodies. This stirred a longing within the man that he didn't understand. The pursuit of this action seemed to be the fuel behind the frenzied energy they had exhibited all day.

The man had no one with whom to seek this type of connection.

His Creator had said it wasn't good that he was alone. He meditated on this. *What did it mean to be alone?* Creatures that he had named today surrounded him. They were here with him, yet none of these were his own kind. His Creator had said He would make a helper corresponding to him, but he hadn't found this perfectly matched helper.

This was what *alone* meant.

He was alone.

The man rolled onto his back and stared blankly at the sky.

Throwing his arm across his face, he covered his eyes. Moisture leaked from them and trickled down his cheeks toward his ears. The back of his throat ached and thickened. His breathing was ragged when he inhaled, and his chest shook when he exhaled.

Crying—that's what this is. Why do I keep crying?

Despair gripped him. He wanted to sink back into the ground.

Is there no one else like me?

He was aware of the Creator's presence. God watched him. The man felt comforted. Peace overtook him as he remembered his Creator's words. He would make a strong helper to supply his lack; He had given him everything he needed. The animals he had seen today were in perfectly matched pairs. If they had a counterpart, surely he did, too.

This seemed to be the order of creation.

Confident that his Creator would meet all his needs, the man relaxed. The love of God soothed him, wrapping him up in His nearness. Weary heaviness grew within his chest, and his breathing slowed. He felt sapped of strength, his body warm and limp, as if he would sink back into the dirt.

Is that possible?

His eyelids grew heavy. They closed.

Blackness.

Nothing.

CHAPTER FOUR

AWARENESS. WARMTH PRESSED against her face. Her Creator embraced her, softly breathing His life into her. Her chest rose, and she drew in God's delectable fragrance. She felt immersed in all-encompassing love and affection.

Passionate joy filled her! *My God!*

Savoring His presence, she tasted God's life breath. His gentle care and delight overwhelmed as He clutched her tightly. Sighing with contentment, her chest fell as His breath left her. Peace and tranquility permeated her being.

Her next breath came naturally, following the first.

A moist scent nearby. A gurgling liquid sound. Faint buzzing noises. Songs and trilling aloft. She opened her eyes. Light.

God's face.

The One, her Creator, hovered over her with tenderness in His eyes. Studying His features, she basked in His presence, cherishing His nearness. *Bliss!*

"You are mine," God said gently. "I made you in my own image."

Love suffused her heart with adoration! She was filled up with Him, overtaken, engulfed in His affection, besotted. He cupped her face, gazing into her eyes.

Softly He pressed His lips to her forehead. Then, tenderly, He lifted her.

She sat, beholding her own flesh. Inspecting herself thoroughly, she smiled, admiring His handiwork. Her skin glowed softly radiant, smooth to her touch; her long hair hung to her waist, black and shiny. Her limbs curved slender and graceful.

Looking around, she discovered a glimmering substance that gurgled as it moved along. The scent of this liquid matter appealed to her. Sweeping her eyes down the edge of the substance, she twisted, curious about where it was going as it moved so rapidly.

Her eyes halted on a being, prone and unconscious on the ground nearby. Warm and inviting, the luminous glow of its skin attracted her.

What is that?

"That is the man," God answered her thoughts. "You are his strong helper. You complete him. Together you have much work to do. You will fight and rule alongside him. He has important information to tell you. Other than my own self, you are the greatest blessing I will ever give him. Stand with him. Love him."

This intrigued her. Her whole being yearned to do this. The woman grinned.

God clasped her hands, and they rose together. Looking into God's eyes, she swayed to gain her balance, surprised by her height. The Creator watched her with patient and affectionate eyes. Eventually, she steadied.

Smiling warmly, He released one of her hands. God now took a step toward the man, leading her to him. Gripping the Creator's hand, her first step wobbled, unsteady. But the second was surer, the third even better. With her fourth step, they stood directly behind the man.

"You are his." The Creator beamed, clearly overjoyed. "And he is yours."

She studied the man. He was alluring and mystifying. *How am I to help him?*

With one arm curled under his head, which was covered with short black hair, he lay on his side, breathing in a rhythm similar to hers. His backside faced her, and she examined the broad shoulders and the back that narrowed to slim hips and buttocks.

Something stirred within, attracting her.

Did she look like that? Curious, she twisted to investigate, deciding her hips looked broader. Everything else seemed similar, though her shoulders appeared narrower. They were similar, but they were not identical. Absorbed, she examined him quietly, contemplating her task.

God released her hand, presenting her to him in his prone state.

She gave herself to the man. Lowering herself to the ground, she sat cross-legged behind him. Tentatively, she stretched her hand toward his body, eager to help him. Gently she caressed the warm, luminescent skin of his shoulder. This touch triggered an emotional jolt in her.

Pounding thrummed within her chest. Excitement rose.

He moved.

Quickly, she withdrew her hand.

* * * *

Consciousness. Something had touched the man. His eyes blinked open, and he found he had rolled onto his side. Confused, he didn't remember where he was. He lay facing the water, his back to the sun. It seemed to be nearer to the horizon; the atmosphere had changed.

The sun's radiance was now soft and warm, rosy and golden, not glaring, as at its zenith. The air felt balmy and pleasantly heavy. All was still and tranquil.

But he was in pain.

When he moved, his side hurt. Something wasn't right.

Reaching for the ache, he prodded his flesh and jerked away from his own touch, inhaling sharply. A part of his body was missing! Something was gone! A deep ache throbbed inside him, and a sharp pain ran down his flank.

What happened to me?

Wincing as he moved, the man pushed himself into a sitting position, gently easing his knees toward his chest. This relieved the pressure. He examined his side. Below his armpit, a raw tender line began at his ribs and ended right above his hipbone.

Were some of his bones missing? It felt as if part of his side was gone! He grew alarmed. Drawing in a deep breath, the man slowly exhaled. It hurt! The calming awareness of his Creator's nearness soothed him. The man relaxed.

All was well. The Creator stood nearby, watching him.

Would He explain what had happened?

Then the man detected the sound of breathing right behind him. He smelled a new scent. Attempting to identify it, he lifted his head, sniffing the air. Something had touched him earlier, waking him. It didn't rumble, chatter, or pant, like many of the creatures he had heard today.

Had one of the animals crept close while he was . . . *Sleeping,* he labeled this missing part of his life that had occurred while his eyes were closed.

Would this happen to him again? Would he awaken to find the same results?

* * * *

The man moaned and caressed his side. The woman glanced down at her waist's symmetry. He wasn't symmetrical. The side that caused him pain dipped in. There was a purplish mark.

What's wrong with him?

She glanced at the Creator, who nodded that all was well.

She looked back at the man. For some reason, his discomfort prompted her to feel concerned. His pain became her pain. Her chest felt heavy, and her throat ached. She reached to touch him again, but hesitated, uncertain. Would her touch hurt him? She pulled back.

The man now sat motionless. It appeared he had heard her. Her breathing accelerated, the pounding inside her increasing.

The man tried to turn his head to peek over his shoulder. But another moan escaped, and his hand cradled his side again. He looked straight ahead and sat still a moment. Then he spun around to face her, keeping his knees pulled up to his chest.

Stunned, she gasped. *He is striking! Incredibly handsome!*

Large, heavy-lidded dark eyes framed with abundant lashes stared at her from under thick black brows. He seemed startled to see her. His eyes gazed out at her from his softly glowing face. Some sort of vigor he possessed tugged at her ever so subtly, inducing her to lean nearer. As she did, he inhaled sharply. Then he seemed to forget to breathe.

Scarcely able to pull her eyes away from his, she made a hasty examination of his face, taking in the straight nose and the faint hue of black that lightly tinged his neck, jawline, and lower face. This slight shading sharply defined his upper lip. His face was so striking that her body reacted to it. Warmth spread across her upper chest and cheeks.

* * * *

The man stared at the most magnificent creature he'd ever seen! This was the one he had been looking for all day—the other of his kind, his *mate*, the other half of his pair.

The promised helper! Thank you, my God!

Astounded by her beauty, his concern about his painful side dissipated.

The soft glow of her skin accentuated her eyes dramatically. Overarched by delicate brows, large, luminous, and insightful eyes studied him. Long dark hair framed her face. Her full lips appeared soft; his eyes lingered. Without willing it, he licked his own lips.

She was shaped differently than he. Of course! She had to be.

As the animals had come to him all day, he had observed the subtle differences between the members of each pair, what he now knew were male and female, two halves of the same whole. She was made to fit him, as he was made to fit her. They were designed for each other.

Their general makeup was the same—head, torso, arms, legs, smooth skin—but where his chest was hard and firm, hers stuck out; she had breasts, which appeared soft and alluring. For some reason he didn't understand, her breasts captured his eyes, arresting his examination to hover over them, visually caressing their ample roundness.

She's exquisite!

He quit breathing.

Recalling the need for air, he drew in a breath and moved his eyes down her form. Her waist curved in gently and was smaller than his. Her hips were broader. Again the movement of his eyes halted, and he lingered over this proportion, which attracted him strongly. She didn't have the same parts as he where her legs joined her torso.

Something about all of this affected his breathing again, and a shot of warmth coursed through his body. He didn't understand his physical reaction to her.

Everything about her body fascinated him; she was enthralling.

As the man took his inventory, he observed her eyes watching him serenely, examining him in turn. Her eyes met his. Simultaneously, they smiled broadly at each other.

A jittery joy raced through him. She responded, her smile widening.

An intangible something passed between them.

He might burst with this happiness! Throwing back his head as the joy erupted, he laughed ecstatically, the sound echoing across the river.

Such a relief! He needed to articulate his thoughts. He needed to tell her how he felt. God spoke. Could he? He opened his mouth and found his voice.

"My helper at last!" he said.

* * * *

Thoughts came out of his mouth!

It pleased her that he already knew who she was and that he had been expecting her. The Creator had probably informed him.

The solid bass sound of his voice resonated. It moved her. Soft laughter bubbled up from her chest. She wanted to hear him speak again.

God's nearness encircled them both, passion flowing out of Him to engulf them in warmth. Taking pleasure in this moment of their shared discovery, He laughed joyfully with them. God's delight multiplied the woman's overpowering happiness with the man.

* * * *

The man realized what had happened. God had created her from his own flesh! The Creator had taken a part of him and fashioned her, crafting her especially for him. She was a gift—a blessing! This was what God had meant. Gratitude toward his Creator overflowed.

He was no longer alone!

An urgent and vital need pulled him toward her. *I have to touch her!* Edging closer, he cradled her face in his hands. With his thumbs, he traced her cheeks' delicate softness as he stared into her receptive, intelligent eyes. *I must name her!*

What joy and honor the man felt as he considered a name for this captivating creature. Because she was made from him, he wanted her name to indicate the attachment he felt. When he named her, he would also rename himself and pledge himself to her. He would choose a name that reflected their bond of unity.

Her arrival had changed everything. She was his—his very own! He gripped her hands.

Poetic rapture burnt within him. *How can I express this?* The words came.

> *You are my own body!*
> *Bone of my bones*
> *And flesh of my flesh.*
> *You will be called 'Ishah,'*
> *Because you were taken out of my body.*
> *You are the woman, my wife.*
> *I am Ish, the man, your husband.*

* * * *

His lyrical proclamation was full of information. She wasn't quite sure what he meant. She had no recollection of being taken from his body. But he had said it so elegantly and with such passion, gazing at her with glad eyes.

"Ish." *I can speak my thoughts, too!* "My husband. I am yours."

Her voice was higher than his, with a light musical quality. His face registered surprise, as she had probably revealed to him when he first spoke. Then he beamed at her. She could tell he liked her voice. This made her happy.

Leaning closer, she gazed into his dark eyes. They urged her nearer. His hands were warm, large, and strong, his fingers long and supple. Tightly, she gripped them in return.

The Creator squatted down and threw His arms around them, pulling both close.

"This is all *very* good!" He proclaimed joyfully.

God then leapt to His feet and threw wide His arms. With radiant face, He spun round and round, exulting and dancing over them with shouts. *Whooo! Hooo! Yesss!*

The Creator then sang in triumphant voice, His passionate eyes fixed upon them:

> *The magnificent story begins—the story of my love!*
> *All praise to the glorious Father for his perfect plan!*
> *All praise to the comforting Spirit for his presence!*
> *We are one, and you are ours! Ours!*
> *You are ours forever and evermore!*
> *I love you with an everlasting love!*
> *I have created you for wondrous things!*

Dropping down beside them, God embraced them closely, smiling wide. With faces so near their breath mixed, their three noses almost touched. They gazed into one another's sparkling eyes. Ish grinned at her and at the Creator.

Ishah basked in their affection, returning it with all that was within her.

"Be fruitful and multiply," God said, "increase in number, and bear many young of your kind. Fill the earth and subdue it. Care for it, tame it, rule over it, and tend it. You are both to rule over all the fish of the sea and the birds of the air and over every living creature that moves upon the ground. I give you every seed-bearing plant on the face of the entire earth and every tree that has fruit containing seeds. These are yours for food. And to all the beasts of the earth, to all the birds, to all the creatures that move on the ground, and, in fact, to everything containing the breath of life I give every green plant for food."

And, it was so. It was, indeed, all very good!

Held tightly within the circle of God's arms, they laughed together for joy.

CHAPTER FIVE

THE CREATOR'S WORDS had a sense of finality, as if something had been completed and He now offered a blessing. Leaning back, He simultaneously cupped Ishah's cheek in one warm palm and Ish's cheek in the other. With a glimmer of love and pain radiating in His eyes, He looked back and forth from one to the other.

Ishah's emotions surged, and her eyes moistened. *Why this tender agony?*

Gently, God stroked her cheek with His thumb, gazing at her.

"Now." His eyes took in both. "Know one another. Listen. Learn. Love."

Then He stood, turned, and walked down the river. But she still felt His nearness, as always. Her chest swelled with the wonder of His presence. All around and within, God remained.

"He's still here," she whispered.

"Yes—whether or not He can be seen, He's always with us, filling us up."

And now the light changed.

Both pivoted as something bright dipped below the horizon, transforming the firmament into gold, orange, and purple brilliance. Perplexed, Ish stared back at her. Ishah realized this was new to him, too. Why hadn't he seen this before?

"All day the sun traveled in an arc across the sky," he said. "Now it's disappeared. I don't know what this means."

As the light vanished he tilted his head. Trust and acceptance eased their way onto his face. Glancing at Ishah, he smiled. She returned his smile. All was peaceful. The scent on the air grew moist and fragrant.

"God designed it all," he said. "This is His world."

Still holding hands, they watched the dusk rapidly descend. As they studied the subtle light-shift, her husband's thumbs gently caressed the backs of her hands. This affectionate gesture warmed her, producing a soft fluttering inside her.

Many noises now sounded forth, increasing and filling the air: songs and chirps and croakings. Delicate lights flashed, floating softly by. The glowing lights seemed attached to miniscule creatures. Pairs of glittering, reflective objects focused on them from the shadows. Small, black living things swooped over their heads, flapping and fluttering wildly and then reeling away through the darkening sky. These emitted small, sharp soundings.

Since Ishah wasn't acquainted with their world, she had no idea what these were, but she enjoyed listening to the music of the darkness and observing all the activity. Ish searched for the source of each instrument in this symphony of sounds. Fixing his eyes on each new sight, he was clearly as fascinated as she by what they heard and witnessed.

Up in the indigo sky, tiny lights now twinkled into view, one by one, cold and sharp, some brighter than others, brilliantly throbbing. And, on the horizon opposite where the sun had disappeared, a new light began to climb—a mottled, illuminated orb. It shed a soft, silvery, celestial radiance that was nothing like the sun. The light was gentle and delicately ethereal. They were captivated as its pearly whiteness glided upward into the blackening sky.

Ish looked down, studying Ishah's face, as if evaluating this new light's effect. Slowly, he moved his eyes from one part of her body to another, visually caressing each part. Reaching to fondle her shoulder, he then examined her face again.

In silence, she focused on his eyes. This soft light caused his skin to have a silvery glow, his dark eyes to appear shadowed, his hair blacker.

After a moment, he met her eyes. Mutual discoverers, they grinned, united in their sense of wonderment. Together both looked back up at the sky.

As this new ethereal light climbed, it seemed to decrease in size and to move farther away. The sharp, twinkling lights increased in number.

"I've never seen this before," Ish said softly, his voice tinged in awe. "When the sun was shining, the sky didn't appear like this. The creatures looked, sounded, and behaved differently. What amazing beauty!" He tipped his head back, examining the splendor. "I don't know whether our Creator just now made this or whether it was hidden by the sun's light."

Then he released one of Ishah's hands and pointed toward the heavens.

"I'm naming the silvery light the *moon* and the tiny lights *stars*. Somehow I know that this is night and that before was day. You do, too, don't you?"

Tearing his eyes away from the heavens, Ish took her hand and gazed at her, awaiting her response. She considered his words. He was right. She nodded. He smiled.

"Some things I know inside myself," she said. "Other things mystify me."

"That seems to be how life is. You were only here for the day's end. If the sun returns, I'll show you everything. Our Creator has crafted a magnificent world!"

"I don't understand what's happening or what God meant when He sang and spoke. Since I've seen only you, I couldn't put His words into any context."

Ish's brows creased. With the dark shadows cast by his brow, his expression seemed serious. Thoughtfully, he examined her face. Then his consternation eased, and he spoke.

"When I first opened my eyes and felt the Creator's breath, I didn't know who, what, or where I was. The sun was over there, but it moved." He pointed to the opposite horizon and traced an arch. "The sky grew increasingly bright. I examined my body and then rose, learning to walk and run as the Creator guided me. I'll try to explain, but some things I'll have to show you. Would you like me to tell you what I know?"

"Yes. I want to understand."

Studying her face again, Ish squeezed her hands. He lowered his knees, sitting cross-legged. As they sat on the earth facing one another, their knees touched. His legs felt warm. They were thicker and longer than hers.

"The Creator made me from the dust. The dust is the reddish-brown, moist substance that covers the earth."

Ishah looked around at the dust, now nearly black in the moonlight.

"In the dust are tiny seeds. God told me to cultivate, work, and tend them. I'm not sure how, but our Creator said He'd make me a strong helper to work alongside me and to help me fight the battle. He said *you* would supply what I lack. All day He brought mated pairs of animals and birds. These I named, looking for my promised helper, my mate—the one who would complete me. Ishah, all day I was looking for *you*. You didn't come, and I thought I was the only one of our kind. I was alone. The Creator told me it wasn't good to be alone, and it's true. I wanted to sink back into the dust."

Something in his last words and tone caused Ishah's eyes to smart. His pain became hers. Crooning a soft sigh, she pressed her palm against his cheek.

Turning, he nestled his face into her hand. Wet against her skin, he flicked his tongue, tasting her flesh. His mouth spread wide in a smile; the movement of his lips and the smoothness of his teeth brushed her skin. Then he pressed his lips tenderly into her open hand. His lips were soft and warm. Deep in her belly, a surge of desire grew. She longed to know him. Returning his cheek to her palm, he stared fixedly into her eyes.

The intensity of his gaze tugged at her, sparking an inner attraction that grew within her core. In response, she moved closer. Silently they gazed into one another's shadowed eyes. Then, keeping his eyes latched upon hers, he continued his story.

"I knew God would provide my helper. He told me He would. The animals all had mates, and I knew God had one for me, too. I lay in the dust and closed my eyes. When I awakened from my sleep, I was in pain. The Creator had removed part of my side to make you, but I didn't know it until I saw you. When I noticed our similarities, I realized you were my own flesh and bones. My side still hurts, but I forgot all about it. You're the most beautiful creature I've ever seen! I waited for you all day."

Pleased at these last words, but troubled that he was hurt, Ishah smiled. There was so much to contemplate. All of this was an enigma—inexplicable. He watched patiently as she considered his words. Then he continued.

"If the sun returns, I'll show you the trees, the fruit, and the water." He gestured toward the dark moving liquid. It reflected the moonlight and the stars. "We'll surely see some of the animals—not all left after I named them, and I'll show you The Forbidden Tree. You'll understand everything when you see it. That is, *if* the sun returns."

"Yes, show me." She grasped his hands again. "I'm sorry it hurt you when I was created. When I opened my eyes, I felt filled with love for our Creator. He helped me sit up. I looked at myself and then saw—what did you call it—the *water*?" She peered at him; he indicated that she was correct. "Then I saw you nearby. The Creator did make me for you. I'm your helper. When He gave me to you, He said we belong to each other."

"I know you're mine, but did He say I belong to you, too?"

"Yes."

Seeming to consider all the implications of her statement, Ish studied her face. "I belong to God. I'm made in His image."

"So am I. It was the first thing He said to me."

"Me, too. So we're both made in His image. We both belong to Him. But we also belong to each other?"

"Yes."

A slow smile spread across Ish's face. "I'm glad. I want to belong to you."

His words moved her. The warmth from her belly spread throughout her body. "I want to belong to you, too." She was barely able to speak.

He lifted each of her hands, softly pressing his lips to them, front and then back. "Tell me the rest. You know things I don't know. I want to hear your story."

Attempting to gather her thoughts, Ishah took a deep breath.

"I sat and watched you in the dust," she said. "I didn't know what you were, but you fascinated me. When I touched your shoulder, you stirred. You seemed to be hurt. Your pain affected me. I felt drawn to comfort and to help you. The Creator motioned that all was well, but I didn't know you were hurt because He made me from your side."

He gave her a quick smile. "It's nothing. I would gladly have this pain to gain you. The pain is decreasing already."

"Now I understand why you said, 'bone of my bones and flesh of my flesh.'"

"We're one body, formed into two people, and created by God."

God's creative design of their unity intrigued her. They were one, yet two.

Contemplating this mystery, Ishah returned her gaze to the night sky. Ish followed her gaze. They gasped at the same moment, overwhelmed by the beauty; then they snatched a glance at one another. Quickly both smiled before aiming their eyes heavenward again.

"Let's lie on the earth so we can see the sky better," Ish said. "Looking at the sun hurt my eyes, but looking at the moon doesn't, nor does looking at the stars. That's interesting."

Together, they lay back on the soft ground.

Ishah rested her head on Ish's outstretched arm. Gently, he nestled her against his side, as if she belonged in that spot. Careful not to press against the hurt place, she kept her arm curved up tightly across her chest. With that hand, she held his hand as he drew her close.

Now it was easier to see the stars, and the warmth of his body comforted her. The night air had grown cool. The panorama was breathtaking. But so was the pleasurable sensation of his body pressed against hers. Simultaneously, each leaned more closely against the other.

"You belong right here," he whispered. "I'm glad you're mine."

She smiled widely. "I feel the same."

Against Ishah, the sharp angle of Ish's hip pressed warmly. The entire length of her body touched him. From within his chest, she felt and heard against her cheek a rhythmic pulsing, strong and vital. It soothed her. He now pointed up at the sky.

"If you connect that star and that one and that one and across to those, it looks like one of the animals I named today."

She tried to comprehend. Of course, she hadn't seen an

animal, so she had no idea. She laughed. Seeming to enjoy the bubbling sound of her laughter, he watched her mouth.

"You laughed." He still studied her mouth. "Why?"

"I haven't seen the animal, whatever an *animal* is. I have no idea what you mean."

He smiled with her. They turned back toward the stars. The night sky changed as the moon traveled across it. The stars all rotated around some axis they couldn't detect. Their breathing slowed. Their bodies grew more relaxed. Ishah felt drowsy.

"I can tell we're going to sleep," Ish said softly. "I want to lie on my side. The Creator must have placed me like that, knowing it would be best. Can you lie down in front of me?"

He rolled so his hurt side was on top, and she slid over him, careful not to jar the wound. Inviting her near, his warm body softly glowed and beckoned. Encasing her with a strong arm, he buried his face in her hair, inhaling deeply. The proximity of his body stirred a tender intimacy within her. She nestled more snugly against him.

Ish drew his other arm under both their heads and then breathed out a small sound of satisfaction, his warm breath soft against the nape of her neck.

"It's good not to be alone," he whispered, pressing his lips to her ear, then into her hair.

"I've never been alone, but it's good to be with you," she whispered back.

With her lips, she caressed his hand, tasting his skin, breathing in his fragrance—virile and warm. Perfect contentment filled her. Snug against each other, their breathing slowed.

Love for the Creator soothed Ishah as she recalled the wonder of waking in His embrace to then discover this striking and affectionate man who now held her in his arms—her husband. She silently rehearsed his poem of love and commitment.

Smiling to herself, she considered the Creator's dance of exultation, His song of praise, and His words of instruction. Their joint mission and God's passion ran softly through her mind. Deep peace and satisfaction surged through her entire self. All was well.

Calm and tranquil, her eyes closed. Ish sighed contentedly.

Blissful sleep.

CHAPTER SIX

LUCIFER CLENCHED HIS fists as he studied the two dirt creatures. They lay unconscious on the earth, their chests rising and falling—sleeping. Apparently, lack of consciousness was essential to them. God had caused the man to sleep, so He could craft this woman.

Luminous in the night, the two glowed with God's presence inside them, His Holy Spirit indwelling them. Yet both had originated in the dust. Lucifer didn't comprehend how God's holiness could have entered them, creatures of mere earth.

In contrast, here *he* was, radiating splendor, dazzling. He occupied the position of prominence over the throne of Yahweh—the Lord God. He was one of the guardian cherubim, blazing with jewels, fiery in his brightness, the most exquisite to behold.

Full of wisdom, he was the model of perfection, the best one God had made. Creating magnificent music in praise of the Creator, he spread his wings wide in the heavens, hovering over the very God of the universe. Of all the angels, he was made first. He was preeminent, the son of the dawn, the Day Star. He shone the brightest.

Why had God wrought this man and this woman? Why?

Dark ruminations filled Lucifer's mind. Restless agitation troubled him. He had been thwarted. He doubted the wisdom of his God. As he watched the two humans sleeping on the earth, he gnashed over the destruction of his plans. Yahweh had demolished his expectations and had stunned him into silence. Bitterness clutched at him. How could he possibly sing?

Lucifer could not accept what was. He was not the center of God's plans as he had supposed. The Godhead's design was not what he had theorized. He had assumed he was the one God would honor with the dominion of the earth. He had thought God was creating this for him.

He was wrong.

As the most brilliant and wise, how could he have made such a flawed and incorrect assumption? Lucifer was deeply offended. Would these human beings rule and have dominion over even him?

As the Son had fashioned the first human being, Lucifer had not been impressed. This was to be a representation of Yahweh, the Lord God? This *thing* was made in His image?

It had lain there in the dust, lifeless, until God the Son had breathed into it. Clumsily, it had risen, awkwardly stumbling around. It knew nothing. *It doesn't even have wings!* Lucifer could have done a better job—he would have created it in *his* image. How could this pathetic creature have dominion? What had God been thinking?

Anger had seethed within Lucifer as he watched God annihilate all his plans. As he gaped at the man rising on its weak and wobbly legs, he had turned to Gabriel and Michael and had grumbled his complaint. They had withdrawn with looks of consternation.

"How do you dare to challenge the wisdom of the Most High?" Michael had demanded. "You are a created being, able only to function within the parameters established for you by Yahweh Himself. You are not God. May the Lord Himself rebuke you!"

Lucifer had known he would get nowhere with them, but immediately to his mind had sprung the names of other angels. He had observed the faces of many when the man had been created; he had heard their thoughts. Ignoring these two, Lucifer had turned away.

Then he had seen his opportunity.

Soon after making the man, God had instructed him not to eat from the Tree of the Knowledge of Good and Evil, lest he die. The man had obeyed immediately. If given the chance, Lucifer had decided this was the weakness he would exploit.

All he would have to do was cause the man to eat the fruit. Then he would be dead—his spirit separated from God and stripped right out of his dirt body, leaving it lifeless, exactly as it had been before God had breathed into it. That would be the end of this travesty.

As powerful as Lucifer was, he could easily bring this about. He could force this fruit down the man's throat, if he chose, and crush the life out of the man.

Lucifer's frustration swelled throughout the day. When the dirt-man had named the creatures, God had relished the names, remarking on each one. *Why had the man been allowed to bestow his pitiful names upon the creatures?*

Lucifer would have chosen better names. He was filled with wisdom.

All day, God had remained engrossed in every movement the man made. He had even wrapped himself in angelic form— the Angel of the Lord—to create him, to walk with him, and to embrace him. In fact, He had never taken His eyes off the man. God watched him even now.

Since the man had been created, Yahweh had been overjoyed with all the man's thoughts and actions. The Godhead had discussed him continually, delighted. God's secret and mysterious plans were all interwoven with the man's reason for existence. The Godhead's joy and love for the man had bounced and echoed in harmony between the Three in One.

Yahweh loved the man so intensely it was hard to bear the fervor radiating from Him as He considered the man constantly—even as the man now slept. Lucifer hated the man.

And, as if one human wasn't more than enough, the Creator had formed this woman. Seeing the man's pain from the wound in his side, Lucifer now knew he could be physically hurt.

He was glad.

But, in spite of his pain, the man was pleased with the woman God had made. As Lucifer considered her sleeping form, he could see why. She was lovely. The woman's presence seemed to affect the man's body. He could scarcely breathe when he touched her. It was nauseating to behold.

Now there were two humans to occupy God's unfathomable mind, two for Him to love with blazing fervor, two to consider and cherish and watch over.

The Creator's song, benediction, and passionate affection for the two occupied Lucifer's mind. God had given them instructions to multiply. This meant there would be more of them. The very thought offended him. God's plan did not include him. *They* were to rule and have dominion. Lucifer hated them both.

When the sun had set today, all the angels in heaven had shouted for joy at Yahweh's creation. Lucifer had led the shouting symphony of triumphant praise, but his mind had not agreed with what his mouth had proclaimed. He had masked his deceit.

Rather, he had calculated how he might destroy the work of God's hands, pondering how he might bring down this man and his wife to death.

As he had observed how the man gazed at the woman this evening, Lucifer had realized what he would do, if given the opportunity. His own genius had surprised even him. He would use this woman to destroy the man. This creature, Ish, was so enamored with her, Lucifer was sure he could exploit that to his advantage. He would continue to watch them carefully, so he could discern how to attack the woman and, through her, to take down the man. Lucifer would be the victor.

However, as Michael had reminded him, he knew his strength was constrained by the will of the Father. Lucifer could do only what God permitted. Indeed, He knew what Lucifer contemplated at that very moment as His two humans lay sleeping on the ground.

Yet the man would not have this advantage. Lucifer was wise. He would watch them and use their very natures to accomplish his plan...if he obtained what he hoped.

Surely, he could destroy them.

CHAPTER SEVEN

REPEATED SHARP CHIRPING poked its way into Ishah's consciousness. *What is that?* A bright light beamed, glowing a warm yellow-orange through her closed eyelids. She popped open her eyes and squinted. The sun had returned! It blazed brilliantly.

An awareness of the Creator's presence filled her with joy. *God, you are near.*

But wait; this was puzzling. Her body had become wet. The fragrance of damp earth assailed her nostrils. Still, her husband lay warm against her—cozy bliss. All was well.

Ishah stretched wide her arms and legs at the very moment Ish did. Their limbs collided, and he laughed softly, his bass rumbling. Ishah's chest filled with happiness, light and free. But then, Ish moaned softly. Ishah's concern eradicated all other consideration. A nurturing response engulfed her. Quickly, she sat up and turned to examine his side.

The wound looked different, now a dark pink color—the hue at the edges of the sky. Gently, she stroked the indentation. Ish's entire side was wet. Running her palm slowly down his hip and thigh, she inspected this wetness, smelling the moisture then licking her hand to taste it, ascertaining nothing.

What is this? How mysterious!

Other than this strange dampness, the wound felt only slightly warmer than the rest of his body. It looked better, too. Reassured, she turned her attention to his face.

Ish had been studying her every movement, his eyes fastened on her. He wore an expression of contentment and satisfaction. Reaching for her, he cupped her cheek in his palm and repeated what he had said before they fell asleep.

"It's good not to be alone."

Since the moment she had opened her eyes, he had been near. "How do you feel, my husband, now that the sun has returned?"

"The pain isn't as sharp as yesterday—the day before this one. My body's healing. God is good!" He smiled up at her from the ground.

Ishah was relieved. But something about his face had altered.

The sharp edge of his jawline rose prominent as he lay flat upon his back. And now, though still radiating soft light, his lower face and neck had a faint shadow. His upper lip appeared more emphasized. Capturing her eyes, this darker tone prominently marked its upper edge.

Caressing his chin, she discovered it was coarse. This slight shading had appeared fainter yesterday—a bare tinge of color, but then his face had felt smooth. Seemingly mesmerized by her nurturing, he lay still. His attention warmed her affections.

"Your face feels different." She flicked her eyes to his.

"Hmm." Looking puzzled, he gripped his chin. "I wonder what that is."

Leaning close, Ishah noticed that the faint black color originated under his skin. She stroked his cheek. The top half of his face felt smooth to her touch, the bottom half coarse. Running one finger lightly along his upper lip, she found the top edge also smooth.

He's so attractive!

The entire time she completed her inspection, she felt his eyes watching her. Now, she looked into them. The intensity of his gaze ignited warmth deep within her, a longing to know him as completely as possible, to learn about him and love him with all of her being.

He was hers, and she was his.

"Your face feels exactly the same." He gently stroked her cheek. His fingertips lingered. Then he gripped his own chin again.

Smiling, she shrugged her shoulders. Another mystery. As Ishah turned this over in her mind, she remembered there were other mysteries she wanted to discuss. Excitement about the Creator's words, song, and blessings bubbled up within her!

"Last night, as we fell asleep, I was thinking about the Creator."

"I think of Him constantly! He's always with us."

"Before I slept, I reviewed everything He said and did."

"I did, too."

Ish laced his fingers behind his head and sang the Creation Song. With her eyes on his, she joined in, weaving her voice in and out in harmony. Grinning at her, he sang with gusto.

The magnificent story begins—the story of My love!
All praise to the glorious Father for His perfect plan!
All praise to the comforting Spirit for His presence!
We are One, and you are Ours! Ours!
You are Ours forever and evermore!
I love you with an everlasting love!
I have created you for wondrous things!

Ish's eyes sparkled as they finished. "Our God is mysterious. He is One, yet Three."

"I noticed that. We are one, yet two."

"Yes! This is intriguing. Everything He says and does captivates my mind." Ish seemed eager for this topic. Rising on one elbow, he became animated. "When I consider His words, it helps me understand. I'm glad I can discuss Him with you!"

He looked happy, as if a deeply felt need had been met.

Together they repeated the words the Creator had proclaimed before the sun disappeared. While they recited, Ishah studied Ish's eyes. They focused internally, as if reflecting on each part of the directive. Joy filled her! The Creator had given them many instructions and a mandate of authority. They looked intently at each other, trying to grasp their responsibilities.

Enthusiastic about their discussion, Ish sat up, wincing. A

small exhalation strained by effort escaped him. Once more, this prompted an emotional reaction. Ishah felt a spasm of sympathy. On some deep level of her being, she was created to respond to him. Stirred by loving emotion, she drew him near, stroking his back soothingly. His skin felt smooth to her touch.

Reciprocating, Ish nestled his head upon her shoulder, nuzzling her neck. There, he gently pressed his lips. An awareness of the warmth of his mouth, the shape of his upper lip, and the scratchy roughness of his jawline flooded her thoughts. She drew him closer.

Contentedly, he returned her embrace, encasing her in his arms.

Then, satisfied, both smiled and sat back, gazing at each other, preoccupied with the other's responses. His eyes were warm and inviting as he leaned near.

"I longed for you yesterday." His eyes twinkled. She studied their depths. "I don't understand all the Creator's words either, so I'm glad we can talk about Him."

Ish lifted his lips to her forehead, softly caressing her skin. She inhaled the fragrance of his mouth, her eyes drawn to his lips, now softly framed by black.

Everything Ish said and did filled her with an inner aching need. Deep in her belly the need enlarged, filling her chest and flushing her cheeks. Both their minds and their bodies were attracted to the other, desiring to be intimately known. They were intricately connected. Ishah felt amiable and expansive. She wanted to talk.

"I wonder about the Creator's words," she said. "First, He said it was all very good."

"I think He meant all of His creation, especially you, created from me and for me. Then He repeated His words about tending the earth. We're to do this together."

Ish's words pleased her. She caressed his cheek, drawn by his intense eyes.

The next part puzzled her. "He told us to be fruitful and multiply, increase in number, and bear many young of our kind. We're to fill the earth."

"That's surely something we can only accomplish together."

"How do you know?"

"He didn't say that until after you were made, so I assume I can't multiply or bear young without you. This must be something I lack. It seems we need to do this together."

"Do you understand what it means?"

"I have no idea." Ish laughed. "I hoped you would know."

"I think in some way we'll produce living beings like us, otherwise how could we multiply and fill the earth?"

"True. But how? I don't know what's required. I can't figure it out."

"How did the Creator show you what to do before He made me?"

"I instinctively knew how to do some things—thinking, breathing, walking, eating, drinking. He spoke to me. He also brought some things to pass, like when He brought the animals and when He gave you to me. At least, that's what occurred on the first day."

"Don't you think it will happen the same way? We'll know how to be fruitful and multiply instinctively, He'll tell us what to do, or He'll make it happen."

"You're right!" Clearly, Ish was pleased. He smiled broadly. "I'm so glad God made you. You're a powerful help with just your words. God will show us what to do."

Ishah felt an inner fulfillment as he spoke. Then he pressed his lips to her hand, looking up at her. Partially veiling his gaze, his hair cascaded softly across his forehead. His eyes demanded some sort of response.

What is it? Everything about his person attracted her, compelling her toward him.

"Let's focus on His last instruction while I show you everything," he said.

"'Know one another. Listen. Learn. Love.'"

"There's no mystery there!" Ish laughed.

"Unless there's more to it than we know."

"Hmm." He paused, tilting his head as he regarded her with respect. "You're wise, my wife! Let's drink and get some food. We have much to do!"

Ish turned toward the water.

Tiny shining beads that sparkled in the sun covered a fine green layer across the dust. Ishah fingered the glittering tops of the growth. The droplets were wet. She had been engrossed in Ish's wound and their interactions, forgetting everything was damp.

"This is new!" Ish surveyed the expanse. "Grass. It wasn't here yesterday. This wetness is dew. See it falling from the mist rising off the river and the earth."

"It's making everything wet."

"The earth was damp when I first touched it yesterday. This must be the cause."

"I wonder why the Creator made everything wet."

"It's another mystery." Ish laughed. "There's much we don't know!"

The tiny droplets shimmered and sparkled in the morning sunlight. The effect was breathtaking. The dew was beautiful, but its purpose puzzled Ishah.

Wincing as he moved, Ish pushed up from the ground and rose. Ishah gaped, amazed by his height. She'd never seen him do this before. With the hand from his unwounded side, Ish grasped her hand, pulling her to her feet.

They stood, looking into each other's eyes while she gained equilibrium. Giving her an encouraging smile, he tilted his head as he watched her.

"We're close by the water," he said. "I was a little unsteady on my first attempt at walking."

"I walked with the Creator, but only a few steps."

Ish strolled ahead to the water's edge. His shoulders were level, and his arms swung freely. All his movements were fluid and graceful. Ishah enjoyed watching his body. Turning, he waited, positioning himself between her and the water.

With her first step, she lurched. He tensed. She straightened herself. They both smiled. The next few steps were easier. When she reached him, he squeezed her tightly. Gently, he lowered her to the river.

"Lie down and look into the water," he said. "You'll see your face."

Baffled, Ishah stared at him. "What do you mean?"

"The water mirrors it. I'll show you."

Ish leaned over the water. Reflected there, she saw his smiling face. From the water's surface, he watched her. She scooted forward until she saw her own reflection.

That's me?

Pursing her lips, she studied herself. Daintier than Ish, with smaller features, her cheeks were fuller, and her brows arched higher. They didn't look the same, but then their bodies didn't either. The face—*her* face—looked at Ish's reflection and smiled. He grinned back.

"You're exquisite! Absolutely beautiful," he beamed. "You're exactly what I wanted. The Creator is so good to me!"

She laughed, filled with happiness at his approval.

Lowering his hands into the water, he sent ripples across their reflections. He drank, and she imitated his actions, relishing the taste as it ran across her tongue and down her throat. The water was cold and refreshing. When they finished, Ish shoved himself up from the riverbank and leapt to his feet— all in one motion. But he grimaced.

"Now come, my wife." He extended his hand. "I'll show you the fruit."

Tugging her near, he laced his fingers through hers and led her up the hill. As they walked, her gait grew smoother. Over all the places they had previously walked and covering this mound of earth, grass sprouted thickly. At the top of the hill they appraised the terrain.

Spread out below them, verdant and peaceful, multitudes of leafy trees of vibrant hues stood stately and calm. Restful shadows cast by the thick foliage blanketed each tree's base. Under the trees in the distance, the soft soil lay placid, brown, and fertile, as if awaiting something.

"This is the Garden of Eden," Ish said. "The Creator planted it here for us. We're to cultivate it, tend it, and care for it. The grass wasn't here yesterday. All the places where the animals and I walked are now covered in it. Look in the distance." He pointed; Ishah peered through the trees. "See the trails of grass coming from all directions? The animals walked there. And see that space?" He indicated the wide, flat area at the bottom of the hill. "That's where they waited for me to name them. It's now covered with grass. The animals and I must have done something that caused the grass to grow when the dew fell on it." Pointing across the Garden on his right, Ish's face grew still and serious. "Over there is The Forbidden Tree." He narrowed his eyes as he examined a distant, dark tree. Then he looked back to her. "Let's go down and eat some fruit."

She wondered about his reaction to this strange tree, but was more curious about the fruit. "I don't know what you mean by the word *eat*."

Ish smiled at her. "I didn't either, but you will. It's instinctive, like drinking."

As they ambled down the hill, he continued to hold her hand. They stepped up to a tree.

"Look at this!" he exclaimed. "This is where I buried one of the seeds yesterday."

A small tree with delicate green leaves sprouted from the earth to their knees' height. It appeared similar to the taller tree. Ish squatted. Thoughtfully, he inspected the plant. Ishah waited patiently, studying his face. He looked off into the distance, surveying the Garden.

Now that they were below the treetops, through the gaps between the tree trunks Ishah detected many creatures in the distance. These had four legs. Heads lowered to the earth, they tore at the new green grass with their mouths.

Comprehension spread across Ish's face. He stood.

"Now I understand what the Creator meant. We need to turn the soil so the seeds are covered by dirt when the dew waters them." He swept his arm, taking in the whole landscape. "Look! Everywhere the soil was turned by the animals' feet, new green things have grown. That was all it took." He pointed at the faraway creatures. "See the animals in the distance? They're eating the grass. Remember the last part of the Creator's command?"

"Yes. 'To everything containing the breath of life I give every green plant for food.'"

"This is what He meant!"

She understood.

He fixed his eyes on hers. "There's no way I could do all this alone!"

As his excitement increased, Ishah responded with enthusiasm.

"I need your help!" he said. "The Creator said He'd bring me a complementary helper, one made just for me. We're interdependent. I need you! First, He brought me all the animals. None of them was a suitable helper. They couldn't talk to me. Their minds are made differently. They're not my kind. I can't accomplish the task God has given me without you. Look!"

Exuberant, his arms spread wide, indicating the entire Garden.

Ishah discerned the enormity of their task. She was eager to begin. With all her being she wanted to help him accomplish everything their Creator had assigned.

Ish grasped her hands, staring into her eyes. "You and I together are to subdue and care for the earth! We're to rule over all the creatures and over all of creation!"

Ish exuded power and strength. Energetic and purposeful, he appeared ready to begin their united mission that very moment. A thrill rushed through her.

"Your desire to work together is good!" The Creator walked up beside them. "This is what you're created to accomplish. You're both made in my image. I work."

Joy washed through Ishah when she saw His face and heard His voice. Love for Him filled her chest and overflowed. She and Ish both dropped to their knees, clasping Him about the waist, pressing their faces against His form, inhaling His life-giving fragrance. Devotion filled Ishah that was so intense she could hardly bear it. Ish wore a similar blissful expression, gazing up at God with happy eyes.

"I love you," God said, looking at each one. "Let me tell you about my creation."

Gently He pressed His lips to each of their foreheads, and then He lowered Himself to the earth beside them. All their knees touched as they sat together at the base of the hill. Around the circle, their eyes sparkled as they smiled at one another.

"In the beginning there was nothing but myself. For all eternity, I am and ever will be. I am Yahweh, the self-existent one."

Spellbound, they listened.

"I am light and life and love. I spoke all into existence. I began my creation with light, separating the light from the darkness on the first day. I named the day and the night. You knew because I placed this knowledge in you."

Ish looked into Ishah's eyes. "I knew it," he whispered. Then he returned his gaze to God. "Thank you for giving us knowledge and discernment."

Encircling them in His arms, Yahweh drew both near, clearly pleased.

Ishah smiled, filled with love for Ish and overjoyed to hear the Creator's explanation. Yahweh was the source of their ability to know and to learn.

"I made this beautiful world for you because I love," Yahweh continued. "On the second day, I divided the water above from the water beneath. The expanse above, I called the sky. On the third day, I made dry land and prepared it to produce vegetation, seed-bearing plants, and the trees you see. The water I gathered into seas; the rivers flow into them. I named the earth and the sea as well. The creation of the sun, the moon, and the stars came next, on the fourth day. They were given to separate the day from the night, and as signs to mark seasons, days, and years. On the fifth day I made the birds and the creatures of the sea. All are to reproduce according to their kind. I began the last day of creation by making the rest of the creatures you saw and named." He smiled His approval at Ish. "It is all good!"

Compelled by the joy in His voice, both leaned closer, eager to hear what He would say next. Anticipation built. Their eyes fixed on God's face, and the Creator beamed at them.

"I created the heavens and the earth and everything in them in six days, and then I created you both in my own image. You are made in my likeness! All of my creation is very good!"

Ish sprang to his feet, barely able to contain his excitement. Captivated by Ish's pleasure and thrilled by God's lesson, Ishah grinned at the two of them.

"Today is a holy day." The Creator's voice held a soft sound of delight at their reaction. It bubbled within His voice. He loved them! "I rest from my labors. As evening brought the end of the sixth day and all of this seventh day, I rest to rejoice in my creation and to take pleasure in you. Today is blessed." The Creator laughed with joy. "Enjoy my rest this day! It is for you."

At this proclamation, their enthusiasm turned to celebration.

The man and the woman threw their heads back and laughed with Him. Ish grasped Ishah's hand and tugged her to her feet.

They danced around and around the Creator and then across the Garden, twirling and spinning, then embracing again, laughing for joy.

God had created this world for them!

Every moment they felt His nearness and enjoyed His presence. Yahweh was their God, and He loved them!

"Well, we're not tending the Garden or cultivating the soil today," Ish exclaimed. "Today God's plan is for us to enjoy His rest. Let's go!"

Pulling Ishah behind him, Ish galloped through the Garden. Hand in hand, Ish and Ishah danced and skipped, weaving among the trees.

CHAPTER EIGHT

CLEARLY ENERGIZED BY their interaction with God, Ish stopped by a tree, still rocking up and down onto his toes. He laughed. "I can barely contain all this happiness!"

"I know exactly what you mean."

Smiling widely, he pressed his forehead to hers, puckered, and planted his lips on her nose. This only added to her breathless wonder. She felt as if she might float away. Could that happen? Throwing her arms around Ish's neck, she giggled as he spun her round and round.

Stopping at last, they stood encased in one another's arms, eyes locked. Ish's breath blew soft upon her cheeks. Gradually their breathing slowed. Ishah leaned near, studying the depths of his eyes. Slowly his pupils dilated. Then his upper lip beckoned to her, trapping her eyes.

"I want to show you the fruit." As Ish spoke, his lips fascinated her. "I ate from this tree yesterday. Yes, look at the ground." He pointed to a small knee-high tree. She tore her eyes away to glance at it. "A little tree has sprung up. They grow rapidly!"

Ishah squatted to examine the small tree. The leaves were new and tender green.

"Look in the branches." Ish pointed at the larger tree. "See the colored globes of yellow and orange, like the sky in the morning and as the sun set?"

"What are those? They're so vibrant."

"That's fruit. It's good! Yahweh our God has given it to us for food."

Ish yanked one off the tree, handing it to Ishah. Then he plucked another. Still rocking up onto his toes, he watched her, clearly overjoyed to share this new experience.

Ishah examined the radiant piece of fruit. Against her fingertips, it felt plush and soft, smooth and velvety. She raised it to her nose, closed her eyes, and inhaled the aroma. *Inviting!* She was surprised at what happened inside her.

Her eyes flashed open.

"See!" He laughed with pleasure. "This is a peach!"

Biting down, he tore off a piece with his teeth. Ishah leaned near to watch. She sniffed the scent on his breath, and her mouth grew moist. Interesting.

He chuckled softly. "You should've seen my first attempt. I licked it first."

The idea made Ishah smile. She bit into the fruit. *Scrumptious!* "It's wonderful!"

"Isn't Yahweh good to provide such delicious food?"

She nodded enthusiastically. "Our God is so kind!"

They each ate their entire piece of fruit. Ish buried their seeds, then grasped her hand and hurried her toward the next group of trees.

This soft scarlet fruit dripped with juice. Its skin wasn't fuzzy like the peaches. Ish called them *plums.* Laughing as the sweet juice ran down their chins, they ate. As if synchronized, each wiped the other's chin and licked the juice off their fingertips.

This provoked peals of laughter and Ish's lips soft upon her forehead.

As they ate, they moved from tree cluster to tree cluster, animated as they discussed the different types of leaves, the variety of fruit, and the beauty of green, purple, orange, and red fruit when offset by the cerulean sky. Ish named each kind. So many varieties, so much good food! They thanked Yahweh repeatedly, filled with His pleasure. The scent, the appearance, and the taste invited them to consume what God had given.

Eventually, Ishah felt she couldn't possibly eat any more. "I'm going to sit here under this tree. I feel . . . full."

Ish grabbed a handful of the tiny mouth-watering fruit—cherries—and sat next to her, the rough bark against their backs. Shoulder to shoulder, they leaned into each other as Ish devoured the cherries. Enjoying the panorama of the Garden, both sighed with contentment.

A repetitive chirking sounded from the treetop. Ishah searched for the source. She had heard this as they had awakened. She discovered the cause—a small creature that hopped and flitted about in the treetop. Periodically, it paused to eat one of the cherries.

"Ish, what's that?" She pointed at the creature.

"A bird—that's a shrike. Did you hear all the birds calling to one another this morning? They sang so joyfully yesterday when I named them."

Ishah watched the interesting little creature for a while.

"There's its mate." Ish indicated a similar bird nearby. They were engaged in bringing little pieces of different substances to assemble something on the lowest branch.

"What are they making?"

"I don't know. They all started doing this yesterday, right after I named them."

Inquisitive about their activity, they studied the birds. After watching the birds' bustling, coordinated labor for a while, Ishah assessed the Garden. The new grass covered the ground here. But in the distance most of the Garden waited expectantly—a vibrant, brown expanse of earth.

The dew was no longer apparent in the grass; it seemed to have vanished. Their bodies and the ground were now dry. *So mysterious!*

Ish became very still. "Do you see that tree?" His tone was somber.

He pointed to a nearby tree, and Ishah studied it. This was the one he had indicated earlier from the hilltop. It had broad dark-green leaves. Crimson fruit peeked through. The sparkling tree next to it was equal in height. The two trees stood taller than the surrounding forest.

"That's the Tree of the Knowledge of Good and Evil," he said. "It's forbidden."

"I know what good is. Yahweh is good. His creation is good. But what is 'evil'?"

Puzzled, Ish stared at her. "I'm not certain. I haven't considered it." He paused, then he looked at her again. "Before God made you, he told me never to eat from that tree. He said, 'When you eat from it you will surely die.'"

"What does it mean to die?"

Ish's eyes glistened. "God said dying is when your spirit—the essence of yourself—no longer has union with His Spirit." He swallowed hard. "And then, your spirit is separated from your body."

"That's frightening," she whispered. Her lower lip trembled.

"I don't understand all the implications, but He seemed grieved. I don't want that to happen. I decided to avoid that tree."

"Did He tell you to avoid it?"

"No," Ish said slowly, "but He said when I eat from it I will die. *When* I eat from it—as if it's something I'll certainly do. When He spoke, His eyes were sad, and I felt like crying. I didn't want to go near it after that. I won't eat from that tree." He narrowed his eyes at the distant tree.

This was puzzling. Ishah couldn't understand it. The Creator had issued a command, and Ish was determined to obey. He listened to Yahweh's voice, exactly as she did. They both desired to carry out all His instructions, recalling His words, pondering them, and obeying. Why would her husband eat this fruit God had said *not* to eat?

Sitting in silence, both stared at The Forbidden Tree, contemplating this mystery.

"Can I eat from that tree?" Ishah asked. "Or was the command only to you?"

Turning quickly, Ish's eyes bored into hers. He didn't blink. His brow furrowed.

"God gave me this command before He made you." Ish articulated each word distinctly, one by one. "But everything He's said since then has applied to us both. You're part of me. You came from my body. We're one. Though He gave the command directly to me, because you're mine, it seems this command is for you, too."

"God said that you had things to tell me."

Ish nodded, rubbing at the back of his neck and fixing his unfocused gaze on some point over her shoulder. He looked as if his mind were preoccupied. There seemed to be more he wanted to say, the implications causing him to grow agitated.

He burst out, gesturing with his hands. "I'm certain the fruit will affect us both—we're one flesh. This is an instruction we should both obey! For some reason, God entrusted this instruction to me. I don't want to die! I don't want *you* to die! Please, don't eat the fruit from that tree. Don't even touch it!"

Ish's eyes were wet and rimmed in red as they stared into hers. His breathing was ragged, and his tone alarmed. Her eyes moistened in response. She grasped his hands to still them.

"Of course, I won't," she whispered solemnly.

Drawing her into his arms, Ish looked steadily into her eyes. With one fingertip, he tipped her face upward. "Thank you. You're my helper. You're made to fight alongside me. Please help me to avoid eating the fruit from that tree." His eyes pled with her. "The words the Creator used make it seem inescapable. I don't want to disobey Him."

"You won't," Ishah assured him gravely. "Neither of us will eat that fruit."

Continuing to gaze at her, Ish ever so slowly lowered his face to hers. Emotion flickering in the depths of his eyes, he paused. Ishah could taste the fragrance of his breath. Ish's scent awakened the yearning again. Studying his mouth and the smooth surface of his upper lip, she lifted her face and leaned into him—pressing her chest against his warmth.

Tenderly, he touched his lips to hers. *A kiss!* That was what she would call these tender expressions of affection bestowed upon her by the Creator and by Ish—kisses.

Her husband's lips were soft and warm, their taste inviting. Savoring the sensation, she closed her eyes. Responding to his mouth's pressure, she returned his kiss. Her arms twined about his waist of their own accord. Softly, he kissed her again and then a third time before he pulled back to look into her eyes. What Ish did stirred her! It was exhilarating!

She gazed back at him. Then she snuggled more closely

against his body. Something inside felt different, energized in some way she didn't understand, both from the connection she had felt as he asked for her help and from the remembrance of his lips.

Thank you, Yahweh!

God's presence seemed very near as they sat locked in one another's arms. Ishah felt God's joy in their satisfaction with each other. Their Creator approved. Ish kissed the top of her head, and she squeezed him tightly, hugging him to herself.

"Baaaa!" a loud bleating sound occurred right beside them. They both jumped. Turning, they looked into the face of a gentle animal with thick, white hair.

"Baaaa!" it said again.

Both burst into laughter. Ishah didn't know why this was funny, but it was. She released Ish and ran her hands through the animal's curly hair. Ish rubbed behind its ear.

"This is the female sheep, a ewe." Craning his neck, he looked around and then pointed. "There's the male, a ram—see his horns. I named them yesterday and was impressed by the thickness and warmth of their wool. I think they'll be useful to us somehow."

The female sheep grazed in the new green grass and worked her way over to the ram, which had a curving hard substance coming from each side of its head—horns, apparently. They touched noses and bumped heads together; then both lay down under the shade tree where Ish and Ishah sat. The sheep continued to chew even after they settled into the grass.

Ish looked down and found Ishah's hand, lacing his fingers through hers. Then he looked into the distance. Several of the animals came closer as they grazed.

"See the others." He pointed at some large animals. "God brought them to be named, male and female. Those are oxen." Then, one after another, he labeled other nearby coupled creatures.

Off in the distance, Ishah noticed even more, two by two. Some were eating. Some were jumping about in play. Others rolled in the grass. Ish indicated various pairs, telling her what they were. Some type of understanding seemed to exist between each pair. Several of the coupled pairs were engaged in an activity that joined their bodies in a way unassociated with sleeping or eating.

"Why do they do that?" she asked Ish, pointing at the joined animals in the distance.

"I'm not certain, but they all seem to do it."

Ish looked down into Ishah's eyes, steadily holding her gaze. She met his eyes evenly. Another mystery. But, as she felt the intensity of his eyes urging her toward him, pleading for some type of unidentified response, she realized that inherent within their natures was knowledge of the action the joined animals performed.

She wasn't sure yet what it was. But, she realized with a start, she *would* know.

Ish leaned toward her and kissed her on the forehead.

Then he told her about the different types of animals he had seen yesterday. Most of them had scattered. She laughed at his descriptions. The ones that had lingered were ones he thought might be useful. He said he didn't know why. It simply seemed it would be so.

They discussed everything God had told them today. There was still so much they didn't know, but He had given them knowledge and the ability to learn. However, because of how He had made them, many of their actions were innate, performed intuitively.

She seemed to be made to respond to Ish on a deep emotional level. A nurturing response rose within her at his words, expressions, or even the sounds he made. Ish exhibited the same emotional responsiveness, delighting in showing her each thing and in seeing her reaction. He seemed protective of her, as she was of him.

He was also clearly designed to organize and categorize all the parts of their world. This was an intrinsic part of him. She longed to work together with him, helping him. All her desires centered on this.

There was far more mystery than Ish thought. They had barely begun knowing, listening, learning, and loving one another. Clearly, there was more they had yet to discover.

Within their cores attraction simmered. As they gazed into one another's eyes, her body responded. She observed this same reaction in him whenever he looked at her and touched her. Some of their interactions were governed by this intense physical attraction—like their kisses.

Yahweh, their God and Creator, had obviously created them to do this.

CHAPTER NINE

RELAXED AGAINST ISHAH'S silken body under the shady tree, Ish pondered each spoken word, joint activity, and enjoyment. He paused on one memory. Overpowered by his love for Ishah, he had yearned to be closer, longing to meld them into one again, to crawl inside her somehow to rejoin his missing rib bones and flank. But this made no sense, for her genesis had been inside him.

Uncertain what to do with this longing he had pressed his mouth to hers. She had called it a kiss. He mused over the taste and smell of her breath, the warmth of her lips, and the awareness of God's joy and approval. Other than their joint adoration of Yahweh, that had been the best part of the day. This day, spent with her, surpassed the previous one. It was much more satisfying than naming all the animals.

The Creator had given him a beautiful world and another of his own kind—the woman, his wife—a mate to complete him in every way. God had given him Ishah, a friend, someone to share the joy of each new day. Everything about her filled him with happiness.

Thank you, my Creator, for all of these gifts!

The fullness of God warmed him, infusing him with joy, and Ish smiled. He might burst from thankfulness. He had felt this way all day. His heart overflowed with gratitude to Yahweh. Today was a very good day. Only the moment of his concern about The Forbidden Tree had kept the day from being flawless, but Ishah's reassurance of help was a relief and a gift.

Now the sun fell toward the horizon, bringing evening again. Ish turned his mind away from The Tree of the Knowledge of Good and Evil. They would avoid it. Tomorrow they would work together! With great pleasure, he anticipated working.

"Let's return to the river," he said. "I'm thirsty."

Rousing, Ishah uttered a small sound of agreement, as if just now recognizing her own thirst. They rose from their restful position, and Ish reflected on all these pleasures as they strolled back, hand in hand. He loved the way her hand fit into his. The interlacing of their fingers met his desire to be nearer to her.

"We need to discern how we can cultivate the soil." His considerations simply popped out of his mouth. He desired to share everything with Ishah.

"Do you have any ideas?"

"We could walk together with the animals where no grass has sprouted yet. I could call them to come help us, but they're now scattered. Not all of them would hear me." He paused. An idea shaped itself in his mind. "I'd like to make a tool—a useful object—to help us turn the dirt."

"A *tool*?" Looking puzzled yet intrigued, she stared up at him, the pursing of her lips lingering over this new word.

Fixated on her puckered lips, Ish bent to place a peck of a kiss upon them, which she returned. "Perhaps we can think of something that will work."

Her eyes sparkled as she smiled back at him.

They topped the hill and paused to survey the river. Some of the larger birds—ducks, geese, and swans—now floated close to the river's edge. Parts of the riverbank were covered with rocks. Other sections had grassy banks, and there were marshy spots with tall grass growing in them. Here Ish detected several types of ducks hiding.

That the grass had grown today was evident. The birds all busied themselves with it, using it for some purpose that caused each pair to bustle about working together. Everything in the Garden buzzed and hummed with activity. All the creatures worked, as if preparing for something. All grew rapidly and abundantly, almost before their very eyes.

"I have an idea," he said. "Maybe the grass can be used to fashion a tool to turn the soil."

But how?

Perplexed, Ishah stared at him, but he couldn't answer her unasked question. He hadn't quite deciphered this yet. His mind turned over the puzzle. The challenge made him happy, as if Yahweh had designed him to be fulfilled by this type of work. He felt as if God smiled at him.

Their God *created*; Ish took joy in creating as well.

Ish refocused on Ishah. "Some idea about rocks and grass is forming in my mind. But I don't have it all sorted out yet. Let's look at the rocks and see whether we can find any that are the right size. Then in the morning we'll see what we can do."

At the shoreline, they separated, considering the few stones by the river. There weren't many, but some had sharp edges, and they looked as if they'd work for his idea. Ish hoped he could assemble the idea that formulated in his thoughts. It intrigued him. They gathered the rocks of correct size and shape—only eight—and placed them on the shore where they had slept last night. This location where Ishah had been formed was precious to him.

"I'm going to drink now," she said.

While envisioning the tool and gathering the stones, Ish had forgotten his thirst. The dryness of his mouth now came to the fore of his thoughts. He went with her.

Both lay at the water's edge, smiling at one another's reflections before dipping in their hands. The day had been warm, so they gulped the water down. Ish felt it sloshing about within. He plunged in his arms to determine the depth. His fingertips just grazed the bottom. The water was invigorating, cool, and inviting.

Yesterday, some of the animals had waded in, staying near the edge where the river ran slowly. And now, many birds floated about in the stream. This seemed like a good idea. Swinging around to sit on the edge, Ish dangled his feet in the river.

Then he stood.

The water reached above his knees and felt crisp, biting, and cold. Enjoying the sensation, he laughed out loud. After the heat of the day, the cool water refreshed him. The river's flowing movement pressed against him, but it was easy to stand his ground. On the bottom, his feet detected pebbles, small rocks, and soil that squished between his toes, muddying the water.

Inquisitive, Ishah studied him. He grinned at her then waded into the river.

The current challenged his balance, especially when he lifted his feet. The river bottom sloped gradually, and soon the water reached his waist. With his toes, he detected the downward slope now dropped off sharply. Farther out in the river, the current flowed rapidly. Deciding not to go there, he turned toward Ishah watching him from the bank.

"Get in! It's perfect after the hot day!"

She stuck her feet in and flashed him a wide grin. "It feels good!"

Wading toward him with sinuous motion, she lithely lifted each foot like one of the long-legged birds, delicate and graceful. Her walking was better than his now, even wading through thigh-high water. She was magnificent! When she reached him, the water leveled right below her breasts, capturing his eyes and intriguing him in a warm and inviting way.

"Now what?" she asked.

He dragged his eyes to her face. "I'm going to stick my head in."

All day, his head had perspired in the hot sun. This would feel good!

Of course, he didn't know what he was doing. In went his head, and up he came gagging and choking as he coughed and spat out water. Ishah's expression had changed completely. Shocked and concerned, she clutched him.

Finally, he could talk. "Do *not* breathe under the water." He coughed deeply one final time.

Relief spread across her face.

Ish repeated his attempt. This time he slowly lowered his body, took a deep breath, and held it. Down he went. Relishing the cold sensation on the top of his sweaty, sunbaked head, he remained under until he needed to breathe. Being covered in the cool water felt glorious. Surfacing, water streaming off him, Ish flicked his wet hair back and laughed heartily. His laughter reverberated across the river.

"That feels fantastic!"

After watching his more successful attempt, Ishah slid into the river. When her chin was even with the water, she breathed in deeply, held it, and dipped under. Her long dark hair fanned out around her, floating on the surface. Soon she bobbed back up, smiling.

"That was glorious!" She grinned widely.

Smiling they jointly experimented, each investigating the moving water, testing the current with their hands and their bodies. Sometimes they bumped together as they moved with the rapidly flowing water or resisted it. Chortling gleefully, they tried to stay upright, often steadying the other or collapsing against one another, overcome by their laughter.

Eventually, Ish took his eyes off the ever-changing water to smile at Ishah. Her lips were now purplish and her teeth chattered. Where her shoulders and arms showed above the surface, there were tiny bumps on her skin.

What's wrong with her? Obviously, it was time to get out.

Grabbing her hand—surprisingly cold—Ish headed toward shore, tugging her behind. Why had this happened? He wasn't cold. Was this because her body was smaller than his? Since she wasn't as tall as he, the water covered more of her body. Maybe this was the cause. As they waded toward the bank, she shivered and shook uncontrollably.

This concerned him.

Ish plucked her out of the river and into the curve of his body, entwining her within the embrace of his arms and legs. As he cradled her upon his lap, he turned her back toward the setting sun. Surely the sun on one side and the heat of his body on the other would warm her.

"The sun will dry us. It's been so hot today, it shouldn't take long."

As he said this, he felt a panicky sense of urgency. He hoped this was true. It had worked with the dew, but he couldn't be certain. Continuing to shiver, she locked her arms around his chest, pressing tightly against him.

"You feel warm" she said.

Wrapping his arms more snugly about her, he drew her even closer.

This effect was unexpected. He felt incredibly careless for suggesting they get in. Why hadn't he taken better care of her? It hadn't been wise to get in the water when the day grew cool. That would have been better when the day was hot. He had so much to learn.

As Ishah dried, she shivered less. Apparently, no damage had been done by his incomprehension of God's rules for His creation. Her long hair was still very wet, though. It dripped down her back. This wouldn't aid the warming-up process.

Lifting each lock, Ish spread the damp tresses, holding each so the sun could shine on it and through it. He enjoyed running his fingers through her hair. She pressed snugly against him.

He liked this. *This is much more pleasurable than the cool water.*

What a joy it was to feel her body touching his. It stirred something within him that he didn't understand—like when they kissed. It made him happy. He wanted to be even closer. He felt a hunger, a yearning, for her nearness. Ish embraced her body more firmly.

He felt God's delight, as if He had designed this to happen, creating her to fill him with joy. The Creation Song came to his mind. Yahweh seemed very near, pleased with them.

With the same pleasure on her face, Ishah gazed up at him. He smiled into her eyes and pressed his mouth to hers. With equal enthusiasm, she kissed him back. Then they both beamed and laughed out loud, elated with each other.

"Warm yet?" he said, laughing.

"Kissing you makes me warm inside!" She smiled widely at him.

"It makes me ecstatic with joy! Yahweh is so good to us! It's good not to be alone."

How could he contain all this happiness? There had to be some sort of outlet for this passionate enthusiasm. What was it? Her bright and shining eyes fixed on his, as if awaiting some sort of action on his part. Gently, Ish nipped her nose with his teeth.

She squealed with laughter. Grinning broadly, he wrapped his arms even more snugly about her.

The sun vanished, and the stars twinkled into view. In warm embrace, they observed the sky. The sharply bright stars peeked out, one after another. Eventually, the subtle moon made its appearance, seeming to rise over the horizon later than the night before, and appearing a little diminished in size. Still, it cast a gentle, silvery glow over everything.

This was interesting. It revealed something about the creation, but Ish didn't know what. Their God had told them the sun and moon would help them keep track of seasons, days, and years. Ish hadn't discerned what this meant yet, but he would watch and learn.

Still warming, they gazed at the heavens, rejoicing in the Creator God and His beautiful world. Elated with each other, they remained with their bodies bound tightly together until it was completely dark. Ishah nestled her head gently against his chest. Breathing in her delicate fragrance mingled with the scent of the river, he layered soft kisses on the top of her head.

"Ish," she murmured against his skin, "the pulsing of your body soothes me."

"Pulsing?"

As she looked up, her brow shadowed her gleaming eyes from the silvery light. "When you held me against your body last night, I felt a steady beat pulsing within you—a rhythm; it lulled me to sleep. I can actually hear it in your chest."

"I wonder what it is."

"Perhaps I have the same thing. See if you can hear it within me."

Falling back in the circle of his arms, Ishah arched and lifted her chin, tossing her now-dry hair cascading over his arm and thigh. Admiring the soft radiance of her skin, Ish leaned to press his ear below the curving bones at the base of her neck, right above the swell of her beckoning breasts. Her skin felt warm. He heard the thumping she mentioned.

"You have it as well!" He peered into her eyes. "A *heart*. It must be the center of the strong emotions we feel. Maybe it also has a physical function. The love I feel for our Creator and for you seems to be centered there."

"For me as well." Sighing contently, she snuggled in tightly against his chest once more.

Thick and bright, the stars covered them, luminous from above.

"So beautiful," she said quietly. "Our God is so creative! Show me the animal from yesterday."

Noticing the stars were in slightly different places, Ish studied them. Then he examined the moon again. Its path looked the same as yesterday, though its size was diminished. The stars and the moon behaved in dissimilar ways in the night sky. Interesting. He would meditate on this.

Pointing to the configuration that reminded him of a particularly hairy, lumbering creature—a bear—he described it, one by one indicating its outline in the stars.

"Hmm," was her only response. She hadn't seen the bear yet.

Enthralled with the beauty of the heavens, each breathed slow and deep, perfectly content.

"How's your side tonight?" she asked.

Ish bent to kiss her forehead before answering. "Still tender, but much better than it was this morning. I'm glad we enjoyed the Creator's rest today. As much as I wanted to work and turn the soil, it was better to rest."

"Yahweh used His rest to restore your body. He's wise."

"Yes. And good. I think I'd better lie with the sore side up again, though."

Gently, Ish laid her down, cradling her before him as he had the previous night. The earth felt warm, and their bodies pressing together comforted him. Blissful contentment filled him.

"We now know more about the Creator God's instructions," he said quietly.

"And, we know more about our earth. Now that I've seen, I can comprehend more of what the Creator first said to us. Tell me again about The Forbidden Tree."

This topic made him uneasy. He shifted uncomfortably.

"It's the Tree of the Knowledge of Good and Evil. The Creator said that when I eat from it, I will surely die. I won't eat the fruit from that tree. Thank you for promising to help me obey. Let's not even touch that tree, or its fruit." His voice cracked. "Please!"

Overcome by intense protectiveness, he broke off and kissed Ishah's shoulder, squeezing her securely to him. She reached back to pat his cheek.

"I'll help you," she whispered. "We won't touch that tree or its fruit."

Her words set his mind at ease. Ish took a deep breath.

"I need your help. You're my helper. You provide what I lack." Gratefulness to their God overwhelmed Ish, and he kissed Ishah's head.

Together, they reviewed every one of the Creator's instructions and the history He had revealed today about the creation. It had been a beautiful day of rest and discovery. However, there were many mysteries they had yet to solve.

"I still don't understand how we're to bear many young and increase our numbers by being fruitful," Ishah said. "How are we to do this? What are we to do?"

"I don't know. I'm not sure about it either."

"Do you think the animals are to do this, too? Is that what the Creator meant when He said they're all to reproduce according to their kind?"

"I believe so. I think His words encompass all of His creation. The animals' response to His command might have something to do with the frenzied way they act around each other."

Ishah lay quietly for a while. "Do you think when the animal pairs join their bodies together it's because of this command? They all seem to do it. What do you think?"

"Yes. I wondered the same thing. But it might be something else entirely."

"Does our kissing have something to do with this? And our lying together right now, as we prepare to sleep?"

"I think it does, but I don't understand this yet. Our physical make-up is different from each other, like the animals. My body responds to yours in an interesting way, like the male of each animal pair. I yearn for your nearness when your body is close to mine like this."

Ish drew her even closer, giving her a tender kiss on the shoulder. There was something more, but he couldn't explain it to her or to himself for that matter. He didn't fully comprehend his response to her.

"But," he said, "I don't know if any of this is related to the Creator's command. I don't know what we're supposed to do."

"We'll learn what He means, I'm sure. He'll tell us what to do, or it will come to us instinctively, or He'll cause it to happen."

He kissed her shoulder again. She squeezed his hand that wrapped around her waist. They both lay silently for a while, pondering all they had discussed.

"It's good not to be alone," Ish whispered to Ishah. Of that, he was very certain.

"I've never been alone, but I know it's good to be with you," she murmured sleepily.

She fell silent again. In low tones, he sang the Creation Song into her ear, barely above a whisper. Gradually her breathing slowed, and she lay heavy in his arms. Holding her near, Ish bestowed soft little kisses into her hair as he mused over these questions.

How were they to multiply and increase in number?

How would they bear young—living beings like themselves?

Did it have anything to do with the joy he felt in her presence?

Was the response of his body and the elation he felt when her body was pressed against his part of the puzzle? Or did it mean something else entirely?

Perhaps they were to use their hands to form creatures like themselves from the dust, as he had been formed. It didn't seem likely; how would these live and breathe? He couldn't figure this out. How could they obey the Creator if they couldn't discern what was required?

Yahweh, my God, please show us how to obey You.

God didn't speak. His silence had always meant that He was going to teach him a lesson experientially. That was how he had learned what it meant to be alone. It had been a powerful lesson. Yahweh knew him better than he knew himself. Ish was eager for God to show him.

Under the canopy of stars, the pleasure and presence of the Creator filled Ish's heart as he held God's most precious gift in his arms. God had made them for each other. Gratitude for Ishah imbued him, filling and overflowing. His eyes moistened. Softly he kissed her shoulder. As he whispered his thanks to Yahweh, his sense of well-being grew within.

God had given him all he needed.

God would reveal how to obey Him. Every day He taught them more, opening their minds to comprehend His world and His instructions. At peace, Ish relaxed and closed his eyes.

Tranquil sleep.

CHAPTER TEN

THE JOYFUL MORNING songs of trilling birds pecked away at Ish's consciousness, but it wasn't until the sunlight illuminated his face that he was dragged into wakefulness. Clearly this regularity of the sun had been built into God's creation.

The nearness of God surged into Ish's consciousness. *Thank you, Yahweh!*

He and Ishah stretched together as they had the day before, noting the dampness of the dew and the warmth of one another's limbs. There was still some discomfort in his side, but it was only tender deep inside, where it continued to heal.

Looking over her shoulder, Ishah said, "You didn't moan. Do you feel better?"

"It's much better than the first day, and even better than yesterday."

As he spoke, he squeezed Ishah and kissed the nape of her neck. Holding her filled him with gratefulness. He wanted to discuss Yahweh.

"Before we get up and start our work," he whispered against her ear, "which of Yahweh's words do you want to talk about?"

"Let's talk about His first instructions again: 'Be fruitful and multiply, increase in number, and bear many young of your kind. Fill the earth.' It intrigues me."

"My mind keeps turning to that, too. I was thinking about it after you fell asleep, so I asked God to show us what to do. I feel certain He will."

"Did He sit down and talk to you?"

"No. I felt overwhelmed with my love for you, so I thanked Yahweh. Then His presence reassured me, filling me with peace. I know we'll discern what to do."

Ishah rolled to face him. He gazed into her captivating eyes.

Each time he beheld her it was like seeing her for the first time. Her beauty enthralled him. He was astounded that God had created her from his own body. *How can it be?* Overcome by emotion, he caressed her forehead with his lips.

"Ishah," he said softly against her skin, "I love you so much."

"I love you, too. Do you think our love has something to do with the Creator's instructions?"

"It seems so. I was so happy to have you sleeping in my arms. My love for you felt intense and strong. I could tell God was pleased—I felt His pleasure. He reminded me that He made us for each other and that He has given me all I need. Sometimes He lets us learn from our experiences. I think this is such a time."

"Yes," she said with calm assurance. "He'll show us."

Ishah's eyes roamed away from his, taking in the other aspects of his face. Gently, she stroked her fingers down the line of his jaw and across his chin. Fixing her eyes on his mouth, she traced one fingertip very lightly around his lips. It tickled.

"The shadow on your face shows more clearly today," she whispered. "This beautiful blackness draws my eyes to your lips."

Looking at his upper lip in particular, she leaned in to kiss his mouth. Engrossed, he returned her kiss. When she pulled back, she tugged gently at his lower lip with her teeth. His heart thudded. Warmth flooded his chest and gut. Tracing his lips with her fingertip once more, she gazed into his eyes.

Grasping her head between his hands, he pressed his mouth hard against hers. A shiver of anticipation washed over him. He closed his eyes and kissed her over and over again. When he opened them, her patient eyes looked back at him eagerly, waiting for him.

What does she want? What is this longing?

He was uncertain how to proceed. What was he to do?

Keeping his eyes on hers, he stroked her cheek with his forefinger. Her eyes studied him, acceptance easing into her expression. He looked at her cheeks. Her face was just as soft and smooth as previously. Ish rubbed his own chin. His lower face was now even rougher to the touch. This was such an enigma! She leaned closer and peered at his chin.

"It looks like small hairs," she said. "Do you suppose this is hair growing from your face? I wonder why it's growing only on your face and not mine."

"It's rougher today. Will it continue to grow each day?"

Ceasing her examination, she smiled into his eyes. "I suppose we'll find out."

Though longing to lie here in the grass kissing her, Ish's thoughts turned to their work. He was eager to try his idea. He sat up. His side was sore, but he no longer felt it tugging at his skin. The scar was now pink. It looked well on the way to healing.

Ishah bent to examine the scar. She looked concerned.

"The Creator did this to make me." She lightly touched the wound. Ish watched her fingertip slowly caress the scar through the dampness of the dew on his hipbone. Again he felt a surge of expectancy, but he wasn't sure why. "I'm glad it's much better, though seeing this makes me feel attached to you. It's a reminder that I'm part of you."

"I'd gladly experience the momentary discomfort again to have you."

Lifting his eyes from the wound, he looked into her eyes. His heart thudded as she smiled at him. The pain of her creation bonded him even more tightly to her. Gently, he kissed her nose.

They both rose, exclaiming over the sparkling sunlight on the dew and then relieving themselves away from the water. This was something they had discovered needed to be done periodically. Apparently, what went in had to come out.

When they lay down on the riverbank, Ish inspected how this newly growing facial hair altered his appearance.

Ishah considered his reflection. "Your face is handsome, my husband."

Meeting her eyes, Ish smiled then dipped his hands into the

water, dispersing their mirrored images. Both drank long and deep from the river. Then Ish turned to the pile of stones they had gathered last night, pondering how exactly to use them. His idea sparked excitement as he remembered all the particulars. He couldn't wait to find out whether it worked!

"Let's gather some fruit and bring it back here to eat." He leapt to his feet. "I want to see whether there are any tree branches we can break off to use for our tool."

"Can we do that? Do the branches break?"

"We'll have to see." As they walked up the hill hand in hand, Ish told Ishah about his idea. "Yesterday, I noticed the ducks and geese using the grass by the river to make something. I thought it might be useful to us as well."

"How?"

"Maybe we can find a forked tree branch. Then we can secure the stones to it with the long grass. This would make a tool for turning the soil."

With a puzzled expression, Ishah stared at him as if she couldn't visualize what he planned. He couldn't explain it—his idea was sketchy, and he was uncertain how to carry it out.

When they crested the hill, they surveyed the Garden spread out below them. The animals were already awake, eating the grass and making their way to the river farther downstream. Trying to detect suitable branches, Ish examined the trees but couldn't see through the thick leaves, so they strolled down the hill.

At each tree Ish evaluated the branches, looking for the right shape and length. Finally he found one, though he'd have to climb the tree to retrieve it. Ready to hoist himself up, he placed one foot in the tree fork and grabbed the trunk.

"I'm smaller than you." Ishah laid a restraining hand on his arm. "And this is a small tree. We don't want to damage the tree more than we have to. Also, your side isn't healed completely. Let me climb up to get it." Awaiting his decision, she looked at him expectantly.

Ish hesitated. This was something neither of them had done before. There were unknown factors, and he felt protective, especially after his blunders yesterday. But as he evaluated the tree and considered her smaller size, he realized she was right. She was made to help him, and it made sense for her to do this.

"You can stand right below me," she said. "Simply tell me which branch you want."

Ish relaxed under her touch. "We don't know all the rules of the Creator's earth yet, so be careful. Remember when I went under the water without holding my breath, and when we didn't realize how cold you'd get at sunset? There may be something unknown about climbing."

Looking solemnly into his eyes, Ishah nodded. Then she hoisted herself into the fork of the tree. She searched for a place to put her foot, made the step, and looked to him for guidance. He pointed to the fork above her. She climbed to the place he indicated.

Ish hadn't seen his wife from this angle before. The view was tantalizing!

Overcome by the sensations racing through him, he closed his eyes and focused on his body's strong reactions. He opened his eyes again. With a quizzical expression, she looked down at him. *My God! Look at her! You made her for me! Thank you!* Her beauty staggered him.

"You're beautiful," he stammered. "I can't begin to tell you how alluring you look."

She smiled with pleasure. "Which branch?"

When Ish pointed, his hand shook. "To the right of your foot. In the fork. See it?"

What was wrong with him? He hadn't reacted to her like this before.

Ishah touched the right limb, and he nodded. As she pulled on it, the entire tree swayed. Ish stood below, so he could catch her if needed. To separate the limb, she tugged at an angle. As it pulled away, the branch cracked sharply. Steadying herself, Ishah yanked. The branch swung down. He grabbed it and finished tearing it off.

As Ishah picked her way back down, Ish wrenched the branch free, surprised by the strength of its attachment. It was difficult to free it from the bark. He dropped it and turned toward Ishah as she leapt from the lowest fork.

She examined him carefully. "What happened while I was up there?"

"I don't know whether I can explain it. Something about

seeing you up there from down here. I felt overcome by it."

"I wonder why." She moved closer.

"It had something to do with your appearance."

Stepping nearer, she caressed the crest of his hipbone. He could smell her hair.

"Do you want to kiss me," she said, "or drag the branch to the river?"

Kiss her!

Ish grabbed her up into his arms. This wasn't like their earlier kisses. Some strong passion impelled him. With one hand at the small of her back and the other behind her head, he pressed her firmly against his body. Urgently, he kissed her repeatedly, parting her lips with his tongue—he needed to be inside of her. His ardor compelled him. He didn't know where this was going. It was as if he had lost his mind and could only taste her breath and feel her body.

Forget the branch and the stones waiting by the river.

Forget the soil that needed to be turned.

Breathless, he pulled away. What was that look in her eyes? She'd never before worn this expression.

"Why did you stop?" Her voice quavered.

"I remembered all I want to accomplish today."

"You kissed me differently. Why?"

"I don't really understand it. It was as if I was thinking with my body."

"I want to kiss you like that again. Can we do that later?"

"Absolutely," he said.

Grinning at her, Ish picked up the branch. With hips pressed together and arms intertwined, they walked back to the river. They forgot the fruit. After depositing the branch by the river, they circled back. Ish didn't want to let go of her. He knew he'd lost his mind. How did he forget the fruit? What was wrong with him?

But he felt as surrounded and filled by the presence of the Creator God as he had in the first moments of his life, as if Yahweh beamed at their delight with one another, just as He had when He blessed them after Ishah's creation. Ish knew they were doing exactly what God had created them to do. Love for the Creator and for Ishah swelled within his chest.

How could he contain all this happiness?

Arriving near the river again, he released Ishah and jogged to the water's edge to gather some tall grass. As he worked, he hummed a melodic bird-like song, creating a tune that sounded as happy as he felt inside. So this was why they sang! Ish tugged the grass stems straight out of their bases, pulling away the pliable inner parts. Humming his melody, he gathered an armful and headed back to his gorgeous wife.

Watching him with an intrigued expression, Ishah stood with her hands on her hips. As she caught his eye, she flashed him a dazzling smile.

Ish felt like those agitated animal pairs he had watched on the first day, rolling around in the grass and joyfully chasing each other. Apparently, they all felt the same. Chasing Ishah across the Garden would be a good use of all this energy. Grinning back at her, he sat down to see what he could accomplish in his half-crazed state.

"I want to attach the rocks to the branch using the long stems of grass." He poked and yanked at the material they'd gathered. "To bind it in some way that connects the rocks, so it can be used to turn the earth. But my mind isn't working. I don't know whether I can figure this out."

Ishah placed her hands on his, stopping his frenzied activity. "My husband, slow your breathing. Relax."

Ish dropped everything to stare at her. Ishah leaned closer. Gazing at her, Ish turned his eyes toward her mouth. One corner was wet, right at the place where her lips met.

"Ishah, I want to spend all day kissing you." He ran his fingertip across her lower lip, gently caressing the damp corner.

"I would love to do that."

Anticipation flushed his face, tingling at the corners of his mouth.

"But . . . I also want to turn the soil so the animals will have new grass to eat. The entire day of rest I looked forward to it. I'm excited to create this tool. I can't quit thinking about it. What should I do? I don't know what I want most!"

"We can kiss later," she said calmly, "when the sun is gone. We've already decided we will. Remember?"

"Yes . . . "

"But when the sun is up we need to work. You still want to work, don't you?"

Ish nodded. She was right.

He jumped up, rushed back to the river, flopped onto the ground, and drank long and deep. Then he plunged his head into the cold water, holding it underwater as long as possible. Very calming. When he lifted his head, he heard her giggling.

She should be giggling, he thought, wiping the water from his eyes. *Her husband has lost his mind . . . Okay, back to work.*

Giving her a sidelong glance, he settled down cross-legged, trying to discern how to connect the stones to the branch. Eating and working together, they stripped off the smaller branches, saving these because they were lighter. Ishah could lift and use these easily.

They discussed how to wind the grass around the branch, so it anchored a rock to each fork. The grass was wet and pliable and worked well, but they couldn't discern how to keep it wound. Ishah concentrated on twisting and wrapping the grass around itself to secure it. Ish worked on positioning the rocks so a sharp edge of each rock dragged along the soil without scraping the grass that bound it to the branch.

"I've got it!" Ishah exclaimed.

She showed Ish how to wind the grass back on itself, tying it into a knot.

"Good! The Creator told me I needed a helper. He's right! I lose my mind, and you calm me down." Ish grinned at her. "I can't tie the grass, but you can."

At his words, a satisfied expression spread across Ishah's face. She dipped her head.

They then took her tying technique and combined it with his rock placement, and they had their tool. Ish named it a *plow*. He was excited they could build this together.

The grass that had dried in the sun while they worked had become difficult to tear. Did all the grass need to dry? Could they use the plow while most of the grass was still moist?

They tried the plow and realized they needed to let the grass dry. Drying seemed to strengthen the bindings. They lay the plow in the sun. Retreating to the shade of a nearby tree to eat more fruit, they waited for the sun to do its work. The sun was nearly directly overhead now, so it wouldn't take long. It was refreshing to sit together in the shade, eating and talking.

But Ish was eager to try the tool. After what felt like a long while, he jumped up to examine the grass. The rocks seemed securely anchored to the branch.

This part of the Garden had been trampled by the animals and was already blanketed with thick grass. So Ish balanced on his shoulder the plow and one of the little branches that still had leaves. He reached for Ishah's hand, and they headed up the hill.

When they arrived at the first undisturbed area, where the soil lay soft and brown, Ish pushed the plow before him, turning the seed-laden soil. Ishah walked beside him, pulling the small branch behind her. They walked a long stretch and then turned to evaluate their work.

The plow was operational—it worked—but turning the soil appeared to have a better outcome where Ishah had pulled the branch. Ish's pushing had shoved the dirt into a heap, so he tried pulling the plow. When they compared the two, it had worked very well.

"I think we should start in the middle of the Garden and work our way out," Ish said. "If I can figure out how, I might be able to fasten the plow to one of the animals. If the ox or donkey pulls it, we can cover more ground by using a bigger branch."

"Good idea!" she said, taking his hand.

****

The Tree of Life and the Tree of the Knowledge of Good and Evil grew in the middle of the Garden. Ish's sense of order compelled him to begin there, but he grew tense as he led Ishah toward these trees. He had avoided this area since the Creator had spoken on the first day. He didn't want to eat from The Forbidden Tree and die. He didn't want anything about their lives to change; he loved his life with Ishah. How could it be possible that he would eat from that tree if he determined to avoid it?

Glancing at Ishah, he observed her peering at the two trees. Seeming to sense his tension, she gave him a supportive smile. As they circled the Tree of Life, she stayed close to him. They went around and around, moving farther out with each concentric circle, until they came to the halfway point between the two.

Then they moved to the base of the Tree of the Knowledge of Good and Evil. Ish had never before been this close to the ominous tree. A sense of foreboding beset him. He didn't even want to look at it, so he kept his head down. The urge to grab Ishah and run nearly overpowered him, but he felt compelled to complete their task, so grass would sprout everywhere.

As they plowed circles around The Forbidden Tree, Ish circled with extra caution. Taking a quick look at Ishah, he discovered she gazed intently at The Tree, studying it and looking up into the branches. Hardly any sunlight touched the ground here. As she looked, The Tree's shade shadowed her face.

"Ishah!" The tension in his voice sounded sharp. "Why are you looking at it?"

"I'm only curious. Nothing will happen. Neither of us is going to touch it or eat the fruit. I merely want to see what it looks like."

Ishah hadn't heard Yahweh's voice when He spoke the command. Ish had impressed on her all that the Creator had said, and he had warned her. But she didn't seem to have the same concern about The Tree. If she had heard the Creator, she would.

"I want to keep you safe. I don't want either of us to die." Ish spoke quietly this time, but he felt desperate for some reason. "Please help me. I don't want us to eat this fruit. We shouldn't even touch it."

She smiled gently at him and shook her head. "Of course, we won't."

Now they intersected their previous work around the Tree of Life, so they enlarged their loop to circle the two trees together, getting farther away with each lap. The more distance they gained, the more relaxed Ish became.

Ishah seemed sensitive to his mood. Her expression cheerful, she smiled at him. At first Ish gave her only a close-lipped partial smile. But the farther away they moved, the more real his smiles became in return. The tension eased from his body now that they were both safely away. With a long deep blast of breath, he exhaled.

It was done! They never needed to come here again. What a relief!

CHAPTER ELEVEN

ISH AND ISHAH continued to work, drawing near the cool shady trees where they had previously rested. Ish turned to peer at the sun. It was about halfway down to the horizon. Since they were both hot and sweaty from their labor, and the sun was still relatively high, this seemed a good time to play in the river.

"How about getting in the water now?"

Ishah didn't answer. She simply took off like a gazelle.

Ish hadn't known she could do that. Together they had walked and danced and skipped, but Ishah hadn't tried running yet. Her long hair whipped behind her. Ish sprinted after her. She had an earlier start, but his running had improved greatly.

Charging from the shade loped the two wolves, rushing as one to Ish's side. Their wolfish grins and lolling tongues caused him to smile even wider. What a surprise Ishah would have.

Ish and the wolves caught her. When they pulled even, her eyebrows shot up and she started laughing. Bursts of giggles made it difficult for her to maintain such a rapid pace. This caused Ish to laugh as he overtook her. The wolves barked and yipped. Together they all raced over the hill, past the spot where they usually slept, and to their drinking place.

Ishah leaped into the water with Ish right behind. Both went under then came bursting back up, peals of laughter ringing over the river's surface.

Back on the bank the wolves awaited them. Tails wagging. Wolfish grins lolling.

"The wolves like you," he said.

"And I like them. Let's do it again!"

Quickly, they waded back, and she raced up the hill. The wolves charged Ishah, yapping and barking around her. Watching her playfully zigzag a trail, he grinned as he ran hard to catch her. At the crest they turned, clasped hands, and ran down the hill alongside their wolf companions. Again, only they jumped in, but this time the wolves charged in a few paces.

The water sprayed around them, sparkling and glinting in the sunlight. Both grinned broadly at the other as they surfaced. Laughing for joy, Ish pulled Ishah toward him, hugging her tightly. Draping her arms about his neck, she beamed.

Into the deeper water, Ish drew her, dipping down so only their heads showed above the surface. Face to face, they glided through the water, Ishah's long black hair floating around them. Gazing lovingly into his eyes, she smoothed back his wet hair. Enjoying the tantalizing pressure of her breasts against his chest, he enveloped her in his arms.

With the river's current, they swayed and drifted, eyes fastened on one another.

Ishah kissed him then pressed her forehead to his, noses touching. They coasted in the current—heads together, bodies entangled in one another's arms and legs. Idyllic pleasure flooded Ish.

"Creator God, thank You for my Ishah," he whispered against her cheek.

"And, thank You for giving me to Ish." She nuzzled him. "And for wolves."

He chuckled.

Peaceful, they floated in the water together, intensely aware of each other and of the nearness of their God. Blissful tranquility!

"This is nice," she said quietly after a while. "It feels good after the hot sun and the dust. But I'm going to lie on the edge now to dry off, so I don't get so cold."

First kissing her, he then released her.

His eyes followed her as she stepped her way gracefully to the bank and climbed out. She lay on the grass with her eyes closed, her hair fanned out around her. Under a nearby tree, the wolves lay against one another, panting and drowsing in a shaft of sunlight.

Ish gazed at Ishah all the while he stayed in the river. *She's so lovely!* She didn't appear chilled, as she had yesterday. Her decision to get out was wise. Finally, Ish pulled himself up onto the bank. Opening her eyes and shielding them from the sun, she looked up at him.

"That was a good day's work, don't you think?" she said.

"Yes! I'm filled with gratitude to the Creator. With your help, I feel as though we're fulfilling our purpose on His earth. It was a good day!"

For a few moments, she lay smiling up at him. His words clearly pleased her.

"I've been thinking about this all day," she said. "I've got an idea that might help next time I climb a tree and you lose your mind."

Jumping to her feet, she grabbed his hand and tugged him along, heading for the tall grass along the river bend. She gathered grass, so he did the same. Soon their arms were full. Then she sat down right on the riverbank, sticking the ends of the grass into the water.

"I have an idea for braiding these together to make something to hold the fruit," she said. "I want to keep the grass wet while we work. Let me try this first. Then, if you can do the braiding, I'll weave together the braids you make." As she gave him these instructions, she sounded excited. Looking over her shoulder, she checked the sun. "If we both work fast, I think we can get it done before the sun sets. Then it can dry overnight."

She crafted her idea, and Ish watched a cord of braided grass take shape. Copying her handiwork with three pieces of grass, he produced the same type of cord. Taking their cords, she wove other grass strips over and under these braids to keep them side-by-side.

Smiling, she glanced at him. "Can you braid more cords while I wind these together?"

Already beginning to braid three more long pieces together, he nodded. "You're amazingly creative! The Creator placed His skill in you. How did you think of this?"

Pleased, she grinned at him. "I don't know. It kept working its way out in my mind as I considered how we bound the rocks to the branch."

While Ish braided, he watched her weave the cords, side by side. When she had it the size she wanted, she wove more grass to bind the side and ends, forming a container that could hold fruit or anything else they wanted to carry. Then she fashioned a long shoulder strap.

"Wife, this basket is wonderful!" She glanced up, cocking one eyebrow at the label he had attached. Ish held it, admiring what she'd done. "What a great idea! Braided grass will make a stronger cord. We definitely can have one of the animals help us; we'll be able to attach the plow with these stronger cords. You're remarkably clever!"

"I think it'll work," she said simply. "Let it dry, and we'll see."

The sun dropped below the horizon. As twilight fell, the stars began to twinkle opposite the sunset. Gathering the basket, they rose and headed back to their usual place. Twining his arm around her waist, Ish pulled Ishah close, his hip against hers. In response, she encircled his waist with her arms, leaning against him.

"I just realized how tired I am," she said. "But I feel satisfied and content."

"I'm happy with what we've accomplished. The more soil we turn, the more grass for the animals. Since God has given it, we need to try some, too."

"Yes. I can't wait to see what the cultivated ground looks like in the morning."

At the place by the riverbank where Ishah had been made— the most precious spot—they dropped into their usual sleeping positions. Ish pulled her close.

"Your kisses after I climbed the tree were the best part of the day," she said over her shoulder. "You promised more kissing."

Ish rolled Ishah onto her back and propped himself on his elbow, pulling her closer. She studied him expectantly. Gazing steadily at one another as the sky darkened and the creatures started their nighttime chorus, they lay pressed together.

Lightly, Ish traced the contours of her face glowing faintly in the darkness, marveling at the softness of her cheeks and her lips. Then, ever so slow and tender, he stroked his fingertips down her neck, over her chest, and across her breast, gently circling and caressing its captivating roundness. *So beautiful!* Grasping her waist, he pulled her nearer.

The moon had started its trek across the sky, and the subtle luminosity of their bodies gradually turned silver in the moon's soft light. They kept their eyes fixed on one another. Ish was struck by how lovely and enticing Ishah looked in the moonlight.

"I adore you," Ish whispered.

Lightly, he planted tiny pecks of kisses on her forehead, down her nose, across her eyelids, and over her cheek, lightly caressing her face with his lips. Then he pressed his mouth to hers. She sighed and nestled closer, twining her arms about his neck. This kiss was long and intense. They were getting better at their kissing, as they were their walking and everything else.

They looked deeply into one another's eyes.

Ishah yawned.

Ish laughed. She was so endearing! He laid his head down beside hers.

"It was a long day." He draped his arm across her waist. "Let's sleep. If the kissing was the best part, was any part of the day difficult?"

"Yes—seeing your tension and concern about that one tree."

"I don't want to eat the fruit and die."

"You won't, and I won't either. Neither of us will even touch it. Let's talk about the Creator as we fall asleep." She yawned widely once more.

In a whisper, Ish repeated all the instructions Yahweh had given. Then he recounted the six days of creation and the joy of the holy day of rest. Softly, he sang the Creation Song, but she remained silent. When he finished, he realized she had fallen asleep.

"It's good not to be alone," he whispered softly. "I'm glad to know you more each day. I long to listen to all you say, to learn all about you, and to love you with all I am."

Then he buried his face in her hair, so he could smell her

delicate fragrance as he drifted to sleep. God was near. Ishah was in his arms. He was a contented man.

Gracious Creator, I love you.

* * * *

When the sun rose, it beamed into Ish's face. Squinting, he opened his eyes and lay still a moment, confused. *What just happened?* Ishah's eyes and breasts and the urgency of her lips possessed his thoughts. A moment before, he had been kissing her passionately, his body pressed to hers. But that didn't seem possible, since she was clearly still sleeping.

Ish closed his eyes again, recalling the pleasure of having her against him, holding her face in his hands, feeling the soft smoothness of her cheeks, and then kissing her mouth repeatedly. Had he imagined that in his sleep? He must have.

A *dream*, he labeled these thoughts that had come as he slept. The heavy, tranquil sleep imaginings pulled him back toward them, but he opened his eyes and looked at Ishah.

Nestled against him on her back, her face pressed against his chest, she was shielded from the sun. The bright light hadn't hit her face yet, so she still slumbered peacefully. Ish studied her face. This was the first time he'd watched her sleep.

Breathtakingly beautiful, she reposed relaxed and peaceful. Full and alluring, her black lashes lay soft upon her cheeks. Her eyelids were dusky, and her lips puckered invitingly. All about him tumbled her long hair, draping his arm and chest. Ish inhaled her tantalizing scent.

Sweeping his eyes away from her face, he gazed at her supine body—her softly radiant skin, her sublimely exquisite form. The Creator God had known exactly how to shape her to captivate his very core. She took his breath away and filled him with desire and some emotion he hadn't yet discovered how to express.

"How is your side, my husband?" She had awakened.

Ish dragged his eyes back to her face. He hadn't even considered his side; he'd been so mesmerized by her beauty. She awed him.

"I didn't even think of it. I was watching you sleep. How I love you! You're dazzling in the morning sun."

"I love you, too." Smiling at him sleepily, she looked pleased.

Propping himself on his elbows, Ish bent over her, burying his face in her hair, inhaling its scent. Softly, she caressed his neck with her lips.

The sensation of her warm lips moving lightly on his flesh flooded him with desire. Responding, he bestowed multitudes of soft kisses on her, starting at her forehead then pausing on her mouth. He lingered there, kissing her passionately, as he had kissed her in his dream. She answered with ardent kisses of her own.

Suddenly aware of her breasts against his chest, he moved his lips in that direction, tasting her delectable skin. As his lips touched her, she breathed out a soft exhalation of pleasure.

That sound! It urged him toward her. He needed his body to be even closer to hers.

Some compelling impulse had been triggered. The sound of her uneven breathing drew him in. He *had* to get nearer. His instincts took over. He found the way. They knew how to do this. Their bodies joined as God had made them to do.

As they were united, a catch in Ishah's breathing indicated discomfort of some kind. Ish pulled back to examine her face. Was she all right? Passionately, her eyes gazed back as she clasped him close again. The exquisite bliss of this act was emotionally overpowering—like the first moments of life as the Creator breathed into them.

Ecstasy! My God! Thank you!

Later Ish lay across Ishah's body. Resting his head between her breasts, he encased her in his arms. She held him near, stroking his hair, her hands soft upon him, soothing and affectionate. The sun crawled up into the sky, and they stayed where they were.

"Bone of my bones and flesh of my flesh," he whispered against her body. "We're one."

She murmured her agreement.

Now Ish understood even more fully what his words had meant all along. They'd had complete unity of purpose since the Creator God had made her. She was his body. She had been created from his flesh. But there was an even stronger attachment now, enthralling him.

The Creator had known exactly how to form their oneness. He had created a place within her expressly for him—a place where they were one and his very core could find expression. He now felt intensely attached to her. They were *truly* one.

Their Creator was very wise, and He was holy.

The majestic and beautiful name—*Yahweh*—ran through Ish's mind like a shout of exaltation as he rendered his fervent praise, adoration, and gratitude. He was completely overwhelmed with his love for Ishah and for their God who had given her to him.

"You've captured my heart," Ish declared softly. "You're Yahweh's gift to me."

Ishah sighed contentedly and kissed the top of his head. "It's as if our hearts connected—they're attached to one another, and the love of Yahweh is somehow all wrapped up with our hearts. I adore you. I actually feel as though I'm part of your body now."

"You always have been. We're one flesh."

She stroked his hair and kissed his head in answer.

How was this gratifying physical union tied to God's instructions and plans? It was obviously a vital part of Yahweh's design. They'd seen the many creatures around them repeating the same act. It was primal, a part of His creation.

This woman God had given filled him with irresistible desire. The passion he felt for her consumed him. He never wanted to leave her side. Desperate to unite his body with hers again, he drew her close.

There was so much work he had planned for them today, but he couldn't pull himself out of her arms. They spent the entire morning in the grass by the river, bodies entwined, repeating this beautiful act of passion. Ish was very aware of their God's satisfaction and joy.

Later, as Ish lay with his head upon Ishah's belly, her stomach twisted and rumbled.

"My wife, you're hungry. Let's rise from here, if we can."

He chuckled softly as he said this. He didn't know whether he'd be able to rise, or if he wanted to, though he was also hungry.

Grabbing Ishah's basket, he sat up. He handed it to her and rose, holding her tightly in his arms. Carrying her, he kissed her face and head and mouth as they walked. He didn't want to let go. Entwining her arms about his neck, she laughed softly. They were delighted with each other. He bore her up the hill and stopped to survey all the work from yesterday.

"Look, Ishah. Everywhere we worked is covered with grass. Let's test your basket."

Smiling, she looked out at their world from his arms. "I hope it works as well as your plow. See all the green!"

"Look at this!" Ish approached the first fruit tree. "The garden grows!"

All around the trees, little shrubs and bushes sprang up with the grass. Giddy with joy, Ish felt elated. Everything before his eyes pleased him. It was all very good.

They gathered fruit and placed it into her basket. When the basket was full, they walked hand-in-hand back to the river, where they spent the day.

All day they investigated one another's bodies, making new discoveries about how they were designed for each other and rejoicing in God's wisdom and love in creating them so.

This was the best gift He had given!

They wondered if this act was related to being fruitful and multiplying. Though the creatures around them repeated the same act, they had no idea. It could simply be a delightful gift from the Creator to bind them even more closely together as husband and wife. If this was related to bearing young of their kind, they knew their God would bring it about.

It was all in His hands. They were euphoric, sensing Yahweh's joy in giving them this gift to enjoy together. They felt exhilarated by His kindness.

When He walked toward them in the evening, they thanked Him profusely for this intimacy He had created for them. Their fourth day together had been the best day of all, they told Him. Embracing the two of them together, the Creator smiled widely and laughed softly.

"Remember," He said. "Know one another. Listen, learn, and love."

Then He walked away into the Garden. As they lay down again upon the grass, they watched the glow of His figure disappear through the trees. His loving presence filled and overflowed within their hearts. He was always with them.

They fell asleep wrapped in one another's arms.

CHAPTER TWELVE

THE NEXT DAY when Ishah awakened, Ish lay gazing at her with drowsy eyes. They had slept facing each other, their arms drawing the other close. Memories of their passionate unity filled her mind. Simultaneously, each smiled softly at the other.

Ishah now knew why her husband's eyes had been pleading. She now comprehended the vital urging that had pulled her toward him. It was a yearning—a need—for this act. She understood more clearly what Ish meant in calling them one flesh.

She'd never existed alone, as Ish had on the first day. He had always been near her, showing her love and consideration since she first became aware of herself and her surroundings. She hadn't known what it felt like to be alone. Therefore, she hadn't experienced the same sense of completion Ish had.

Sliding her arms around his waist, she drew him close, yearning for this intimacy again. He was equally eager. Afterward, he lay across her body, his head cradled against her shoulder.

"Are we rising today, my wife, or are we spending another day lying here?"

Ishah considered. Lying together all day yesterday had been sacred. This was a holy act specifically designed by their Creator to draw them nearer to Him and to each other. It was beautiful, the pleasure exquisite! She wanted to spend another day in this way, yet she knew how Ish had anticipated turning the soil. She also wanted to help him do this.

"Can we do both?"

"Certainly." Smiling at her, he rose on one elbow. "Yahweh has blessed us so thoroughly. I sense His pleasure in all we do." Pausing, he traced the shape of her upper lip. "We can plow the earth and sample some of the grass and green plants. Perhaps we can explore down the river, and I'll take you into my arms and make love to you anytime you desire."

Ish's white teeth flashed at her. Noting the label he had attached to their passion, she grinned back. The phrase was apt.

"Let's go farther down the river first," she said. "I'm curious."

Ish rose, held out his hand, and pulled her up. As they walked along the river, they ate their morning fruit and repeated the Creator's instructions and words to one another. They rejoiced in this confirmation of His love and care, this newly demonstrated evidence of His design for their physical unity.

Puzzling over the meaning of His words, they talked about each part of His directive, wholeheartedly desiring to fulfill it all, both the parts they understood and the parts that remained a mystery. They wanted to comprehend so they could carry out those as well. The recitation of His words and their considerations of Him excited their hearts. They smiled widely and spoke animatedly as they discussed Him and His plans for them.

Ishah noticed that they seemed to be especially affectionate today, touching each other repeatedly and bestowing kisses often. As they walked and talked, they encircled one another with their arms, keeping their hips pressed together. They kissed the hands and arms and face and head of the other, periodically pausing to clasp in loving embrace.

Neither of them wanted to let go. They both felt a need—a hungry desire—to stay connected physically. It was difficult to separate for even a moment. They decided this was inspired by the greater sense of oneness this act produced. Now they seemed completely interconnected, as if they truly knew one another. This deeper knowledge prompted the desire to listen, learn, and love even more wholeheartedly, as Yahweh had reminded them.

Their conversation was repeatedly interrupted by their affection and by their adoration and praise of God for what He had given. Continuing their loving walk along the river, they turned their discussion to the six days of creation, repeating the sequence of Yahweh's acts back and forth to one another, smiling and kissing frequently.

They danced together as they sang God's Creation Song.

Rounding a curve in the river, Ish stopped. "I haven't seen this before."

Looking about, Ishah noted more varieties of fruit trees. Near the river bend, one tree bent low, comprised of long winding branches with sharp and vividly green leaves. Little round purple fruits grew in clusters.

"These look interesting," she said. "Let's try them."

As they first bit, they both laughed. Then they leaned in to kiss. The little purple fruits had skins, and inside each was a soft, juicy part that burst in their mouths. They enjoyed the sharply sweet taste and the squirt of the juice.

"*Grapes*," Ish stated.

Ishah loved it when he did that! She laughed.

As Ish studied something, his thought processes were reflected on his analytical face. His mind turned inward, his eyes indicating he had chosen a category where similar items had previously been assigned. Then, he stated the name matter-of-factly, as if it were an obvious thing.

Puzzled, Ish stared at her.

"I love it when you name things," she said.

Giggling, she smiled at him. He popped a grape into her mouth.

"Eat the grape!" Ish laughed and pulled her against his side.

They meandered through the vines, feeding the grapes to each other, laughing when the juice squirted, and kissing. Ish tore off a grape leaf and chewed it thoughtfully. Yahweh had also given these for food. Ish took the first taste.

"Hmm" was all he said.

Ishah ate one, too. It was different with a sharper taste, not sweet like the fruit.

As they came out from the vines, they scanned farther down the river.

The banks narrowed, and the water flowed faster, spraying up into the air and rolling rapidly over rocks buried below the surface. The volume of the churning water increased as they walked toward this narrow place. This was intriguing.

"Let's follow the river and investigate why it flows like that." Ish laced his fingers through hers, and then bent to softly kiss her head.

For some distance they walked along the riverbank, observing the water's movement. It grew more violent as the banks became increasingly narrow. Finally, the riverbank became too steep and rocky for them to traverse without the possibility of falling in.

White and agitated now, the water looked as if it could harm them. The ground rose up sharply on each side of the waterway, leaving only a narrow passageway for the stream to flow through. The river seemed to disappear in the distance, and there was an echoing rumble somewhere over the hill.

Ish helped Ishah up the side of the rocky banks. With great care, he guided her gently. The rocks were all damp here, and they had to step carefully. Ish kept one hand protectively on her elbow. When they reached the top of the hill, they surveyed the scene.

Smooth and glassy, the river plunged over a rocky ledge, spilling over the rim. Through the clear water, they could detect the stream's depth as it slid smoothly over, falling a great distance. At the bottom, it churned violently. Awestruck, Ish turned to her, gaping as she was.

River mist fell upon them, wetting their bodies.

Peering through the mist, Ish pointed. "Look there!"

Downstream, the waterway widened and the water flowed more calmly again. An entire unexplored expanse of the Garden lay below them as they surveyed the landscape.

"The waterfall and the pool beneath are awesome!" he yelled over the falls' turbulence, gesturing toward the panorama. He had labeled all of this, and she knew what he meant. Nodding her head in agreement, she smiled.

For some time, they stayed there gazing at the monumental hills, gray in the distance. From the majestic waterfall and wide turquoise pool beneath, the flat plain broadened into a serene and tranquil valley dotted with trees and pairs of animals. All of this, coupled with the faraway hills, provided a breathtaking vista. Ish gestured and smiled animatedly at Ishah.

Pulling her into his arms, he spoke into her ear, "Look at the Creator's magnificent world. God is so kind to us. He's given us each other and this remarkable place. Do you want to go down there?" He pointed to the base of the waterfall.

She nodded enthusiastically. He kissed her.

With their fingers laced, Ish bent his elbow, pulling her close against his side. They made their way carefully down the rocky hill. The rocks were slippery. Wearing a look of concentration, he often steadied her with his free hand.

As usual, Ish's gentle consideration multiplied the love Ishah felt for him. Affection and warmth filled her. *I love him so much!* Silently, she thanked Yahweh for creating her and for giving her to Ish to be his wife.

At the bottom of the hill, they turned to look back, transfixed by the falls' grandeur. It was white and looked as if it were solid, no longer transparent but opaque. However, it moved and misted, and they both knew that it was water and that they could place their hands through it. The cascading water captivated their vision. They couldn't pull their eyes from it.

As the waterfall hit the rocks below, its pounding noise deafened them, vibrating their bodies to the core. They couldn't hear each other, so they simply smiled, shrugged, and pointed out their observations, each responding with a smile to the other's silent, yet elated, discoveries.

Ish pointed to one side of the cascading water. Ishah turned to look at what had captured his attention. The rock wall over which the river plunged was comprised of different shades of rock—vivid tans, greens, and oranges striped in bands of stone. She hadn't noticed before, because her eyes were fixated on the enchanting sight of falling water.

Along the river's edge ran a narrow pathway of black stone that curved behind the waterfall. The wall of rock along this pathway was a different stone than she'd ever seen. Ish caught her eye and gestured toward this shimmering black stone.

When she nodded, he brought their joined hands to his lips, kissed her hand, and then led the way toward this mystery. Navigating their way carefully over the wet rocks, they walked toward the waterfall. They couldn't speak, but their eyes met frequently as they edged along the wall of black rock, heading behind the waterfall itself.

The smooth black stone supported the other rock strata of varying colors. It was the base, the foundation that held up all the other layers. Though striped with thin lines of lighter stone, its predominant feature was the deep blackness that seemed to capture and absorb the sunlight.

As they stepped alongside this stone wall, Ish ran his palm over its smooth surface. Then he pointed above his head. Ishah looked up and spied a thin vein of glistening golden rock embedded within the black stone. Glittering veins interlaced at irregular intervals in the black wall. The golden rock reminded her of the sun as it sparkled.

First with her flattened palm, she stroked the black rock. It was smooth, hard, and cold. Then she stretched to touch the stripe of golden rock above her head. When she poked, it gave slightly against her pressure. Ish's hand probed and investigated as well. Wonder was reflected on his face. The gold intermingled with the black stone was striking!

Ishah felt along the deposit, engrossed in the shimmering, soft appearance of the gold stone in contrast to the smooth hardness of the black. Ish had pressed his back against the stone wall and now looked toward the waterfall. She glanced at his face. He was mesmerized, so she turned, following his gaze.

They now stood behind the center of the waterfall on a smooth, black ledge of rock. The power of the cascading water overwhelmed, vibrating their entire bodies, the roar of sound deafening. The water shimmered with sunlight.

Piercing the constantly moving water, the sun's rays glimmered and glinted, distorted as they radiated a pale illumination. The light twinkled and shimmered as it hit rocks of various brilliant hues set high in the black rock and in the overlying strata.

Because the glittering water poured down continually, the color of the light constantly altered, casting a spectrum of pale green hues. These tones reflected onto the soft glow of Ish and Ishah's bodies. Fascinated, each studied the reflection of the shimmering colors on the other's face. Then, looking around, they observed the moving light bouncing off the embedded streaks of gold and the many jewel-toned rocks embedded within the black stone.

It was one of the most amazing and magnificent things they'd seen in God's world. What a wise, creative, and holy God they had! Ishah's eyes met her husband's in wonder. They both smiled broadly.

Then Ish extended his hand, cautiously sliding it into the sheet of sparkling falling water. His arm was flung down. Water sprayed in all directions, wetting both their faces and bodies. Surprise showing clearly on his face, he gaped at her.

She tried it as well and was astounded by the water's force as it cast her arm down, spraying them both again. The mist and this spray from the falls wetted them thoroughly. Ishah's hair dripped down her back as they stood pressed against the black wall, watching the pounding water hit the rocks at the waterfall's base.

Feeling Ish's eyes upon her, Ishah turned to meet them. With a concerned expression, he gazed at her, his head slightly tilted. He pulled her close against his body, and she stood between his feet. Pressing her tightly to his chest, he wrapped both his arms about her.

It was then she realized she was cold—she shivered slightly. He had noticed first.

Reluctant to leave, they watched the splendor of the waterfall a while longer. They needed to get out into the sun so she could dry and grow warm, but they lingered in this beautiful place watching the play of light and falling water.

Finally, Ish released Ishah, took her hand, and tugged ever so gently. Moving them away, he led her out from behind the waterfall and carefully along the rock ledge. Several times, both peeked back over their shoulders as they walked through the mist and down the river.

"What was that?" she said, as soon as she thought Ish could hear her. "What did you name the stones?" Bouncing up and down with excitement, she eagerly awaited the labels he would attach, so it would be easier to discuss.

"Let me warm you while we talk." Ish pulled her snug against his body and kissed her forehead. Then he looked into her eyes.

"The place behind the falls is a cave. The smooth black bedrock that runs along the wall and into the cave is onyx. The colored stones are ruby red, topaz, emerald green, sapphire, beryl, jasper . . . There were so many! The golden substance embedded in the onyx I'm naming *gold*. Its very appearance sums up the name."

"I agree. The onyx is smooth and hard, the gold . . . soft. That surprised me! The other stones were too high in the wall to touch. But they were so beautiful!"

"The Creator is amazing! His design of the world is too intricate to comprehend. It's obvious the colored stones extend back out of our sight into the ground itself. I wonder why." He paused, contemplating what they'd just seen.

"Maybe He made them simply because He loves us and knew we would find them beautiful. He delights in giving us good things."

Ish smiled at Ishah, tipping his head to survey her face. "You're probably right."

Why had the Creator made these remarkable, colorful rocks? Why create a hidden cave behind a stupendous waterfall? Was it just for their pleasure and enjoyment?

The beauty captivated their eyes and thrilled their hearts!

With Ish's arms wrapped around her, Ishah stood observing the amazing sight. Then they turned to continue their journey through this new and exotic territory. They stopped to look back again, capturing one more view, exclaiming again about the glorious creation and the kindness of their God to put them here.

CHAPTER THIRTEEN

THE SUN WAS now high in the sky as they headed back toward the field to plow. Ish kept his arm circled around Ishah's waist, cradling her close against his hip as they walked. They circled around the hill over which they had earlier climbed.

On the back of the hill they found unusual trees. These stood tall and slender, only wearing long leaves that fanned out at the top. There were clusters of fruit at the base of these leaves. Ish could barely reach the lowest cluster. He grabbed some of the fruit and yanked it down.

"*Dates.*" He handed some to Ishah.

They sampled and smiled, exclaiming over the tastiness of this fruit.

Continuing to circle the hill, they now headed back toward the Garden's center. Far in the distance, Ishah spied the Tree of Life and the Tree of the Knowledge of Good and Evil—their tops towering over the other trees. The Tree of Life gleamed in the morning sun. Ish took her hand and, of course, aimed them to eventually pass it, rather than the other tree.

They spotted animals that Ishah hadn't seen yet. Telling her their names, Ish pointed to various creatures, detailing some of their characteristics and recounting how exciting it was to name them. She hadn't seen all the animals because they had scattered after being named.

A large contingent of these unfamiliar animals paced toward them, as if in greeting, and Ish and Ishah ran their fingers through the creatures' coats as they trod along on soft paws. Ish told her their names. She loved the names he had bestowed. He was brilliant.

One of the animals, a powerfully built cat with a golden mane, cuffed Ish gently with its big furry paw. He and the lion rolled across the dirt together before righting themselves. They then dodged back and forth in play, stirring up the dust. Ish buried his hands in the lion's mane and pinned its head to the ground, then he laughed loudly.

Ishah leaned against the lion's mate, stroking the sleek head of the lioness, together watching the game their mates engaged in, amused. Ish grinned at Ishah when he met her eyes, triumph and joy playing across his features. With a parting shove for the lion, Ish turned and grasped her hand, pulling her away from the lioness. The lions streaked off together.

"They were the first cats to come to me on the first day."

"I'm glad to meet all of these new friends."

Squeezing her tightly, Ish draped his arm about her waist, and they continued toward the Tree of Life, surrounded by a group of the other animals. These nudged and bumped their sleek coats against them in turn, nickering and rumbling greetings.

"This is a fun and convenient way to get the soil turned here." Ish still grinned broadly from his fun with the lion.

Ishah nodded her agreement, smiling back. She loved seeing him with the animals. It informed her how he must have spent his first day.

As they travelled through the Garden, they spotted some of the comical monkeys Ish had mentioned earlier, chattering at them from one of the nearby trees. These were small ones with black hair and little flesh-covered faces. As the monkeys jumped from branch to branch, they seemed to be laughing at them, and the monkeys amused them as well.

By the time Ish and Ishah reached the far side of the Tree of Life, the sun had reached its blazing zenith. They were hungry and hot, so they reclined in a nearby tree's shadow after pulling down some of its fruit. Most of the animals continued on their own trek, but a few lay under the cool shade of surrounding trees.

Ish pulled Ishah onto his lap, facing him. Looking at her intently, he leaned back, resting his head against the tree's trunk. Gazing into his intense dark eyes, she examined his handsome face. Tenderly caressing his head, she ran her fingers through his shiny black hair. With one fingertip, she followed a trickle of perspiration that traveled under his hair and along his jawline into his newly growing facial hair. His eyes watched her.

Cupping his face between her hands, she met his gaze and pressed her lips to his. The black hair now growing on his lower face framed his delicious mouth. She pulled back and studied it, entranced by the smoothness of his full lower lip. Then she kissed him again.

"I'm perfectly content," he said. "I don't think I could be happier. I love you so much."

"I feel exactly the same. Everything you do causes me to love you more deeply. Our love is interwoven with my awareness of Yahweh's nearness, His love for me, and my love for Him. I don't know if I can hold all this love."

Ishah encircled Ish's waist with her arms, listening to his heart beating, blissfully happy simply to rest against his body under this tree. He lifted her face to his, and they made love in the shade. There was nothing to distract them from their joy in each other and their satisfaction in the unity of their bodies. They lingered.

"The pleasure I feel in your body, our companionship, and the constant presence of God—all of these fulfill me. I feel as if I'm going to burst with happiness."

"I don't think that's possible, husband of mine." She laughed softly. "But I know exactly what you mean."

He held her close. They felt perfectly satisfied in every way.

Eventually, they ate the fruit they had gathered and rose to continue their journey around the Garden, stopping to peek into a bird's nest they found on a low branch. This was what the birds had been building as they worked together so frantically. Within the nest sat one of the paired birds. Peeking out from under it were sky-colored objects that looked like tiny rocks.

The bird stared at them in an annoyed manner, as if they were intruding.

"*Eggs,*" Ish whispered to Ishah.

She nodded. It seemed they shouldn't disturb it. They walked away, discussing the nest, but neither of them could comprehend what the eggs were or why the bird sat on them.

Now that they were back near the place where they slept by the river, the grass grew thickly—verdant swells of hill and meadow, and more varieties of vegetation. Many animals had clustered here to eat the various types of grass, flowering greenery, and shrubs growing in abundance. Some of the taller animals nibbled the plentiful fruit or green leaves from the low tree branches. They all enjoyed what God had declared was theirs to eat. To everything containing the breath of life He had given every green plant for food.

Ish and Ishah sampled some of the green plants they found between the Tree of Life and the hill. Some tasted sharp; some were bland; some had a biting flavor. They all tasted vitally green and nourishing. Each would add variety to their diet of fruit.

Back near the river where they'd left their plow, they worked the soil around the base of the hill opposite where the animals had trod. As He often did, Yahweh walked up the river to talk with them, and they showed Him their work.

His eyes sparkled with delight as He laughed and talked, praising their efforts and their creativity. They thanked Him for the waterfall and the gorgeous landscape. He embraced them closely, telling them He loved them.

His nearness made every day a joy! His physical appearance was an extra blessing.

After He walked over the hill, they finished plowing. Then Ish laid the plow down, grabbed Ishah's hand, and raced with her to the water. They played and splashed, and then climbed out to dry before sunset. They lay on their backs, with their heads together, contemplating the sky. Ishah's heart felt completely full of God and Ish and the beauty of the day.

"An interesting day of discovery!" Ish gazed at the heavens. "Our God is so good to us. What a magnificent place. We have so much to do and so much to see."

"Other than talking with God, the best part was the cave behind the waterfall. The gold in the stone wall was incredible. No, wait—the best part was watching you play with the lion."

"Other than seeing Yahweh, I thought the best part was making love to you under the fruit tree." He fixed his smile on her.

"Maybe you're right." Leaning close, she kissed his mouth, smiling back at him.

"You're the most beautiful part of God's creation."

Ish rolled onto his elbows, poised above her, fixing his passionate eyes on hers before kissing his way down her neck and pulling her body toward his. He satisfied her in every way. Nothing could be better. They suited each other perfectly and loved each other completely.

They were surrounded by the beauty of God's creation and by His creatures, all of them harmoniously learning about His world and engrossed in the mates He had given. Their world was exquisite, and they had everything they wanted and needed. Their work was satisfying and fulfilling, and they enjoyed each other in work and in play.

Yahweh—their artistic and gracious Creator—hovered over them, filling them, embracing them, lovingly present at all times, appearing to walk and talk with them, rejoicing with them in each discovery of their surroundings and of one another.

What more could two people ever want? Absolutely nothing.

CHAPTER FOURTEEN

FOLLOWING THE HOLY day of rest, a day Lucifer had filled with music in praise of God's glorious work of creation, Yahweh had permitted the angels to examine His work more closely for the first time. However, they had been instructed to remain unseen and unheard.

With all the other angels, Lucifer had streaked through the newly made atmosphere. He had alighted near the man and the woman, as had a host of the other angels. This crowning achievement of the Godhead had drawn the most curiosity.

Crowding around the man and the woman, they had watched them closely. Talking among themselves about the two humans, their angelic thoughts had traveled from mind to mind, undetected. The bodies of the man and the woman had fascinated the angels—angels were spirit, not physical. Their spirits were clothed in light, not in flesh.

Why did the humans need these bodies? What did God have planned for them?

As Lucifer had eavesdropped on the others' ruminations, he had overheard here or there a voice of complaint like his own. Covertly he had noted these other disgruntled angels.

After a thorough examination, most of the angels had gone to investigate other parts of the creation.

But Lucifer and a few others had remained—Samyaza and Azazel were in total agreement with him.

They had examined the two humans constantly, remaining near them day after day. Lucifer had hoped to discover their weaknesses so he could exploit them. Day and night, he had followed them everywhere, observing them carefully, becoming intimately acquainted with their interactions, their uncertainties, their strengths, and their naïveté.

Most of the time, because he could not discern their thoughts, he had hovered within arm's length, his arms folded across his chest, glaring at them as he regarded them with contempt and disgust. He had analyzed how their actions affected their breathing, their eye dilation, the blush on their cheeks, and the beating of their hearts, detected from within their bodies. Yet they had been entirely oblivious to his presence.

As the days had passed, he had grown increasingly envious. Not only had God given them dominion, but He had also given them these bodies.

Why would Lucifer—the most beautiful and wise angel in heaven—envy these human beings? Because of their weak and puny bodies? Surely not.

Yet day and night Lucifer had pondered how fulfilling it would be to possess a body, to have a home for the spirit, to have sensory awareness. What must it be like? This was something about which he had no experience. He longed to inhabit a body like theirs. Disgusted with himself for even thinking this, Lucifer had become increasingly discontented.

* * * *

On this day, Lucifer had shadowed the man and the woman on their trip through an unexplored portion of the Garden, watching as they discovered the waterfall and the distant mountains. Now he stood, studying their unconscious forms in the moonlight. The two lay entangled, embracing after uniting their bodies sexually before sleeping. Their affection sickened him. He didn't understand it, yet it also intrigued him.

Lucifer longed to comprehend their passion, and why they wanted to unite their bodies. All their actions from the previous days had built up to this, like a crescendo. They committed this act frequently. It affected them intensely—physically and emotionally, but also spiritually. It had a different effect on them than the same act when performed by the animals.

If something had this strong an impact, surely he could exploit it, break it, and corrupt it to harm them. That this was an intrinsic part of their makeup provided him a target, an opportunity for a foothold. As the days went by, he continued to scrutinize them each time they engaged in this act, each time they kissed, each time they touched. He planned to manipulate this attraction for his own purposes.

Lucifer's absorption with his destructive plans consumed him. He never took his eyes off them, never ceased his machinations. Night and day, day and night, he watched.

* * * *

With all the multitude of angelic sons of God, Lucifer returned to the throne of Yahweh, assuming his assigned position above the throne with the other guardian cherubim. The clear, ringing voice of the Creator summoned him.

Before the throne, he dropped down, falling to one knee. But within his heart he was unbowed. He regarded God with disdain, His created humanity with derision.

"Lucifer, from whence have you come?" God the Father asked.

God knew exactly where he had been, but he would play this game and tell Him what He already knew. Deceitfully, Lucifer projected the correct tone of deference and reverence.

"From looking at Your new world and watching the man and woman You have made."

"Have you considered the obedience of the man concerning my instruction about the Tree of the Knowledge of Good and Evil?"

Of course he had, but God knew this. Lucifer merely nodded.

"He has no guile," God said. "With all his heart, he desires to obey me."

"Why should he not? Have You not given him a perfect world, a beautiful woman, and everything he needs? But stretch out Your hand. Let me try him to see how obedient he is. He will eat the fruit and shake his fist in Your face. Let me show You what he is really like. He will no longer adore You or worship You."

And then, Lucifer snickered to himself; the two humans would die, and he would again be elevated to his rightful place of dominion.

"Because of my great love for humanity, you may test the man and the woman."

The Three were unified, always acting as One. Focused on some mysterious purpose, the Father never wavered. He locked eyes with the Son at His right hand. The Son remained steadfast and resolute, the Spirit in unity. The intensity of Their unfaltering love and commitment to the man and the woman thundered through the throne room. It shook the heavens.

Lucifer felt it move through him, but he braced himself, remaining unaffected. Baffled, he narrowed his eyes as he studied the Godhead. What was going on here?

"But you may not touch them or harm them in any way." God laid out the parameters within which Lucifer must operate. "You may not lay even a finger upon them."

Lucifer nodded. God dismissed him.

Again, Lucifer assumed his position above the throne, spreading his wings and leading the songs of praise. But his mind was otherwise occupied.

This had been almost too easy! He couldn't believe it! He had obtained exactly what he wanted: the opportunity to test the man and the woman. Now he could destroy them.

However, the ease with which he had been granted this gave him pause. Was there more to this than he knew?

But then it began to dawn on him, growing and swelling in his mind—he could outwit Yahweh! Though God knew what he was thinking, evidently Lucifer had tricked Him. Clearly, he understood God's humans better than God did. Lucifer detected their weaknesses with clear-eyed objectivity. His view wasn't colored by love. Hatred clarified Lucifer's view.

He should be God.

Perhaps Gabriel and Michael would not join him, but others would. He had already noted the voices of dissent. With others who had glowered at the humans with equal scorn, he had stood on the earth observing them. His plan now involved more than destroying humanity. Lucifer resolved to form a rebellion.

He would seize Yahweh's throne.

He would make himself like the Most High.

He would be God.

In the throne room of heaven, he already possessed the position above God's head. All the angels could see him as he directed the singing. From this position of influence he could easily persuade other angels to join him. Together, they would steal Yahweh's throne and exterminate these ludicrous human beings He had created. Lucifer would then reign over the universe.

Capturing the attention of Samyaza, Azazel, and others who had observed the man and the woman with him, Lucifer nodded, thinking his plan in their direction like a light beam. He had been correct in his assessment; they were outraged at God's plan for these humans. They all agreed, and then sent their own thoughts out to those who were under their influence. And so it went. With the speed of light, they amassed one-third of heaven's angels on their side.

The organization of his coup distracted Lucifer. There were many egos to soothe, many promises of rank to vouch. However, though his thoughts were otherwise occupied, his mouth continued to sing, producing the glorious music that filled the throne room. Now he looked down at the Godhead and was startled when he met God the Son's eyes fastened upon him.

The Son pointed up at him.

"You dare to make yourself the opponent of God!?" the Son stated firmly, the voice of absolute authority. "You are filled with slander and deceit. Because of your magnificent beauty, your heart has become arrogant. For the sake of your splendor, you have corrupted your wisdom. You seek to place yourself above the Most High God. You have sinned, forfeiting your station and your name. You will now be called *Satan*—the *Accuser*."

With one swift gesture of His arm, God the Son hurled Satan to the earth, casting him down from his position above the throne.

"I expel you," the Son proclaimed. "I find wickedness in you and cast you out."

Catapulting down from heaven, Satan and his cohorts in rebellion hurtled toward the earth. In the glimpse he caught through space as he spun through the atmosphere, his wings completely worthless as they flapped against his face and whipped out from his body, Satan detected that from each mutinous angel blazed a trail of fire through the black.

Tumbling and flailing, he attempted to gain control of his descent, but faster and faster he plunged.

Satan landed with a thud, flat on his back. The earth reverberated with the shock wave. A thick cloud of dust mushroomed. Prone, he watched this thick dust mingle with the trail of fire and smoke that had consumed him. Then it all floated down to where he lay flattened, ash settling onto him and the earth around him.

Raising his arm to shake his fist at God, he discovered it was charred. He was no longer beautiful; no longer did he shine like the stars as he wore his clothing of light. He was an unclothed spirit. He had forfeited his shining name, his eminent standing, and his brilliant beauty.

The heavens opened and myriads of angels viewed his shame, appalled by his exile and the destruction of his beauty. Within the throng, Satan spied the silent condemnation worn on the stern countenances of Gabriel and Michael.

Unyielding, the Son stared intently upon him and the other fallen ones. Having seen the One God in all His radiant holiness, they had yet rebelled against Him. The breach was eternal. Yahweh's judgment was swift and effective. God had caught Satan completely unaware. Even though he was now fallen and cast out, Satan realized that he still brought glory to Yahweh by exhibiting God's wisdom and justice. The Lord God could not be tricked or outwitted.

Wrath surged through Satan as he realized he had been thoroughly thwarted. A shriek of murderous rage exploded from within him, a bellow that increased in volume and fury. His exquisite singing voice appeared to be scorched. Satan curled his ashy spirit hands into fists and raised them both in defiance, shaking with the ferocity of his anger.

"So be it!" he shouted. He would make God pay.

But Satan clearly had to operate within the parameters God had established. He was not as powerful as he had thought.

But what powers did he still possess? Could he make himself have an appearance of bodily form? If not, he would twist the natural order of God's creation. Might he possess the body of a creature in the Garden to accomplish his work? As unclothed spirit, he assumed he could slide into and out of at least one creature, if not more than one. He would experiment with this.

Satan formulated his revenge. He would obliterate all Yahweh had made that was beautiful, just as he had hoped and planned to do all along. He had permission to *test* God's humans. He would start there. He would *tempt* them toward evil. The boundaries would be breached, the limits chafed, and the exquisite annihilated.

Every minute fraction given would be seized.

He would damage them as much as possible.

Satan would kill God's crowning achievement—the humans made in His own image.

It would be simple. The man was pathetically weak and naïve. His agitated words about the Tree of the Knowledge of Good and Evil had provoked curiosity in the woman. She was now inquisitive. This was almost too easy! He already knew how he would attack the man.

Satan would deceive the woman and tempt her to eat the fruit.

CHAPTER FIFTEEN

ISHAH SAT UNDER a shady tree, weaving strong grass cords and peering into the distance, studying the Tree of the Knowledge of Good and Evil. She wasn't as concerned about it as Ish. But, being inquisitive, she studied it from wherever they worked.

Ish never even looked at The Tree. But it was so beautiful that it was difficult for Ishah to resist taking peeks. She saw no harm in looking. She wasn't going to touch it.

This tree had the most beautiful fruit in the Garden, a deep crimson red, emitting an enticing vibrancy. The surface of each fruit looked firm and shiny. Next to it was the Tree of Life with its sparkling golden fruit. But as far as she was concerned, it was exactly like the rest of the trees in the Garden. There was no mystery. They could eat from it, as they could from all the other trees—except the one.

Nothing else was forbidden them in the Garden.

In spite of her husband's explanation, Ishah couldn't comprehend what it meant to die or lose unity with Yahweh's Spirit. What would happen if their spirits left their bodies? Every day Ish repeated the Creator's warning as they reviewed all of His instructions, again asking her to help him obey God's command. Of course, she agreed.

They'd now been in the Garden fourteen days.

Ish had talked about it every single day.

Her curiosity had grown as she attempted to understand his reaction. As completely as they sought to heed Yahweh's words, Ishah couldn't imagine why they would ever eat from this tree. Their life in the Garden satisfied them in every way. They loved Yahweh and desired to obey Him. Why would either one even consider disobeying Him?

Because they had plowed here first, luxuriant grass, little shrubs, and flowering plants had already sprung up around the trees, making this the loveliest part of the Garden. The center was now filled with this lush vegetation, but the rest of the Garden contained only trees surrounded by the fertile reddish-brown soil.

There it all lay, awaiting their cultivation. The work was simple and gave them pleasure. They had woven thick grass cords strong enough to attach the plow to the donkey or the ox. They also bound more branches to the plow to enlarge it. Now Ish could walk alongside the animal, guiding it, talking to it, and stroking its head as it dragged these heavier branches.

Overnight, everywhere they plowed, living green things sprang from the soil.

Each day, the Garden grew more green and lush.

Each evening, they walked and talked with Yahweh, showing Him their daily work, their faces shining with joy in His presence. Clearly delighted, the Creator smiled as He listened to their enthusiastic explanations. He then walked with them to examine their work and to delight in all they had accomplished. He listened to their new ideas, and He always affirmed His love.

Thank you, Yahweh! A surge of love permeated Ishah's heart—God's presence!

Since Ish had the animals' help with the plow, her work had changed, taking her far afield. The grass cords frayed and broke easily, so now her tasks included weaving baskets and grass cords. While she braided the grass under nearby shady trees, she talked to Ish from afar or watched him in the distance. To help him, she carried his favorite foods from various trees and plants, walking back and forth. Her assistance helped him accomplish more.

She had also discovered how to carry water to him in a tightly woven basket, saving him the long walk to the river. The basket was braided in one long piece that coiled from the center and was thickly lined with long grasses and broad leaves. On the inside, she had sealed it with the sticky sap from the tree they had broken when they made the plow. As she carried it to Ish to relieve his thirst, water dripped slowly all the way, cooling her.

But I miss walking beside him all day, my God. Leaving his side is difficult.

Immediately, the warmth of God's nearness comforted her, and she smiled.

As Ish plowed farther out from the Garden's center, Ishah walked with him. When she left to retrieve water, Ish always took her into his arms, saying he'd long for her in her absence and asking her to hurry back. Then he watched her as she walked away, his eyes pained by their short separation. When she returned, his smile beamed wide, and he hugged her to himself, thanking her for bringing the water, and then pausing to drink.

Occasionally, as Ishah went back and forth, she walked by The Tree.

The leaves of The Tree were large and broad. Almost no sunlight touched the ground under it. There the shade was cool, the grass soft under her feet, and the flowers sweet and fragrant. She enjoyed this part of the Garden.

If Ish paused in his work and saw her near The Tree, he stopped plowing and watched her as she came toward him. There was always a crease between his beautiful dark eyebrows, which she detected more clearly as she ran toward him.

Today he was working on the other side of The Tree, far from the river. She planned to carry water to him so he didn't need to travel back and forth and interrupt his work. Because this day promised to be particularly hot, she decided to walk under The Tree as she did occasionally. It would be faster to return this way. She wouldn't linger. She would only enjoy the coolness as she passed.

Ishah laid aside the weaving and hurried toward Ish to tell

him her intentions. After his usual embrace and instructions, she left his side and quickly made her way to the river. She felt his eyes upon her and turned to wave as she passed under The Tree. She was fine. Waving, she reassured him. He waved back then stood watching her. She moved so rapidly, the sun hadn't traveled far when she returned with his water.

She drank when Ish was done and then walked beside him. Nearby, she saw a bushy tree that they hadn't eaten from yet and dashed to gather some fruit. Now that they were farther from the river, they were more likely to see different types of fruit trees. They always stopped and sampled the fruit from these.

"Taste this one," she called to Ish, running back with a piece of the fruit. She was surprised when his face puckered.

"That's a *lime*." His face still twisted from the bite. "It's sour."

Ishah passed him the water to rinse his mouth. Then she grabbed his favorite fruit from her shoulder basket and handed it across, replacing the sour lime. He thanked her and kissed her head. Pushing aside the dirt with his foot, he tossed in the lime and covered it.

Examining his face, she noticed the sweat on his brow. "I've been considering how to weave a covering for your head. It would keep you cool and shade your eyes while you work."

Dipping into the water basket, she scooped up some water. She felt his eyes fixed intently on her face. With the cool water she bathed his sweaty forehead, smiling into his eyes as she stroked her wet fingertip down his nose. Then she poured a tiny stream onto the top of his head. Standing motionless, he closed his eyes and smiled broadly, enjoying the sensation.

"*Ah!* Ishah! Thank you!"

He shook his head rapidly, flinging water onto her face. This was what the wolves did to dry themselves after they got out of the river. She laughed as the droplets splattered her.

Grinning, Ish opened his eyes and kissed her. Then he turned back to the plowing. He kept one arm around her waist and one around the donkey's neck. As she walked beside him, she peered at his head, stroking it periodically, trying to determine how to weave what she envisioned. Exactly how would she make it? Creating things filled her with joy.

"Maybe I can work on the head covering tonight." Speculatively, she studied his head.

He glanced at her and smiled. "That would be nice. I'll help you with the braiding."

At the end of each day's work, they felt tired but satisfied. In the cool of the evening, they sometimes continued to make items from the grass. They loved to create things. It renewed their energy. This was what the Creator had made them to do. Often they talked with Him as they sat weaving in the evening. Tonight she would show Him her idea to cover Ish's head.

There were only three days when they hadn't accomplished any work. Two had been holy days of rest, beautiful days of rejoicing, and the other was the day they had discovered how to unite their bodies.

Smiling, Ishah gazed at her husband. Ish glanced back at her and returned her smile, and then looked at her more intently.

"What are you thinking about?" he asked.

"Our fourth day together."

He released the donkey and grabbed Ishah, lifting her into the air. Grinning at her, he spun, turning them round and round.

"That was the best day!" He gave her a dazzling smile as he lowered her to the ground. "Every time I hold you in my arms I'm filled with joy. You're my very own—my own flesh and bones. I thank Yahweh for you every day."

Ishah wrapped her arms around Ish's waist, looked into his eyes, and squeezed him tightly. "I'm glad to be one with you. I love you so much."

"As I love you, my wife." He bent down to kiss her. "Let's take a break."

Ish untied the donkey, setting him loose to wander and graze.

Laughing, Ishah took off running toward the nearest cluster of fruit trees. Ish pursued her and scooped her up, kissing her as they tumbled into the shade. They were in a playful mood today, and their lovemaking was playful as well. Afterward, he cradled her in his lap, and they ate their favorite fruits, grasses, and plants from her basket.

Now that so many green things were growing, they had discovered a variety of plants they enjoyed eating. They ate some, feeding them to each other as they rested together in the shade.

They discussed how far they'd come from the river and what they'd accomplished since learning to connect the plow to the donkey. The beautiful green grass and abundant plants flourished, providing more food for the animals and for them. The work made them happy!

When they drank the last of the water, Ishah knew her drippy water basket needed refilling. She would miss Ish, but she discerned that he was still thirsty. His work in the beaming sun was taxing. The sun had risen to its zenith, so the walk would be hot.

She rose. "You need some water. I'm going to walk under The Tree again where the shade is dense. I'll travel from shade tree to shade tree on the way to the river and back."

Ish stood, keeping his eyes on hers. "Please don't linger under The Tree." He leaned in to kiss her forehead. "Walk by as quickly as you can."

"I will. My husband, neither of us is going to eat that fruit."

Certain of this, she placed her hand on his cheek, watching his eyes as she stroked his short black facial hair. With her thumb, she smoothed the crease between his brows. He smiled then, and hugged her tightly before turning to find the donkey.

Ishah walked toward the river. As she passed under The Tree, she looked back. Ish still stood where she had left him. By his shoulder, the donkey waited to be tied. Ish waved. She returned his wave and walked quickly through the shady spot and on toward the river.

As she went up the hill and then down, she felt so happy! Joy in the Creator and in her husband filled her. When she saw their favorite place by the river—the place she had been created—she recalled everything they had done together there, and she thanked Yahweh. Gratefulness filled her. Smiling at her own recollections, she drank deeply from the water and then refilled the water basket.

On the way back, Ishah passed under The Tree. She noticed Ish walking to meet her, so she paused in the shade, placing the water basket on the ground and smiling at Ish as he came.

"*Ishah.*" Like a whisper, her name was quietly hissed.

Startled, she jerked her head toward the strange voice.

Peering into the branches, Ishah met the piercing eyes of

a glistening creature. It had iridescent purple-and-green-scaled skin, and its thick serpentine body coiled round The Tree, over and under the branches.

Had the creature spoken? Do some creatures talk?

From its shoulders spread wings—arched and stiff. Its short legs sported sharp claws that stabbed into the tree's bark. A high collar of thin skin rose around its long neck, framing a sly face. Slanted eyes sloped toward its nose, which consisted of large holes just above its mouth. From between its teeth, a black forked tongue flicked rapidly.

Tantalizing! It was the most unusual creature she'd ever seen.

Though she'd never before met this particular animal, it appeared somewhat similar to some she had observed. She peered higher through The Tree's branches searching for its mate, but saw none.

The pounding of Ish's feet vibrated her soles. She glanced in his direction.

Looking warily at the creature, he rushed up beside her, grasped her hand, and tugged her back a step. From its perch, the talking creature didn't acknowledge Ish in any way. It kept its cold, hard eyes focused directly on her.

"Ishah," it hissed, "*did God really say, 'You must not eat from any tree in the Garden.'?*"

"Yahweh isn't unreasonable. He is kind. We may eat the fruit from the trees in the Garden. But God did say, 'You must not eat fruit from the tree that is in the middle of the Garden,' this tree here, 'and you must not touch it, or you will die.'" Ishah repeated her husband's words. Since he had restated them daily, she felt well prepared for this peculiar conversation. She glanced at Ish who frowned sharply at the mate-less talking creature.

"*You will surely not die.*" Shrewdly, it flicked its tongue.

This was the opposite of what Ish had told her. But the creature seemed to be filled with the wisdom of the ages, as if it knew things she had never seen or heard.

"*God knows when you eat this fruit your eyes will be opened.*" Its tongue flicked again. "*And you will be like Him, knowing good and evil.*"

Ishah remembered how she had felt when she had first been created. She had been confused. Was Ish confused? Had he heard the Creator correctly?

The command he repeated to her was unlike any of the Creator's other instructions. It puzzled her. She'd never heard Yahweh forbid them anything.

Contemplating the creature's words, Ishah stood motionless. The name of The Tree *was* the Tree of the Knowledge of Good and Evil, so the animal's words made sense. Eating from The Tree would give them knowledge. They would be able to distinguish between good and evil.

Ishah wasn't certain what *evil* was, but she was curious.

She stared at her husband. He peered suspiciously at the animal, as if trying to discern why it had spoken these words. Ishah looked back at the creature.

Insinuatingly, its eyes gleamed as it leaned closer, releasing a disdainful hiss.

Ishah inhaled sharply. *What is this creature implying?*

There were many things God hadn't told them, but which they had learned by experiencing the creation and each other. Had He omitted the fact that they should know both good and evil? Surely He would want them to be like Him, wouldn't He?

Is Yahweh keeping something from us?

The thought stunned Ishah. Didn't God want them to be like Him? They were made in His image, after all. If the fruit on this tree would make them wise, why wouldn't He want them to eat it? Why was He keeping knowledge and wisdom from them?

Ishah eyed The Tree. *It looks very good for food. It would be nice to gain knowledge.*

She felt as though she knew nothing. Ish surely was wrong. The creature was right: God wouldn't keep this from them.

Ishah grabbed the nearest crimson piece and took a bite. A rush of sensations swept through her. Stunned and confused, she turned toward Ish.

He recoiled, as if he'd been hit in the chest. The color drained from his face. Horrified, he stared at her. Until this moment, he had never looked at her like this.

"What have you done?" His voice rose. "The serpent lies. It twists God's words."

Ish's expression frightened her. She looked at the bitten fruit. Its flesh was a deep purple, almost black. Dark juice trickled down her hand and forearm, dripping onto the ground, but the fruit was delicious. The fruit of The Tree hadn't caused her to die.

"Husband, I'm fine. It's delicious. Try it. I didn't die. You're mistaken."

"You can't see it!" His eyes searched her face. "You're dying!" His voice cracked, rough with emotion. "I heard the Creator's words! I know what He said. He always speaks the truth. The serpent lied."

"But why wouldn't Yahweh want us to be like Him? He would want that. He would want us to discern both good and evil. He would want us to be wise. He gave us knowledge and would be happy for us to gain more. Here's an easy way to do it."

Violently, Ish shook his head, as if trying to negate her words.

Ishah frowned and rushed on. "We've made so many mistakes, because we don't know anything. Remember when we got in the water late in the day and I grew cold? Remember when you didn't know to hold your breath when you went under the water?"

Ish stood motionless, hardly breathing. Hurriedly, she continued.

"Every day we try to discern the rules of the Creator's earth and what He meant when He gave us our instructions, but we can't understand it all. Being wise would be good! We would gain knowledge. The Creator would want this. Why else would He make this tree, the Tree of the Knowledge of Good and Evil, if He didn't want us to eat from it?"

Ish drew a deep breath and let it out slowly.

"Then why did the Creator instruct me not to eat from The Tree?" Ish put the question to her firmly. "And why did He tell me I will die when I do?"

Now thoroughly confused, Ishah held out the dripping fruit to Ish.

As he stared at the bitten hole, some harsh reality dawned on him, the horrific certainty spreading across his face. Focused on the juicy cavity, Ish seemed paralyzed by this horror. His face blanched of all color, and he dragged his hand down his face, as if to wipe away the decision she held out to him.

Distressed, he opened his eyes and resolutely lifted the fruit from Ishah's hand. Staring at her teeth marks, he clutched her to his chest. Then he looked into her eyes.

"I was alone before the Creator made you. You're my body, bone of my bones and flesh of my flesh—my very own. We're one. I love you." A single tear coursed down his cheek. "Since you must now die, I don't care what the Creator said—I choose to die with you. I'll seek this knowledge and eat the fruit with you." Fixing his tortured eyes on hers, he sunk his teeth into the fruit.

The moment he bit, everything changed.

A shadow fell over Ish's face, snuffing his radiance. The fruit in Ishah's stomach, though it had been sweet in her mouth, turned to bitterness. The cold certainty of impending death crept through her. She no longer felt the nearness of the Creator.

Instead, empty hopelessness left a gaping dark hole.

Where has our God gone?

She realized she'd been tricked. The new rush of emotions began their destructive work.

Her cheeks tingled. A sense of panic tightened her chest. She had disgraced herself. She hadn't realized that anything but the truth could be uttered, and so she had believed the serpent's lies. She had doubted God's instructions and Ish's repetitions. And now they would both die. It was certain. They were already dying. She felt her lack. Fear twisted her gut.

The serpent hissed a subtle laugh and climbed higher into The Tree.

Everything was wrong now. Something had broken within her. Her heart pounded. Defeated, she covered her head, collapsing to the earth. Even the hot sun overhead felt cold.

"Where is my God?" Despair ached in Ish's voice. "He's left me! Yah . . ." He broke off into a wailing scream.

Huddled on the ground, Ish's tormented cry of anguish stabbed at Ishah's heart. He had known the serpent was lying— he had even told her so. Yet he had eaten the fruit, choosing to disobey the Creator and to die with her.

"Why did you do that?" Ish aimed his pain at her. "Why didn't you help me?"

Glancing up, Ishah stared into her husband's desperate eyes, his face twisted in torment. Quickly she dropped her head, shame flushing her cheekbones. Daily, Ish had pled for her help.

She had promised, but now she hadn't helped him at all. She had actually tempted him.

How could I have betrayed him like this?

Her heart felt ripped inside her. It must have torn in two. The aching in her chest felt unbearable.

"Why didn't I stop you?" Ish sobbed raggedly, his voice filled with pain and regret. "Why didn't I protect you? Why did I eat it? I failed. I destroyed everything."

Ishah could barely make out his words. They seemed to be muffled, perhaps coming from behind his hands—she can't bear to look at him again. Overwhelmed with agony, she kept her head bowed. She heard him run out into the field.

Dragging herself off the ground, she pursued him. He stumbled blindly, gripping his head. He bent over, and the contents of his stomach splattered onto the ground. He collapsed onto his knees. She dropped beside him, putting her arms around him.

He shrugged away from her touch—he'd never done that before.

"I'm so sorry! I was tricked. The serpent sounded so wise, as if it knew more than we knew. I believed it. I doubted you. I was wrong."

Devastated, he stared up at her. "Why didn't you believe *me*? I love you."

"I know. I ruined everything." Ishah wept bitter tears.

"No, I ruined it. Nothing changed until I took a bite. God told me not to eat it, but I deliberately disobeyed him." He dragged in a heavy sob. "I couldn't stand for you to die. I didn't want to be alone again. I chose you over Him. Now it's all over. He's gone!"

The absence of Yahweh, this unexpected and crushing result of their disobedient act, seemed to be destroying them both. Ishah felt overcome. She couldn't even *think* His holy name. Ish covered his face, hiding his despair from her. Their oneness felt as if it had been severed.

Why had the serpent done this to them? Why would it want to deceive her, provoking Ish to choose this way? Why had the Creator left them? She didn't understand any of this.

"Did Yahweh see us do that?" She pulled Ish's hands from

his face. "Surely He saw us! Is that why He left?"

Her husband had no answers. He stared back at her, crushed and speechless.

"Now what do we do, Ish? Tell me! What will God say to us when He comes back? I'm afraid to be in His presence." This reality struck her momentarily speechless.

She'd never been frightened of the Creator before, but now she was. She didn't want Him to see them. They stood and stared at one another's bodies. Ish blushed. They were naked. In front of all creation, they stood bare and ashamed.

Why hadn't they noticed this before?

They had run around in front of all the animals, even wrapped in each other's arms as their bodies become one, right under the sky with the heavens, the birds, and the animals watching all they did. How could they have been so foolish?

"We need to cover our nakedness," Ish whispered.

"Let's hide!"

Ish turned and bolted for the river. She raced hard after him, as if death pursued them.

CHAPTER SIXTEEN

ISH COULDN'T BELIEVE his wife had listened to the serpent. She hadn't seen this creature before, but he had when he named it. It hadn't looked like this. Neither had it been able to speak. Somehow, it had become grotesquely enlarged and deformed, its nature distorted and sinister.

How? How could it speak? Why had it tempted Ishah? Why had he simply stood there listening to the thing talk? Why had he eaten the fruit?

Ish couldn't understand any of this. He needed to reorganize his thinking. He didn't want to talk to Ishah. He wanted to be alone. God had said it wasn't good for him to be alone, yet *this* was what he now desired. Had eating the fruit destroyed his relationship with his wife?

The Creator's words came to his mind again. *You may eat freely from any of the trees in the Garden of Eden, but you must not eat from...the Tree of the Knowledge of Good and Evil, for when you eat from it you will surely die.*

Was this why God was now gone? Was this what God had meant when He said Ish's spirit would no longer have union with His Spirit? This hurt too much.

Ish knew the Creator would find them, and he would have to answer for this. He didn't want to face Him. He had tried to obey. He hadn't even looked at The Tree and had hardly ever gone near it. He had instructed Ishah. She had promised to help him avoid this.

She promised!

Why hadn't she listened to him? And why hadn't he stopped her? Why hadn't he rebuked the serpent, grabbed her, and hurried them away? God had given them the right to rule and have dominion over all the creatures. Why hadn't they ruled?

They were dying. Of this he was certain. He could feel the difference. He was embarrassed when he thought of God. The remembrance of His beauty and His holy name was painful. For the first time in his life, Ish felt separated from Him. God had left him—His Spirit was gone.

Within his chest, Ish's heart clutched.

Would God now tear his spirit out of his physical form?

Would their lives end? Is that what dying meant?

Terror gripped him, causing him to shake. He felt cold to his core. He didn't want his life to end. He didn't want his relationship with Yahweh to be over. The very thought made him sick.

Ish collapsed onto his hands and knees. More of his stomach contents spewed onto the ground. While he was bent over, Ishah caught him.

"My husband." She breathed heavily. "Let me help you."

Flinching away, he glared at her. Spitting out his words, he demanded, "Why did you do that? Why didn't you listen?"

Rising to his feet, he pinned her with his stare. His eyes felt cold and hard. He breathed heavily. He'd never before looked at her or felt like this. She staggered back.

"Why?" He lashed her with his question.

"I thought you were mistaken." She looked down, her voice quiet. "You said this was one of the first instructions God gave you. I remembered what it felt like when I was first made. I knew nothing, and I was confused. The serpent seemed wise, and I thought it would be good to acquire knowledge. I thought you'd gotten it wrong."

"I obviously hadn't, had I?"

"No." She glanced up to meet his eyes, and then bowed her head.

"How long have you doubted me? Did you plan to do this all along?"

"No! No!" Quickly she looked up, shaking her head. Her eyes reddened. "I didn't plan this. I'd never even thought of it! I didn't think anything could make us eat that fruit. I simply thought you were being overly cautious. I thought The Tree was beautiful and the fruit looked good to eat. I was curious, but I wasn't ever going to touch it. I didn't doubt you . . . until the serpent spoke."

"I don't believe you."

Ish spun around and sprinted away. He heard Ishah crying behind him. He didn't care.

She had doubted him. Well, she was wrong. He couldn't stand this. Lowering his head, he ran as hard as he could. He hoped he hurt himself.

Racing over the hill, he glimpsed the place Ishah had been made. It was as if he'd been hit in the stomach. Heaving and coughing, he gagged up a bitter liquid, and then wiped his mouth.

The beautiful memories of this place now hurt him, making him physically sick. Nothing would ever be the same again. He didn't want to see Ishah. Would he ever want to hold her again? At this moment, he didn't think so. It was all over.

The end was here. The Creator God was gone. Dying hurt terribly.

Ish raced down the hill toward the tall grass. They needed to make something to cover themselves. How had he not recognized that they were naked, that they walked around in only their skin? Stupidly, he had paraded around in only his flesh, completely nude, exposing his wife and himself to shame under the sun.

Why hadn't he covered their nakedness? He was a fool!

Gathering armfuls of the long grass, he hurried up the riverbank. Ishah still hadn't appeared. This concerned him. Where was she?

He was angry with her. He'd never felt this way before.

Part of him was furious, yet the logical part remembered how he had treated her every moment before they'd eaten the fruit. They had never acted like this. None of these feelings, actions, or words had burst forth. They had experienced perfect harmony since the moment they had first beheld each other. But now, everything was changed.

Ish knew he still loved Ishah; she was his body. But he didn't know how to manage these emotions and the anger that seethed within him. Eating the fruit seemed to have broken everything. But he needed to go back. If he was still the man he had been this morning, he would. It sickened him to admit that he wasn't that man any longer.

Even so, back up the hill he sprinted. Shielding his brow from the sun, he spied Ishah in the distance. With her knees drawn up and her head down, she huddled against the sprawling base of a large fig tree. This was because of him. He had never before hurt her.

Something inside smote him.

A lump formed in his throat, and his eyes grew gritty. Remorse. He rushed to her and knelt down. But he couldn't take her into his arms, for he still shook with anger.

"Wife, I'm hurt and angry. But I shouldn't have spoken to you like that."

Why could he hurt her so easily now?

"But I did doubt you." She didn't raise her head. "I should have listened. I should have walked away. I ruined everything. I'm so sorry."

"Well, I ought to have stopped you. Or one of us should have rebuked the serpent and taken authority over it. The Creator gave us the mandate to rule." Ish felt sick again. It was true. "I shouldn't have eaten the fruit either."

Mirroring his feelings, she gazed up at him in despair, her face dull and flat.

Nothing would ever be the same. They couldn't change what they had just done, even if they hid from God and covered their nakedness. Ish saw this clearly. They were dying. Soon their spirits would leave their bodies. Would their forms lie lifeless upon the ground?

The horror and regret tore through him—more new emotions.

"Ishah, I can't face Yahweh." Desperation and fear unnerved him. His voice quavered. "We need to cover ourselves and hide. Can you come and help me?"

Dubiously, Ishah peered up at him. This was the first time she had looked at him with distrust. He had run from her, shrugged off her help, and shouted angry words at her. She now had reason to doubt him—more destruction.

"Please, help me." Ish rose and offered his trembling hand.

Hesitantly she took it, allowing him to pull her up. Ish laced his fingers through hers and squeezed her hand. Cautiously, she half-squeezed his.

How much had he hurt her? He seemed to have damaged the way she responded to him. Unplanned and unbidden, the angry words and actions had spewed out, as if asserting his own rights rather than thinking of her first was now his natural way of interacting.

He despised himself for his behavior, yet within his angry heart he felt justified.

How could he keep this from happening again? Had his disobedience made him evil?

"Please, forgive me," he said softly. *Forgive.* There had never before been anything to forgive. This was a new word. He hoped she understood. "I don't seem to be able to control the way I feel and act anymore."

"I'm trying, but something is hurt inside me, and I can't explain it. This is all new to me, too." She studied him. "I hope you can also forgive me."

"Like you said, this is new. I'm also trying. We're weaker than we ever knew. We both made horrible mistakes today. Come." Ish tugged her hand. "Let's cover our bodies and hide. It terrifies me to face Yahweh. I feel frightened and sick when I think about Him."

But it was more than terror. There was something else in his heart, something that had never been there before, and Ish couldn't figure it out. He didn't want to think about God. It hurt too much. Maybe, if Ishah stayed beside him, he wouldn't have to consider these new feelings. He wouldn't have to think these sickening thoughts.

"There are so many new emotions," she said.

Ish groaned at her statement and pulled on her hand.

But Ishah wrested free and reached for the tree's leaves. "I think we can use these."

Though the fig tree was filled with fruit, he felt no hunger. Instead, he grabbed as many leaves as he could hold. Ishah stuffed leaves into her basket, so he crammed his leaves in with hers. When it was full, he grasped her hand, and they both raced for the river.

As they crested the hill, she dragged on his arm. Then she stopped. "I can't go down there." She swallowed hard. "It was so wonderful there with you, but it won't ever be the same."

"I know." And he did. "But, Ishah, I still love you. I hope you still love me."

He did still love her, even though love didn't feel as it had this morning. Then, he had loved her with the most passionate, pure, and selfless love. But this new broken love required effort and was but a shadow of the morning's love. This love was tainted with anger, disappointment, distrust, and broken promises. Was this what love had become? He wanted the unbroken love back, but he didn't think that was possible. This made him sick with regret.

"Come on." He tugged on her arm. "Let's get this over with so we can hide and die."

"I can go down there and die if you're beside me. I still love you, too." She glanced at him, and he glimpsed the truth in her eyes. Somehow his words seemed to have repaired the wounds he had inflicted. "Do you think this will continue to hurt so terribly?"

Ish groaned. "Well, we're already dying, and I can hardly bear it. So it will probably hurt more to die completely." His throat ached, and he blinked hard. "I'm afraid our unity with the Creator has ended. When He takes our spirits out of our bodies, I believe our lives will end."

With alarm in her eyes, Ishah stared at him.

Clearly, this hadn't occurred to her. Ish turned his mind away from the thought. It scared him too much. Better to focus on their task. He pulled her toward the river. With glazed eyes, she stumbled along beside him, unseeing.

"Let's see what we can do with the leaves," he said as they ran.

She didn't answer.

Working side by side would help. She could distract him

from these terrifying considerations. They raced down the hill. He led her to where he had laid the long grass and pulled her down to sit cross-legged on the ground.

"Ishah." He nudged her. She startled and gaped at him with unfocused eyes. Then, seeming to come to herself, she considered the grass before them.

"Can you pull the long grass into thin strips?" Her voice was barely above a whisper.

Taking one of the stems, she demonstrated. His hands copied her actions. Then, with a small stick, she poked little holes into each of the fig leaves.

"Talk to me!" Urgency caused him to be abrupt; she startled. "I don't want to think about facing the Creator. I've disappointed Him, and it makes me sick to consider it."

"I feel the same about you. I disappointed you, and I feel as if my heart is broken."

He hadn't considered this. Yes, she knew how he felt.

Compassion for her washed through him. She was as miserable, too. He remembered her under the fig tree, clutching her knees. Alone. He grasped her chin. She flicked her eyes to his.

"I still love you," he said.

"As I do you."

Her pain-filled eyes bore into his. They sat staring at one another, each experiencing this new kind of love with all its pain. Yes, he would want to hold her in his arms again. But he didn't know if he would ever again do so. They would soon die, and all of this would end.

Would *they* end? Would they simply cease to exist?

Ish tore his thoughts away. It filled him with dread. He needed to work.

"Do I have enough grass torn?" Ish lifted the grass.

"I don't know. Hold up one of those strips. See if it goes around your waist."

It did. Taking the strip of grass from him, she poked it through the tiny holes she had punctured in the leaves, threading the strip of grass through leaf after leaf. Ish took another strip and repeated the same action. They would need two of these— one for her and one for him.

Ishah then wound piece after piece of grass around the strip, securing it firmly. This bound the top around the waist. Winding them together like this made it stronger.

"You're wise," he said. "I never could have designed this. I still need your help, and you're still my helper. That didn't get ruined when I ate the fruit." This reassured him.

Quickly she glanced up at him, as if she also needed his affirmation. She seemed to require things from him that he'd never had to give her before.

"That's true." She smiled faintly then looked back at her work. She exhaled, and her shoulders relaxed some.

When she finished weaving the grass, she knelt before him. Covering his nakedness, she reached around him to position the long string of leaves, a *garment*—this was something new.

Ish rotated, and she fastened the back. As her hands smoothed all the way around the garment, he turned slowly. Again, he was reminded of his stupidity. How had he not realized they needed to cover their nakedness?

"This works well."

"We need to make one for me, too."

They worked silently, both absorbed with their thoughts. Ish pondered his failure. Eating from The Tree hadn't made him wise. He was now overwhelmed by his own stupidity and had lost his God. He dreaded the coming confrontation. What would he say to Him?

Yahweh's words come into his head, "When you eat... When..."

God had known this would happen.

Why didn't He stop me?

Ish had thought Yahweh was the source of wisdom, but now he doubted His character and His love. God could have warned him again. He could have intervened. Why hadn't He?

Never before had he distrusted the Creator.

This separation from Him hurt. It damaged Ish to even think these things. It made his heart feel hard and maimed. All of these emotions were new.

Ish was angry with God, as he was with Ishah. He was still wounded by her betrayal and her lack of trust. Now Ish felt anger and distrust of Yahweh tear at his heart as well. Until the moment he had eaten the fruit, he had trusted the Creator implicitly and wholeheartedly. When he ate the fruit, his confidence in the Creator had died.

This realization made him sick again. Expecting to gag up more of the bitter liquid, he dropped the grass and crawled toward the river. Nothing came up. He felt broken, as if there were a mortal injury to his heart.

The essence of him felt damaged. His thoughts, emotions, desires, intentions—his very self—had been destroyed. This was an internal wound to his spirit. Damaged as he was, it would be easy for God to peel his spirit out of his body.

How could he live like this?

If dying meant their lives would end, maybe it would be a blessing to end this misery. Burying his face, Ish flattened himself on the earth as despair, frustration, and regret pummeled him. His partner in pain, Ishah placed her hand on his shoulder, soothing him.

"I'm so sorry, husband."

His voice breaking, Ish whispered into the dust, "I can't bear this."

"Let's finish with the leaves and find a place to hide."

Though he heard her continue to work, he couldn't move. Instead, he pressed his face into the dirt, anger and distrust growing and burning within him, doing further damage. This hurt even more than his distrust of Ishah and the anger he felt toward her.

Maybe this would be what killed him.

CHAPTER SEVENTEEN

GOD THE SON had known that this would hurt. He had designed this blueprint before the foundation of the world. Knowing this would happen, the Godhead had created humanity with volition and curiosity. This was all part of the plan.

By definition, real love hurts when sin becomes part of the story. God knew.

He yearned for the intimacy He had experienced with them.

He despised the fact that they now misunderstood Him.

He wanted to ease this misery they now experienced.

He knew what this was doing to them, and thus, He wept.

Because of their human sin, the Holy Spirit had departed their carefully crafted bodies, no longer filling them with God's presence. The two were immediately aware of His absence and felt terrified, lost, and confused.

The first human argument had erupted. The two didn't know why.

They felt ashamed of the beautiful bodies He had created. They were now afraid of Him and tried to hide. The man was angry, no longer trusting Him. Both were filled with regret.

They thought He had left them, when actually He was very present. He saw everything—both inside and outside of them.

He heard their thoughts; He sympathized with their emotions. He would *never* leave them. He loved them with an everlasting love.

But, for now, the two were turned against Him.

The plan was unfolding exactly as designed.

Humanity was not easily contented; they were brilliant; they became bored; they had to be tested, and permitted to rise to the challenge. They needed triumph and celebration. They craved the bliss of being pursued. They yearned to be won. They would settle for no less.

And so, the Spirit would woo them. It was a romance.

God's love was irresistible to those He had chosen. They just didn't know it yet.

Only His presence and glory could ever fully satisfy them. He had set eternity into human hearts. Therefore, His plan would guarantee them eternal bliss and contentment.

The certainty that those who belonged to Him *would* spend eternity with Him eased the torture and heartache of this first separation. Indignant over the pain Satan had brought upon the human family, God's righteous anger demanded justice for them.

Restoration would occur. A war had begun.

The hosts of heaven had to be mobilized. God would prevail.

The fallen ones knew they had no hope of winning, but they would try. Though they had to work within God's parameters, they would destroy as many lives as they could, in hideous, painful, and devastating ways, crafted by their evil minds. They would take delight in doing so.

They hated the human family. The carnage had only begun.

God would orchestrate all things for His benevolent purposes and for the good of those who would love Him. God would turn even the fallen angels' corrupt actions, causing them to produce good, working their evil deeds contrary to their intentions.

God would redeem it all. Nothing could thwart His plans.

But for now, mankind was separated from Him.

Only God the Son's passionate sacrifice would save and satisfy them.

Now He would go talk to the man and the woman. The consequences had to be explained. The promise of future redemption had to be vouchsafed to them verbally for the first time. God the Son would now promise His future arrival as one of them—fully God and fully man.

Later, He would live a sinless life as the Redeemer, the only one qualified to pay for their sinful action. He would die for them, paying for their sins with His own blood, and He would rise from the dead, crushing the evil one, so His beloved ones could be justified and declared righteous. Like all the promises He would make before He came, this one would be given in an obscure way to shield His intentions from the knowledge of the fallen angels.

They were at war.

God now directed the strategy and the mobilization of the holy angels. The hosts girded themselves as their individual assignments were received. Angels with immense power poised for action, ready to assume their positions against Satan.

The Tree of Life must now be guarded; the man and the woman must be protected.

The hosts of angels winged their way toward the earth, streaking down at the speed of light, taking their protective stances around the man and the woman, facing off against the fallen ones who surrounded them. All was done according to rank, authority, and dominion.

The first act was complete. The wooing would be successful.

It began.

CHAPTER EIGHTEEN

ISHAH FINISHED THE leaf covering for her waist, but she couldn't reach behind to tie the strand. Uncertain about what to do, she stood. Her husband lay prostrate in the dust, his fingers grasping and tearing at his hair.

Obviously, he sensed she had completed her task, because he raised his head. Shoving himself up from the riverbank, he examined her leafy garment in a preoccupied way, his face hard. His eyes didn't meet hers. He appeared angry again.

Internally, Ishah withdrew, shielding herself from the emotions Ish would soon unleash. He looked sick and pale but determined on some course of action. Without a word, he secured the leaves at her back and then seized her hand.

Here it came.

Running up the hill, he jerked her behind him. Sprinting toward The Tree, he pulled her in his wake. She didn't want to go back. As she withdrew, she slowed. He yanked on her arm. He was faster and stronger. She couldn't keep up. She stumbled against him, but he didn't ease his pace.

Why was he doing this? What propelled him back toward The Tree?

As they approached the two tallest trees in the Garden, Ish hurried straight for the Tree of Life, practically dragging her. Ishah could hardly breathe.

The sun was close to setting. Evening drew near. The day began to cool.

Ishah heard the Creator walking in the Garden as usual.

Leaves thrashed noisily. The trees whipped and swayed in a mighty wind. God had never before arrived in this manner. Flashes of light blazed forth, blinding Ishah's eyes. A deep rumbling echoed, vibrating her chest, causing the ground to tremble.

Ishah wanted to prostrate herself before Him. She'd never felt like this.

Dropping her head, she hunched, cringing away from His approach as she stumbled on weak limbs behind Ish, who darted behind the nearest cluster of bushes and shrubs. Ducking, he wrenched Ishah's arm as he yanked her down beside him. It hurt.

She kept silent, shocked by his rough treatment and Yahweh's approach. The swiftness of Ish's running speed had taxed her. She clutched her weak knees and burrowed her head into the shelter formed by her limbs. Hot trembling breaths puffed rapidly against her bare abdomen as she attempted to catch her breath.

Peeking out from the shelter of her arms, she peered at Ish. Looking annoyed, as if he'd been thwarted somehow, he stared intently at The Tree of Life. His brows were drawn together, his expression dark as he fumed over some inner frustration.

What is he thinking?

His stern face frightened her. Normally, he told her all his thoughts, but a silent barrier now stood between them. With dark and glittering eyes, he stared at her. There was something stealthy about his gaze. She'd never seen his eyes look like this. Ishah flinched.

* * * *

Ishah gaped at Ish. With wide eyes, she shifted away causing him to wonder, *What do I look like?* Had something changed his appearance? She furrowed her brow. Her chin trembled.

The remorse Ish had experienced earlier smote him again. She was afraid of him! Rather than dragging her against her will across the Garden, he should have explained. He should have spoken. The man he was this morning would have.

"I won't let this happen," Ish whispered. "I'm going to get us to The Tree of Life to eat its fruit so we won't die."

"*Adam*, where are you?" God called.

The Creator had altered his name. *Why Adam?*

Now God stood next to where they hid. He knew exactly where they were. Yet, He called for him. That fact tugged at his heart, drawing him toward God in a familiar way.

The flashes of brilliance, the warring of the trees, and the echoing thunder caused his body to shake. His teeth chattered. It was difficult to breathe. A sour taste rose in his throat. Sullenly, Adam shoved away the fearfulness and stood tall.

Glaring at God, he braced himself and crossed his arms. "I heard You in the Garden, and I was afraid because I was naked. So I hid."

That was only a partial truth. Apparently, he could now lie, exactly like the serpent.

All around him, God's presence wafted and floated, fragrant and full of life. This was the breath that had filled his lungs. But God had clothed Himself in light, and no aspect of His Person could be seen. It was like gazing at the sun, looking painfully at God's shining radiance. Still, he kept his eyes locked hard on the brilliance that emanated from God.

His anger compelled him. Though he wanted to fall on his face before Him, Adam stubbornly stood his ground, glowering, consumed by his wrath.

"Who told you that you were naked?" Yahweh asked. "How do you know that?"

God's tone surprised him. Adam had expected harshness and ire, but the Creator spoke gently and lovingly, a kind sympathy in His voice.

"Have you eaten from The Tree from which I commanded you not to eat?"

Defiant, Adam practically spat his words. Apparently, this was how he spoke when he was angry. "The woman *You* put here—the one *You* gave me as my mate—*she* gave me some fruit from The Tree, and I ate it."

He felt justified. If his wife hadn't eaten the fruit and tempted him, he could easily have kept God's command. None of this would have happened. This was her fault. The serpent's words hadn't deceived him. He knew what the Creator had said.

Out of the corner of his eye, Adam detected Ishah. Rocking back and forth, she clutched her arms about her body, as if holding herself together, as if his words had destroyed her.

Again, regret and the pang of guilt smote him. Why did he keep hurting her? He couldn't help it. It now came naturally, pouring out of him like water. But he wouldn't back down.

Yahweh turned His attention to her now. The wind died down.

"What is this you have done?"

God spoke gently to her. *Why?* She had eaten the fruit first and had tempted him. He thought God should be furious with her. Ish waited for her to blame him as he had blamed her.

She would say he hadn't protected her. His directions had been poor. He had exaggerated. In his zeal to protect them he had established extra restrictions—they weren't to touch it, and he hadn't even wanted her to look at The Tree or its fruit.

He had made it a curiosity to her. He just now realized this. His tension about The Tree had produced the opposite effect than he had intended. Then, standing there under The Tree with her, he hadn't silenced the serpent or protected her in her moment of weakness.

He hadn't ruled over the creature, demanding it cease its lies.

Remorse struck at him again. What *was* that? He ignored it. Tense and rigid, he stood. *Blame me, wife. Go ahead.*

* * * *

Ishah felt as if she'd been hit in the chest. The shame of it overwhelmed her.

How could she ever look her husband in the face again?

No longer was he glad that God had created her for him. He was angry with God. He wanted to be alone. She felt torn by grief. Would she break into pieces?

Her vision blurred as everything around her slowed. Gradually it occurred to her that God's gentle voice had been aimed at the place where she hid. This fact soaked into her heart and mind: He had spoken to her. She didn't think she could move, but she rose, her knees knocking and her body trembling, terrified to contemplate His face and to hear His verdict.

Glancing up briefly, the blast of His wind caressed her face.

His brilliance emanated in all directions, the light so intense that none of His features could be seen. He wrapped Himself in this radiance. She could no longer behold Him. Overcome by her guilt in contrast to His holiness and divinity, she fell face-down and stammered out the truth.

"The serpent deceived me, and I ate the fruit."

The wind eased—now blowing in another direction. She lifted her head and detected the serpent. As it flicked its tongue, its cold hard eyes remained fixed on Yahweh's light-wrapped form. Until then, Ishah hadn't realized the serpent was still nearby.

"Because you have done this," God said to the creature, "you are cursed more than all the livestock and all the wild animals!"

The Creator spoke in the firm voice of absolute authority. He didn't question the serpent as He had questioned them. Instead, He immediately pronounced His judgment, a thunderous noise rumbling and reverberating across the Garden as He spoke.

"You will crawl on your belly and eat dust all the days of your life."

As God spoke, so it happened. The serpent's body transformed. The legs with the claws fell away and withered upon the ground. The wings and the collar of skin seemed to be absorbed by its long, slender body, which shrank in size. An angry *hiss* and a foul odor escaped as these changes occurred. The green-and-purple-scaled body now squirmed in the grass.

"I will put strife and enmity between you and the woman," God proclaimed, "and between your offspring and hers. Her seed will crush your head, and you will bruise his heel."

Bright light split the sky as the serpent slithered away.

A crack of thunderous noise echoed through the heavens, reverberating in the earth. Ishah clutched her head and squeezed her eyes shut, trembling with fear. Yet, she felt hope. She didn't understand what the Creator's words meant, but still

His proclamation uplifted her.

If God intended her to bear offspring, He would not strike them dead on this day. Their spirits would not be stripped from their bodies. Maybe her husband had been mistaken when he thought that dying might be the end of their lives.

There would be offspring of their kind, one of her seed. That offspring would crush the serpent's head. The serpent had tempted her, and she had failed. But, retribution would occur on her behalf. God would use the fruit of her body to destroy the serpent.

"Ishah." God's gentle voice aimed at her once more. The wind and the flashing light ceased. "I will greatly multiply your pains in childbearing, making it more difficult. It will be hard work. With pain you will give birth to children. Yet, you will yearn for your husband, desiring him, and he will govern and rule over you."

Why did God place this burden upon her? She would bring forth one who would crush the serpent's head. She would bear children. But now, it would hurt. Why? Was this to be a reminder of what she had done? Would she now have greater pain, because their intimate union and Adam's need for her had prompted his disobedience?

This was mysterious. Could it be fathomed?

Ishah didn't understand what childbirth would be like, but she now knew her body had been created to bear young of their kind. This was how they were to multiply and fill the earth. God had now made her task more difficult.

But He hadn't pronounced a curse upon her as He had the serpent.

Ishah felt as if she had a duty now to produce this one who would crush the serpent. By carrying this out, perhaps she could somehow atone for what she had done today.

But still, what had once been beautiful was now broken! Adam would govern and rule over her. Until he ate the fruit, Adam had showed her gentle consideration. Now, his actions were angry and erratic. She had experienced a taste of this pronounced judgment already.

Adam was stronger than she. Therefore, she hadn't been able to resist when he had dragged her through the Garden. Neither had he asked her, as he would have in the past. He had simply imposed the running and hiding upon her. He had ruled.

Would this be the norm—the new way he would treat her?

As she huddled on the ground, she squeezed herself more tightly, rocking back and forth in her agony. There seemed to be a hole where her heart had been, where her emotions were centered. A hollow ache filled her chest. Tears ran slowly down her cheeks.

"I was direct with you, Adam," Yahweh said. "I spoke plainly and clearly."

Ishah looked up. Adam's shield of anger crumbled. He was afraid.

* * * *

The trees thrashed and groaned above Adam's head, and the sky darkened as he faced God. The wind hit him with full force, and he braced against it. Now it was his turn to listen to God. All of God's words had surprised him. Even after all he had said and done today, his wife would still yearn for him, yet he would continue to act the same. Since that was the case, why would she desire him? Could he even treat her as he had before? Could he act lovingly any more?

The remorse again.

This time he allowed it to soften him. He would try. More pain, more hard work, but children. Not only one child, the crusher of the serpent's head, but more than one.

They weren't going to die on this day, though he knew something had died inside.

Adam's anger at God melted away. He feared what God would say. He was now going to get exactly what he deserved. He had done this. What would have happened if he hadn't eaten the fruit with Ishah—if he had obeyed the Creator regardless of what she did?

He couldn't comprehend that decision.

He had made his choice; she was his body. When she ate, it was as if he had already eaten. He ate. He couldn't live without her. He had chosen her over God, eating the fruit with her rather than obeying His command. He had chosen to die with her. He hadn't wanted to lose her.

However, it felt as if he *had* lost Ishah, in spite of his actions.

The very thing he had done to try to keep her seemed to have taken her away.

"I commanded you not to eat from the fruit of the Tree of the Knowledge of Good and Evil." Yahweh's voice was firm and measured. "You listened to your wife and ate from it. Therefore, the ground is now cursed because of you, its fertility taken from you. Through painful hard work you will eat from the fruit of the ground all your days. It will now sprout thorns, weeds, and thistles. Your breath will come hard as you sweat and labor to grow your food . . . until you return to the ground. For you are dust, and to dust you will return."

Adam was a dead man.

His work was now going to be backbreaking and strenuous. It would be difficult to get their food, not easy as it had been in the Garden. Every day he would toil and labor simply to eat, and then he would die and become dust again. His life would eventually end.

Adam's mind flashed to his first moments in the dirt when God had breathed life into him. Before God had breathed, Adam had been mere dust, lifeless, unaware. His body would again dissolve into nothingness—dust—and blow away. This was why God had labeled him *Adam*. The name's very meaning—the man made from the dust—would remind him of his mortality.

He was Adam. He was but dust. To dust he would return.

He would be reminded every time his name was spoken.

Overwhelmed by God's words and the events of this day, Adam turned away his seared and watering eyes, sank to the ground, and covered his face. The shape of the light that surrounded Yahweh burned behind his eyelids.

Adam was in shock, his reactions wooden. His emotions and thoughts couldn't keep up with this. But there was more. A bleating sheep brushed by him. Uncovering his face, Adam detected the stately ram along the edges of his vision. It walked straight to Yahweh, and He killed it.

The ram collapsed to the ground—dead. Adam was stunned.

A red substance spurted from the ram's body, soaking the ground. It was the color of The Tree's fruit, *blood* he categorized it. Yahweh labored over the carcass and crafted something from pieces of the ram's skin. Then He approached them. Blinded,

Adam could barely discern God bending over Ishah.

His heart thumped against his ribs. *What is God doing to her?*

* * * *

Desperately Ishah glanced about, her throat tight and her mouth bitter. The ram now lay lifeless on the ground, its tongue hanging out, and its eyes glazed and unseeing. This was what it meant to die. One day this would happen to Adam and to her. This horrified and sickened her. She shrank from the coming certainty. Unable to watch any longer, she covered her eyes. She could take no more. Heartbroken, she squeezed her eyes tight.

Yahweh's hands alighted on hers and slowly lowered them. She flinched, pinching her eyes more firmly closed. The glow of His appearance showed orange behind her eyelids, occasionally peeping between her lashes in flashes of brilliance.

Gently, God caressed her cheek, His hands warm and nurturing.

Though He stood right before her caring for her body so tenderly, she felt far from Him, as if she had distanced herself. She remembered the moment He had breathed His life into her. Since then, she had always felt as if He embraced her closely to Himself.

Until now.

Their God hadn't left them. Their own actions were what had separated them from Him.

Sobbing, she contemplated living without His fellowship. How would she survive?

She inhaled the fragrance of God as He gently removed her leaf garment and carefully clothed her nakedness. The new garment weighed upon her shoulders and smelled like sheep.

Opening her eyes, she squinted down at the sheep's wool. The garment covered her breasts as well as her lower body. Crumpled and weeping, Adam hunched on the ground beside her. Her own tears ran silently down her cheeks.

* * * *

God's blazing brilliance moved near to Adam. Then, tenderly, God removed his leaf garment—Adam's scalded eyes could see nothing. God's own hands wrapped him in another portion of the ram's skin, securing it with cords also made from its body. These smelled of the sheep and its blood.

Remembering the day when he had first buried his hand in the sheep's hair, Adam squeezed his fingers into the wool. He had felt it would be useful to them, but He had never dreamt it would be for this calamitous purpose. He recalled the tilt of the ram's head with the curling horns.

A sob broke from Adam's aching throat. This was death. The ram was no more. All that remained of him was his butchered body, and his skin covering their nakedness. The ram's living essence had departed. It should have been him, Adam—dead on the ground.

The Creator had given him volition. He had the ability to think, decide, and act. He had acted in a way that had destroyed their lives. And now they and all their offspring and, apparently, all of creation would suffer the consequences. The ram was now dead, the earth cursed, and they would return to the dust. They were now fallen.

"The man has now become like one of us, knowing good and evil," Yahweh said quietly. "He must never be allowed to eat fruit from the Tree of Life, or he will live forever."

Of course, God had known of Adam's plan to get fruit from the Tree of Life. He had prevented it and would continue to do so. Adam realized that living in this fallen state for all eternity would be a curse. Why would they want to live like this forever?

God's action to prevent it was a kindness.

"You are banished from the Garden of Eden," He said. "This place of delight, this foreshadowing of paradise here on earth. Cherubim will guard the way to the Tree of Life with a flaming sword so you cannot eat from it."

So it was over. Whatever "paradise here on earth" meant, it was lost to them now. They were being sent away. God's voice was sad, but He was firm. They would leave their beautiful home where all their needs had been met and where they had communed continually with their God. They could never come back.

The Creator stationed Himself directly in front of the Tree of Life and stretched wide His arms, thrusting them from it.

Wind blew forcefully out from Him, as if to blast them away. The ground shook with the thunder.

Adam didn't want to leave.

He yearned to return to the way they were before they ate the fruit, so he could stay here with his wife, living out their days, enjoying each other's presence, always aware of their God. But he was spun around, and the inherent force of God's Person propelled him forward, his feet stumbling. In front of him, he couldn't discern anything but the shape of the light that had surrounded the Creator. Would the shadow of this light remain burned into his eyes?

Stunned, he walked through the gloom. In the night sky, everywhere he looked, the light from the Creator floated before his eyes. But his eyes gradually adjusted to the darkness. God's seared image slowly faded.

Stay! Stay with me! Adam pleaded with God in his mind. *Don't make me leave You!*

Could God even hear him now? With anguish and despair gripping his heart, Adam trudged along. He ached for God, yearning for their former intimacy, but God was firm and relentless.

Adam had forgotten his wife.

That had never happened before—another first illustrating the destruction of their oneness. Where was she? God's image had faded, Adam's vision mostly returned. He looked for his wife.

Stumbling along, her arms wrapped about her body, she walked beside him. Tears ran silently down her face. He had wounded her deeply. He didn't think he could repair this wound. How would he even begin? He had lost everything. How would he begin to do *anything*?

Relentlessly, Yahweh's force pushed them out from the Garden. Would they be forever separated from Him? It seemed so. The reality of that cold certainty was what hurt Adam the most.

He had no idea how to repair his relationship with Yahweh or with his wife. He didn't know whether it was even possible. Having broken fellowship, Adam couldn't comprehend what to do next. Staggered and bewildered by the consequences of his actions, all he could do was stumble along, tripping over unseen obstacles in the dark, his hands hanging lifelessly at his sides.

The moon, now barely visible as a thin crescent, hung above them. The stars still filled the sky, but everything else had changed. He was not sleeping by the river with his wife in his arms, slumbering peacefully in anticipation of another perfect day together rejoicing in God's gifts.

He was now trudging through the night, not knowing his destination, having no hope.

* * * *

Ishah glanced at Adam. His head and shoulders slumped as if he had no will to live. She contemplated his pain and devastation—he felt as she did. But he didn't turn to her for sympathy or comfort. He didn't share his pain. He no longer turned to her for help. She squeezed herself tighter, the tears coursing down her cheeks.

She had lost Adam. Her heart felt flayed. Was there a hole inside her?

As God's power propelled them, they stumbled forward, away from the Tree of Life. They walked on and on, tripping in the deep darkness. No word passed between them. Ishah's heart hardened toward Adam. Something cold and bitter gripped her. All she could think of was her pain and how Adam had hurt her. All seemed hopeless.

For the first time she felt completely alone, though the Creator's presence was nearby, moving her onward. Alone, though Adam staggered through the night beside her. This was beyond alone. This was abandoned and forsaken. She was broken.

No encouragement or sense of hope could penetrate her heart. The dearest loves of her life, her Creator and her husband, were now outside her reach. *Can I ever be restored to either one?*

Engrossed in these thoughts, overwhelmed with the pain of her loss, she lurched through the darkness, not mindful of where they were or how long they had journeyed.

Near dawn they came to a large river. It was over.

* * * *

A rush of moist air blew across Adam's face, and he detected the sound of flowing water. The sky grew faintly lighter up ahead.

God's force drove them at great speed, carrying them across a river, their feet barely skimming the water, and depositing them on the opposite bank.

They stood outside the Garden.

Turning back, they looked at the place they desired most to be.

On the far bank, blocking their way, were two massive beings of enormous size and blinding brilliance. *The cherubim!* Each appeared to be three times as tall as Adam with six enormous beating wings, which spread as wide as they were tall. The movement of their wings whipped the air, causing the trees on that side of the river to sway and thrash. He could feel a faint breeze from their wings, even on this far side of the wide river.

They blazed forth light and seemed covered with quick, stern eyes, which scrutinized everything in all directions, ever watchful. One of them held high a flaming sword in his outstretched arm. This sword he flashed back and forth and then pointed at them.

Overcome with terror at these astounding angelic creatures, Adam collapsed to his knees.

They couldn't possibly go back.

CHAPTER NINETEEN

SATAN EXAMINED THE cherubim stationed in the Garden of Eden on the river's far side. Because they were all created on the same day, they were well acquainted. He was glad they guarded the Tree of Life—there was now no way for the man and the woman to eat its fruit and live forever. Of course, in their current state, if they did eat that fruit, they would forever be his allies and not God's. In fact, they were his allies right now.

The man and the woman had destroyed one another. It was beautiful to behold.

They weren't physically dead yet; that was true. But they *would* die. They *were* dying. Although their bodies would apparently live for a time, they were spiritually dead.

Walking corpses. Separated from God. His Spirit no longer filled them.

Satan guffawed. He had not predicted this result when he deceived the woman! He had thought they would simply fall down dead, and that would be the end of it. He wasn't sure why they were spared.

Watching them in this state entertained him. *They are miserable!*

Earlier in the day, the man had physically overpowered the woman. Satan had snickered as he watched the man drag her through the Garden. The man's violence had given Satan many ideas for the future. He had observed how the man's behavior affected the woman.

Every time the man opened his mouth, he seemed to inflict more damage. She withdrew into herself, her heart cold and hard. It showed on her face. Division between the two of them was good. Strife was lovely! Satan decided to whisper even more resentful thoughts to the woman to keep her heart embittered.

However, as he stood on the riverbank considering this, a highly problematic issue could no longer be avoided—God the Spirit was already working. He encompassed the man and the woman, whispering into their hearts and minds. Immediately after their first bites of the forbidden fruit, He had started His wooing. His words sickened and angered Satan.

Why did God want them back? Did God's love for the humans compel Him to desire to restore them? For Satan, there was no returning: once it was made, his angelic decision to sin had been for all eternity, entrenching him forever as God's enemy. But could the humans turn back?

Surely it was impossible! God's holiness and justice prevented the tolerance of any sin in His presence. Wickedness could not exist alongside pure, blazing holiness. God's purity obliterated corruption, repelling it, meting out justice. Satan, of all beings, knew this experientially.

Then, why this wooing? What did God have planned?

The Spirit cooed reminders of God's love to the man and the woman, remembrances of the joy and delight they had experienced when near Him, offers of mercy, and reminders of the promise. This pledge implied a coming defeat for Satan. But he would consider *that* later.

The Spirit also aimed convicting jabs at the man every time he mistreated the woman. These were hitting the mark. God the Spirit reminded the woman of His tender love and care for her, holding her up with these remembrances. But Satan could do nothing to prevent any of this.

After all, the Spirit was God, whereas *Satan* was not. Satan was merely a fallen angel.

Then there was the other issue. Two heavenly angels now faced off against every one fallen angel who had rebelled. Only one-third had been cast down. Satan and his cohorts faced former comrades who knew their strengths and weaknesses. These were not good odds. Satan eyed the two stern holy angels who stood arrayed against him now—Gabriel and Michael, of course. They shielded the two humans.

Additionally, every angel, both celestial and infernal, was under the sovereign rule of God. They could only operate within the boundaries established by Him.

Satan found he was very much hindered and constrained.

And then, there was the primary issue—he could no longer avoid considering it—the promise that his head would be crushed. *What does this mean?*

The Almighty's voice had been triumphant as He had announced it. It was certain. God was omniscient and omnipotent. Obviously, He had known He was going to make this promise when He had allowed Satan to test the man.

Therefore, Satan's head *would be* crushed.

The rebellion he had instigated would be put down.

He would lose. It was guaranteed.

He didn't understand how. God must have kept something hidden from him. So Satan decided to focus on the fact that this vow involved the woman and her seed. He would be allowed to bruise the heel of this offspring of the woman.

Bruise.

He would continue to foster strife between the man and the woman. Then they would not want to lie together, and there would be no children. If he failed in this, he would bruise all their children. Being born into a strife-filled family would be the beginning of their bruising. He had no idea who this one—this crusher of his head—would be. So, he would attack them all.

Perhaps God would speak more on this later. Then Satan would narrow down his target. He hated the man and the woman. He was certain he would hate all their offspring. So, regardless, it would be a joy to bruise and harm any or all of them.

He and the other fallen angels would consult together. They needed to determine how to proceed. But these celestial angels who now scrutinized them, along with God Himself, would see and hear all they plotted. God was omnipresent.

Even though his crushing would occur in the future, Satan felt as if he had achieved a victory. Still, God had allowed it. Therefore, there had to be a purpose Satan could not comprehend.

Had he played right into God's hands? This gave Satan pause.

Had this really been *his* victory, or God's victory?

Satan felt uneasy and uncertain.

CHAPTER TWENTY

ADAM WOULD BEGIN. This was his responsibility. He would initiate. He had to repair the damage he had caused. It had taken him a while to recover his senses, but now he was cognizant. He didn't know how long he had remained sunk to his knees, struck down with terror at the sight of the enormous angelic creatures and the horror of his own loss.

But now, rising to his feet, he deliberately turned away from the cherubim and the Garden behind them on the other side. Adam sought his wife.

Down on the riverbank she stood. Catching a glimpse of his movement, she glanced sidelong in his direction. Then she returned her eyes to the appalling sight of the cherubim, twisting her body ever so slightly away.

He waited.

After a moment, reluctantly, she directed her eyes toward his, fixing him with a stare, though still not turning to face him. Adam stepped toward her and pulled her into his arms. Stiffening, she leaned away, resisting his embrace. She clutched at herself, as if her own resources were her only source of comfort now. Still, he held her tight, contemplating what he should do now.

Their last warm interaction had occurred as they had created the leafy garments. Then, sickened by his actions, he had crawled away from her, gnawing on his anger at the Creator. Without explanation, he had then yanked her roughly across the Garden to the Tree of Life—a futile attempt. And, finally, he had indicted her and had criticized God for creating her.

That was probably the moment he had lost her. Their relationship would probably never be completely repaired. This grieved his heart. Just yesterday their unity of purpose and mind had been blissful. But now, an enormous obstacle stood between them.

What should he say? What would the man he was yesterday morning have done, the one who had loved her unbrokenly?

Adam pulled her down to the ground facing him. Cross-legged, he sat studying her solemnly. She wouldn't meet his eyes. Her eyes looked flat and lifeless, her lips pressed together. The river flowed silently at their side, and the sun began to rise.

Beginning simply seemed best. "I'm ashamed of everything I've done since I failed to protect you from the serpent."

She gave him her full attention. Silently, she regarded him with wounded eyes.

"I dragged you through the Garden without telling you my intentions or asking if you wanted to go. I injured you as we ran. Then, in my anger, I distanced myself, closing you out, blaming you and the Creator God. I've been so wrong. I'm very sorry."

Her eyes were like stones, hard and unyielding. It was clear she no longer trusted him. Coldly, she examined him. This was bad. He hurried on with his confession.

"I know I destroyed everything between us when I implied that Yahweh's creation of you was a mistake."

She snorted, and her expression hardened.

Unfazed, he continued. "I saw your reaction, where you lay on the ground. You wrapped your arms around yourself, as you have them now. I felt overwhelmed with remorse, but I made myself hard and resistant, because I expected you to blame me. I waited, but you didn't do it. Then I felt even worse for what I'd said about you."

Still nothing. Just the cold, hard eyes.

This was how he had stared at Yahweh yesterday. Ishah

was justified in her anger. He, however, had not been. God had clearly warned and instructed him, but he had chosen to disobey. He waited, keeping his eyes fixed on Ishah.

No response.

He plunged back into his apology. "I want to do all I can to restore our unity and to regain your trust. I'm patient. I'll do whatever it takes. I love you. I was angry, and my heart was hard. But I need you now more than ever. I hope you can forgive me."

She appeared as if she doubted that would ever happen. Clearly, she despised him.

With cold fury in her gaze, she sat a moment longer. Then she shoved herself up from the ground and stormed up the bank. Stopping some distance away, she turned her back to the rising sun and cast her eyes on the cherubim across the river. Adam wished he knew what she was thinking. Waiting, hoping she would speak, he sat watching her.

Nothing.

The sun moved higher into the sky.

After a long period of continuing silence, Adam leapt to his feet and stalked off down the river in the opposite direction— away from her—walking hard and fast. He couldn't merely sit there. He had bared it all to her, humbling himself, but he had received no response.

So that his anger wouldn't ignite again, he needed to leave.

She was treating him unfairly. He wanted to demand that she accept his apology. This was his new post-fruit-eating nature— he knew this. He determined not to let it win. He walked away so it didn't.

As he strode along the river, Adam sized up the land. His stomach still felt unsettled, but he knew they would be hungry soon. When that happened, Yahweh had said he would have to labor strenuously for their food.

This certainly wasn't Eden.

But there were a few fruit trees sprinkled randomly here alongside the river. The Creator had known they would need them. Gathering as many pieces of fruit as he could carry, Adam continued to walk.

The earth seemed to have faded, the colors no longer vibrant. Everything appeared dull and flat, with a gray, almost monochromatic tone. Dead. The soil here didn't appear as rich, and the mist that watered the earth each morning had caused thorns and thistles to sprout, as God had said. They looked tenacious. Nowhere on this side of the river did Adam detect any of the plants they had enjoyed eating in the Garden.

He named the river the Tigris. It seemed to be a different river than the one in the Garden—it was wider and flowed faster. Recalling that river in the middle of Eden, he named it the Pishon. He now knew there was more than one river.

He sought for a good location by the Tigris, one like their place in the Garden.

That also hurt. Thinking of Eden nearly broke his heart. There, he had awakened to find Ishah studying him, trying to discern who or what he was. There they had laughed and played. There they had talked with the Creator and had loved each other.

Could they ever have that again?

After seeing his wife's recent reaction, Adam doubted it. His only hope now was that Yahweh had spoken about children. So, in time, their relationship would surely improve. Even if he saw no evidence, Adam decided to believe the Creator's words.

Choosing not to believe and heed His words had disastrous consequences.

Rounding a bend, he came upon a possibility for a new home. Surveying the entire area, Adam studied this potential location. Where the Tigris curved, it had a rocky beach. Walking through the rocks, he found some that would be suitable for a plow. Of course, there were no animals to assist them that Adam could see. How would they get across the river?

Tall grass grew along the bank near the rocky beach. They would need this grass for baskets and cords to bind rocks to the plow. They'd have to find a suitable branch for a new one. No grass grew around the trees yet, but young thorns and thistles sprouted thickly.

A small hill had several trees growing against it, one with long branches that touched the ground all around the base. It was not like the fruit trees. Adam labeled it a *pine*. Under this tree they would shelter. God had made it for them when He had created the world, knowing they would live outside the Garden.

Adam walked back to the rocky beach and gathered stones to mark the place. Gathering up the fruit, he headed back to find his wife. He was now prepared to endure her hostility.

But when he returned to the place opposite the cherubim, Ishah was gone.

He peered in both directions. She wasn't in the water or on the shore. Since he hadn't seen her depart, he had no idea. Her feet had left no tracks on the hard earth. He'd have to wait.

Maybe she'd never come back!

The sun's journey, ever higher into the sky and then past its zenith, bore witness to his patience. While he waited, his hope slowly faded. He reviewed the events of the previous day and became heavy with grief and despair.

It occurred to him that this was again a holy day of rest. It had begun last night. This was the fifteenth day since they had been created. It crushed his heart to consider what he'd lost.

Could he honor God on this holy day, out here away from His presence? Was there anything he could do to restore his relationship with Yahweh or with Ishah, *if* she returned?

It all seemed pointless.

Ishah was gone. He didn't expect her to return. Why would she? He had destroyed their love. He was alone again. But this was worse than at first, because he now felt her absence. Without her, it would be impossible to carry out the mission the Creator had given them. And, even if she did return, he had corrupted the innocence and joy of the life they shared.

But the absence of Yahweh grieved him even more than the loss of the woman. His chest remained tight with anxiety and his shoulders tense. He felt desperate, frightened, and lost. The loss of God filled him with hopelessness.

The longer he sat, the more he realized how utterly exhausted he was. Sinking down into the dust, he contemplated the brilliance, size, and strength of the cherubim on the river's other side. Eventually, he fell asleep while looking with longing at their former home.

A troubled and fitful sleep.

CHAPTER TWENTY-ONE

ADAM DREAMT OF beautiful days in the Garden with his wife. Awakening, he stirred restlessly, wondering why he felt hollow and uneasy. Then, the horrifying truth came crashing back. They were not in the Garden. They had lost everything. It was gone. She was gone.

Despondent and crushed, he stared at the cherubim across the river. The sun neared the horizon, blazing brilliant from behind the angelic beings. The unobtainable Garden lay at their backs. His first day of misery neared its end.

Hearing something behind him, Adam rolled over. Ishah sat there in the dirt, exactly as she had in the Garden when she was first created and he had awakened to discover her. Of course, now she was clothed in the ram's skin, and tears had left trails down her dusty cheeks.

Forlorn, her entire person was permeated by a look of despair and loss.

"I thought you'd abandoned me," she said quietly. "So I went in the opposite direction. But I longed for you and came back, hoping you'd return to me." Her desolation was complete.

"How could I ever leave you?" He touched the indentation in his side—the place where the Creator had removed a part of him to make her. "You're my own body. We're one flesh."

She started to cry. Her tears shattered him. He had already felt he was on the verge of breaking. Pulling her into his arms, he cradled her against his chest. She wrapped her arms around him, instead of holding them locked about her own body.

"I love you." His heart ached for behaving as he had. "In my anger I did and said stupid, foolish things. My heart was hard. I hurt you, and I *knew* I was hurting you, but I kept right on. I'm so ashamed. I was so wrong. Please forgive me, Ishah. Please. I can't stand to lose you."

She wept, her tears wetting the shoulder of his garment. He wept with her, both of them emotionally devastated. Letting their sorrow consume them, they held each other.

"When you left I realized how much I need you," Ishah said. "I love you. I'm so sorry I didn't help you. Instead, I tempted you to eat the fruit. Please forgive me. I violated my promise and your trust in me."

Something stabbed at Adam's heart. He recalled the care and concern he had taken to keep her safe and how he had failed. Pulling Ishah up with him, he sat, cradling her in his lap.

"Of course I forgive you. We were both foolish. This will hurt us the rest of our days." A plan formed in his mind. "Let's make a commitment to talk and to forgive. It will be difficult because our natures have changed. Do you know why I walked away?" He ducked down, looking into her wet, swollen eyes, wanting to reassure her. "I wasn't abandoning you. I felt angry because you wouldn't forgive me, so I walked away. I was afraid of what I might say. You saw what my temper turned me into yesterday. So I'll have to fight it. I'll battle this with all my strength. I will! I promise you. Can you forgive me when I fail?"

Solemnly she stared at him. At last, she nodded. "Yes. I'll try. I've now seen my own weakness. When you're harsh with me, I become cold and indifferent toward you. My heart grows embittered." She looked down, her voice barely above a whisper. "I felt as if I hated you, as if I wouldn't care if you died."

Ishah's words hurt, but he couldn't condemn her. *Hate* was a new word, but he knew exactly what she meant. Basically, he had told God that he wished Ishah didn't exist, that He shouldn't have created her. It was the same thing.

Still, her confession skewered his heart. The urge to be alone rushed through him.

He needed to think.

Covering his face with his hands, he turned inward. How could two people who loved each other feel hatred toward one another? They had never felt this way before they sinned. That was what their actions were—*sin*. He knew this instinctively, like he had known day and night.

They were now sinners. This was what they had become when they fell.

They were now selfish beings. His first thought had been for Ishah, as hers used to be for him, but now, they had to make the conscious choice to put the other first. Sadly, it didn't come naturally anymore. Not only was their love broken, a dim reflection of what it had been, but their every thought, emotion, and action seemed broken and ruined as well.

Sin had poisoned them.

With a start, he realized this was more evidence of the Creator's knowledge.

God had known they would fall. Not only had He prepared a home for them outside the Garden, but He had also given them self-awareness of their new inner brokenness. He wanted them to recognize this change. Why? Would God have more to say? Would He ever speak to them again? Was there any way they could get victory over their own natures?

They had been given the mandate to rule and have dominion over the earth. Now it seemed their biggest challenge would be simply to govern themselves. Could they? They could try. He lifted his head and looked into Ishah's eyes, releasing the hurt caused by her confession.

"I understand," he said. "We're determined to overcome what we've become. Let's attempt to rebuild our trust in each other. I want you to trust me again."

"And I want you to trust me. But what will we do if we fail?"

"Admit our faults, make an effort to understand the other's weaknesses, forgive, and try again. Can we do that?"

"Yes. But what if we don't succeed?"

"Then we'll probably have many days like this." Adam sighed, despondent over the lifelong trial that stretched out before them, compared to their former state. "We're different inside now. We must learn to know each other all over again. Listening, learning, and loving will be difficult."

Her eyes met his; she nodded. "Yes, something inside me feels broken."

"We've now become sinners—I can't seem to stop sinning."

"Neither can I. That first sin changed me."

"Sin is now sickening us, breaking us up inside, causing us to be selfish. Distancing us from the Creator. He feels far away. I know you've felt this, too."

She nodded. "So, I'm right. We'll fail again."

"I'm afraid so. We'll have to be restored to one another again and again, but I'll never forsake you. You're my own body. If I can't speak when I walk away, it's because I'm trying not to let anger destroy me. Can you let me walk away? I'll always return. Can you trust I'll never abandon you?"

"I'll try. Can you remember that when I'm embittered and look as if I despise you, I really don't? My heart will become cold if you're harsh, but I'll still love you, no matter what you say or do."

"I'll try to remember."

Adam dropped his head, afraid to meet her eyes.

"Can I kiss you again?"

She answered by lifting his face to press her lips gently against his. He returned her kiss. Drawing back, they stared into one another's eyes, each measuring the other. They were reconciled. At least one thing felt somewhat in order now.

"I want to show you something." Still holding her, he rose. "I slept. You didn't. I'll carry you, if you'd like."

She put her arms around his neck. He almost forgot the fruit.

"I gathered some fruit for you." He grabbed it up.

She only nibbled, but she looked pleased.

Carrying her, Adam headed up the river toward their new place. As he walked, he told her about the names he had given the two rivers, and he described their new home.

Eventually they arrived. He hadn't realized he had walked so far. His anger had propelled him, and he hadn't been mindful of the distance. As he showed her everything, he could tell she compared it to their original site and felt the same pain as he did.

"I know," he whispered. "I feel the same. I want to be back in the Garden with you."

Adam carried her to the small hill to show her the shelter. At the base of a sharp rise there, the trees clustered against the small bluff set into the hill. The drooping branches of the pine formed a sheltered space. It would be the right size for a sleeping chamber. Under it they would be shielded. They wouldn't exhibit their nakedness to all of creation.

Ducking through the branches, he carried Ishah inside. He knelt before her, peering timidly into her eyes. After all that had happened between them, he lacked any self-assurance about how she would respond.

"Ishah, can I lie with you? I need the closeness of your body and the physical reassurance of your love. I feel as if I might break. I need you to keep me whole."

"I feel the same," she said softly. "I need your body, too."

Adam breathed a sigh of relief. In spite of everything, she hadn't rejected this intimacy with him. Their garments' fastenings appeared as if Yahweh had designed them to be removed. His knots were similar to the ones they used. Surely, He meant for them to come off.

It occurred to Adam that this was more evidence of His care. Maybe He hadn't abandoned them when He drove them out. Could they have unity and fellowship with Him again?

They removed the skins, and Adam spread them on the ground.

Gratitude filled him when he gazed upon her body, his own flesh and bones. Knowing her intimately was essential, like food and water and air. He felt restored to her as they become one. Maybe their world hadn't been completely destroyed. Perhaps there was hope.

After all that had transpired, the emotional release of making love caused them to weep. Kissing each other desperately, they wept the entire time their bodies were united, each seeking consolation in the other. This had never happened in the Garden. Tears seemed to be part of this new life. Later, lying in the darkness, they clung to one another.

"Yahweh made it clear that you'll bear young—our children." Adam smoothed her hair from her face. "We now know how we'll increase in number. It *is* related to our bodies joining together and to our desire. Because of that, Ishah, I want to give you a new name."

Gauging her response, he studied her face. Awaiting his next words, her eyes glinted at him in the darkness.

"God changed the name I'd given myself. He called me Adam—it means the man made from the dust. This is similar to what He always called me, but now *He* has chosen my name. Every time I hear it, I'll be reminded that I'm made from dust, and to dust I will eventually return. This name forces me to recall my approaching death."

Ishah crooned softly, her eyes soft and sympathetic. She understood. He felt comforted.

"*Eve* means 'life,'" he continued. "I want to call you Eve, since you'll be the mother of all the living. It's a name of hope. It will remind us of God's promise. He didn't strike us dead. Rather, He promised you will bear children, and one will crush the serpent's head. With your body we'll carry out His command to be fruitful and multiply. While my name will remind us of our death, your name will remind of us that life will continue."

He awaited her response.

"*Eve*." She tasted the name. "It's full of promise and the expectation of something good. I need those reminders. Thank you, Adam." She buried her face against his shoulder. "Do you think the Creator still cares for us?"

"Yes, I think He does." He caressed her head. "At first, I felt we were out here all alone. I thought our actions had caused Him to reject us. But then I found evidence that He'd prepared a place for us. There are a few fruit trees here. This place by the river is similar to what we had in the Garden. And just now, when we removed the ram's skins, we found He'd used the same knots, so they'd be familiar. He arranged these details to ease our way. He cares for us. But I'm still not certain whether we can ever have true unity with Him again. That grieves me."

Eve was silent as Adam watched. He stroked his fingers through her hair—she, the future mother of all the living.

"I agree with you," she said. "There's evidence that He might still love us. When I returned and saw you lying asleep by the river, exactly like the first time, I thought my heart would burst.

It was like a gift from God that you came back to me." She choked back a sob. "I've also been thinking about His words. His promise that the serpent's head will be crushed demonstrates His concern for justice on our behalf. It seems to me that He still cares for us."

"That's true. I was glad to see the serpent cursed. I wonder why it tempted us and what its relationship is to the Creator. I'm glad one of our offspring will crush its head."

"So am I. Very glad."

"That one will have to be far wiser than I. Everything I did was flawed."

Motionless and silent, Eve lay in his arms. After a long while, she lifted her eyes to his. "Regardless, I'm sorry I went under The Tree at all, listened to the serpent, and then ate the fruit after promising you I wouldn't. My actions tempted you. I'll always blame myself."

Stroking her hair, he said, "Since we love one another, I think blaming ourselves is better than blaming each other. We're going to keep sinning. So maybe admitting our faults and taking the blame is what love looks like now, because love is broken, a mere shadow of itself. It's now tainted with pain and remorse and broken promises."

"You're right." She sniffed. "We'll keep making mistakes and hurting each other."

"But," he said quickly, wanting to encourage her, "if we're quick to take the blame, then admit our faults, and ask for forgiveness, maybe we'll win our battles with anger and bitterness. Maybe we won't inflict pain on each other."

"Maybe you're right. I hope we gain more evidence of the Creator's love." Her voice broke.

"I think we have it already." He nuzzled into her hair, kissed her head, and drew her closer. "He planned ahead for us, we have the promise of coming children, and we have each other. You help me to be strong. It's good not to be alone."

"I've now been alone, and it's good to have you back." She wrapped her arms firmly about him. "I couldn't bear this without you."

Bound tightly in one another's embrace, feeling heartbroken yet glad for the other, they spent their first night together outside of Eden.

CHAPTER TWENTY-TWO

THE NEXT MORNING, even before Adam opened his eyes, the obstinacy of his damaged nature asserted itself. This surprised him. Irritability was a new morning emotion. How could he listen, learn, and love in this condition? The absence of God left a ragged hole.

When they stepped out into the morning sun their struggle began. Surrounding them were unplowed fields and the hard-packed earth. As Adam scrutinized the soil, it became increasingly evident that they would now be enslaved in a continual battle with the unyielding earth. The seeds here were scattered sparsely, the thorns and thistles anchored firmly.

Nothing was going to be easy. This wasn't the Garden of Eden.

After eating the fruit he had gathered and drinking at the river, they decided to use sharp rocks on the thorns and thistles. Weeds were something they'd never before encountered. Additionally, Adam now recognized how the burdens of their new life and the difficulties of their labor affected their newly changed natures.

In Eden, their work had been a joy. Obviously, not so here.

There, they had been surrounded by an abundance of fruit. Adam had turned the soil to provide green things for the animals with no thought about their own food. But now, a panicky urgency tightened his chest. He must provide food. It rested entirely on his shoulders.

He suspected that green plants wouldn't simply spring forth from this hard soil overnight, as they had in the Garden. God had cursed the ground. Strenuous labor would be required to coax what he could from the dust. The seriousness of the situation made his decision particularly weighty about where to till the soil. Their lives depended on his success.

Silently, he surveyed the ground over the hill from their sleeping shelter. It looked level there. A wide-open area received the sun. Back in the Garden, he had noted that the plants in the sunlight grew faster. Maybe this area would be good, too. It looked like a much better location than the area between their shelter and the river, which needed to be left open for daily activities. That strip of land, unlike this wide field, was too narrow to grow much food.

"I think we should start up there on the level place." He strode toward the broad, flat field.

"Are you sure?" Eve didn't move to follow. "We'll have to walk up and down the hill to get water as we work. Wouldn't it be easier to start by the river?"

"The flat area up here is better." Adam continued to climb the hill.

Behind him now, she still hadn't moved. "But the soil looks easier to work right by the river. Are you certain?"

Why did she question him? He had made up his mind. This irritated him.

Her suggestions in the Garden, before they ate the fruit, hadn't provoked him. But now, for some reason, he felt annoyed that she questioned his decision. He tried to answer calmly.

"This area is better for a field." Inflexible, he threw his answer over his shoulder as he continued walking. "Let's begin up here."

From the flat area above their shelter, he now looked down on her as he moved to the area he had chosen. Her face looked resistant, as if she thought her idea was better than his. But she didn't say anything. Instead, she silently followed him up the hill.

Adam felt annoyed that she didn't concur wholeheartedly as she would have in the Garden. Decision-making had been easy there. Each of them had yielded to the other, their intents unified.

But now he had a responsibility. He had to feed them. If he failed, they would have no food. He couldn't even comprehend that. He'd never had to be concerned about it before.

Why did she resist him? Was he being rational? Adam attempted to examine her suggestion calmly. Why did she think her idea was better?

Turning it over in his mind, he understood her reasoning, but he still felt his plan was superior. He stuck to his intentions. Asserting his right to make this decision, he inspected the flat field, studying the thistles and thorns spread across the surface. How to begin? She had come up beside him now, though she still didn't speak.

"Let's try to hack these weeds out with the sharp edges of the rocks," he said.

Squatting down before one batch of weeds with rock in hand, Adam struck the base of a particularly luxuriant thistle, hitting it repeatedly. There was still no response from Eve, but she squatted down beside him and worked on another.

They toiled in silence.

As he chopped at the thistle's base, the soil loosened, and the plant's substructure was exposed. A *root*, he labeled it. How far below the soil did it extend? The deeper he hacked into the subsoil, the farther down the root grew.

Finally, he seemed to have loosened it. He grasped the thistle to yank it out. Sharp spines all along the plant's shaft pierced his skin, drawing blood. Quickly, he dropped the weed and examined his hand. Unlike the ram's blood, his didn't spurt. It merely beaded on his skin, so he grabbed the thistle again. It hurt, no matter how he repositioned his hand.

Inexplicably, the pain in his hand sharpened his irritation with Eve, who remained silent.

He wrenched the weed free, tossed it aside, and moved to the next plant, working his way through thistle after thistle.

There was still no word from Eve. Adam decided he wouldn't speak either. With each thistle he attacked and each sharp prick to his hands, he grew increasingly annoyed with her silence.

The next thistle he assaulted was solid and sturdy. He had to dig and hack for a long while before he could wrest the root loose. The spines were particularly sharp. As he tried to grasp the plant, it pricked his skin repeatedly. Each stab of pain increased his aggravation with Eve. Blood from his palms smeared the plant's stalk, making it slippery. Seizing the stubborn thistle, Adam yanked it out, threw it aside, and then turned on her.

"Are you going to be silent all day long?"

She merely raised her eyebrows and stared at him.

"Eve! Do you know how hard this is? If I make the wrong choice, we won't eat! This isn't Eden. Our work here isn't play. For the first time, I'm worried about food. And I don't have any guidance from the Creator. Your silence makes this more difficult."

Mutely, she contemplated him, her lips pressed firmly together.

He couldn't stand this! The sun was only a short distance above the horizon, and already he had to stalk away. He didn't want to say something he would regret, but he felt like yelling at her.

Why is she doing this?

Adam stomped far across the field and dropped down behind a tree, so he couldn't see her. Faintly, he heard her continue to work behind him.

He questioned himself. *Why does this irritate me so much?*

He truly felt his decision was best. Why did her disagreement bother him? Was it because they'd had only harmony until two days ago? Could he make a decision she didn't agree with? Was that allowed? This was complicated. Did unity mean he had to yield, even if he believed his plan was best? What happened if he yielded, it was a disaster, and they had no food?

In addition to these unknowns, he couldn't ask Yahweh. There was a barrier between them. Adam didn't know if he could turn to God for help out here. Had God stayed in the Garden? Could Yahweh even hear him? If so, did He care? This separation added to his frustration.

He didn't know what to do about either quandary.

Adam realized he had to do what he thought best, but he wanted Eve's agreement. He desired to move forward in a unified way. Having her concur would give him more certainty about his decision, since he no longer had the calming reassurance of God.

At least he had their experience in the Garden to compare with his current behavior. Sin, selfishness, and discord hadn't marred those first weeks—they hadn't fallen yet. Their natures had been yet unaffected by disobedience, and they'd treated each other as they should. He could measure what he would have done then against what he had determined now.

Considering how he had treated Eve before his nature was broken, Adam recognized that he hadn't articulated his decision this morning. He hadn't really listened to her. He had dismissed her idea without giving her any explanation. Maybe, if he clarified his reasoning, it would bring her into agreement.

But why was she silent? This angered him. Was there a reason? Maybe she wanted to say something hurtful, and she was guarding her mouth. Could he grant her that? Yes, he could. He would go back and try this again.

Adam walked back across the field toward Eve. She was still bent over, chopping out the thistles. When he drew near, she stopped working and looked up at him expectantly. Her eyes didn't look stubborn. Her jaw wasn't set, as it had been earlier. She wiped her dusty hands on her sheepskin-covered thighs and sat back on her heels.

"Adam, I didn't speak because I felt argumentative. I wanted to have my own way, but I was trying to see your perspective. I didn't want to fight, so I kept silent."

He squatted beside her, examining her pile of thistles. Her confession had knocked all the anger out of him. He felt the sting of remorse again. They had talked about doing this yesterday—in fact, he had even reviewed and reaffirmed his intentions first thing this morning, but he hadn't realized how difficult it would be.

"You did better than I." He glanced up at her face. "I wanted your immediate agreement with my decision. When you didn't give it, I got angry. I wanted my own way. I'm certain this is part of our fallen natures. It seems to be what's driving us now."

Eve nodded. A contemplative look crossed her face; her focus turned inward. Then she fixed her eyes on him, waiting for him to speak further.

She always seemed to know when he had more to say. She had done this in the Garden, he remembered, but he now understood the importance of her perceptive nature. When he was uncertain, her quiet patience made it easier for him to get his words out.

"Let me tell you why I want to turn the soil here. I owe you a better explanation." Point by point, he enumerated his considerations. "I should have explained more thoroughly, but I was stubborn. I didn't even think about giving you reasons or asking for your input. I should have listened to you. Will you forgive me for not including you in my decision-making?"

"Certainly." She smiled. "Will you forgive me? I couldn't speak to you without being angry. I felt so resistant, as if I had to insist on my own way. I'm sorry."

"Of course I forgive you. Do you agree with my decision?"

"Yes." She nodded. "I do."

Adam chuckled, caressing her chin between his thumb and forefinger. "I think we're going to have to do this frequently. It seems I can't do anything without thinking and acting contrary to how I behaved before, in the Garden."

"Neither can I." She nodded in agreement.

Now they were allies, companions in a struggle with their own natures.

Rising, Adam picked up his rock. They still had most of the morning before them. As they worked together now, they talked periodically, comfortably conversing about their efforts. He was hopeful. Maybe they could accomplish something without another argument.

Since he wasn't irritated with her now, he didn't feel angry when he grabbed the next thistle, even though it hurt his hand. It was mysterious how physical discomfort and strenuous work affected their new emotions. He was certain they'd be surprised by this combination again.

It was a grueling morning. Their bodies ached when they stopped to rest at the sun's zenith. Dust and smeared blood daubed them, and their legs cramped when they finally stood and trudged down to the river. They were already exhausted, and the day was only half over.

Slowly, they lowered themselves by the river. Before plunging their hands in the water, they stared at one another's reflections. Their eyes met. They didn't smile. With grim faces, they washed the dirt and blood off their torn and aching hands, and then cupped them to drink. After drinking, Adam splashed water over his face and neck, washing off the dust.

Adam grasped Eve's hand, helped her up, and led her along the river.

They needed to search for food. They'd eaten all he had gathered the previous day. As they walked, Adam rubbed his thumb reassuringly over the back of her hand. He knew she felt discouraged and probably blamed herself, just as he felt personally responsible. But they needed to put this behind them and move forward to face the challenge. Their lives depended on it.

They walked some distance before they found fruit trees. They gathered as much as they could carry and then started back.

"Eve, can you make some baskets?" Adam broke the silence. "Then we can carry more fruit. That would be helpful."

"Yes, I can do that." She looked at him and smiled weakly.

He knew she could tell he was attempting to encourage her with his reminder of her basket. It had been left behind. If they could gather some of this fruit and store it near their shelter, they wouldn't have to make this long walk each day. As tired as they were after only a half-day's work, any extra effort they could save would help them get through each day.

They returned to the field and continued their backbreaking labor over the thorns and thistles, toiling in silence, side by side. Sometimes their shoulders touched, and they leaned into one another, grasping a moment of comfort from the other's presence.

Finally, the sun dropped to the horizon. Adam straightened, stretching his aching back.

He evaluated the work they had completed. Compared to what they had accomplished in the Garden with great ease, this entire day's work seemed as nothing.

How would he ever feed them?

They had to discover more effective methods for removing the weeds and turning the soil. Again, he felt panic clench his chest. Terrified that he would fail, he swallowed hard.

Would Yahweh let them die? What then would be the point of their existence? Could he ask God for help? Merely recalling His holy name hurt. How could God possibly hear if He remained across the Tigris with the cherubim? Was there any hope?

"Eve, I'll be back." Adam caressed her shoulder, giving her a grimace of a smile. "Please, go on down to the river and wash. Don't wait for me to eat."

Adam spun away and sprinted across the field. He wanted to be alone. When he was out of her sight, he threw himself face down on the ground.

For some reason, he felt closer to the Creator when he lay in the dirt.

It was there he had first opened his eyes and basked in God's nearness, drawing his first breath. Though God was far from him now and Adam didn't know whether he could ever commune with Him again, being facedown in the dirt somehow made God feel near, as if he had returned to his own genesis, and the possibility of encountering God still existed.

Adam needed him.

CHAPTER TWENTY-THREE

EVERY WAKING MOMENT, Eve's guilt increased. Everything reminded her of the cost of her sin—their work, their interactions, and their days. The burden of her culpability pressed upon her, compounding the difficulty of their work this side of the Tigris.

Here they battled the weeds and hard soil constantly. Using their God-given creativity, they experimented with various methods. All their strategies were strenuous and exhausting, leaving them covered with dust and sweat, a salty substance on their skin, their hands torn and bleeding.

Kneeling in the dirt, grasping a sharp rock in both hands, they hacked the weeds, attempting to dig them from the soil. Searching for a more efficient method, they utilized woven grass cords to attach a rock to a sturdy branch. Wielding it as a tool, they chopped the weeds loose, but the tool was awkward and fell apart rapidly. One day, they rose right before the sun cleared the horizon, while the mist still wetted the earth, and they yanked the stubborn weeds out of the damp ground with their bare hands.

They made another plow, and Adam experimented with ways to turn the cursed earth. He pushed the plow, but this proved much too difficult, because the soil was unyielding. He tried various ways of pulling it, but it bounced along the top of the hard earth, rather than tilling it. He chopped and hacked with the tool they used for removing the thistles. This was tedious and slow. It didn't allow him to turn much soil each day. His regal brow creased with frustration.

Using his own strong shoulders and many grass cords, Adam attached the plow to his body, since he had no oxen. Following behind, Eve guided it. This worked best. She was glad to assist him, but the work was grueling. Walking behind him as he strained, gazing at the sweat and blood trickling down his back when the cords cut into his flesh, and hearing his heavy breathing always reminded Eve of what God had said: "Your breath will come hard as you sweat and labor to grow your food until you return to the ground. For you are dust, and to dust you will return."

Adam returned to the dust before her very eyes. It hurt to look at him.

They had grown thin. There was nothing green yet to eat. Adam's physical splendor faded—his cheeks sunk in, the marked ridges of his rib bones protruded, and his eyes were beleaguered and filled with pain. One day, both of them would disappear into this dust, but until then they had to work hard to gain their food.

As she watched Adam strain in his labor, Eve loathed herself, disgusted with what she had done to him. Crying tears of frustration, she guided the plow behind him. Occasionally, she turned her bitterness toward Adam, remembering his inaction as the serpent had deceived her.

But mostly, she directed her guilt and shame toward herself.

Her emotions caused Adam to react in various ways. Often, he was able to walk away without saying anything harsh. Other times, he saw her face, knew she blamed herself, and comforted her. In addition to dealing with her reactions, Adam had his own frustrations and exhaustion to battle each day.

Their emotions seemed so variable now, dictating most of their responses. The trials they endured sharpened their reactions to each other and to the work itself.

And their bodies had changed. Along with their increasing

gauntness, their skin's glow had diminished each day since the initial fading of their radiance. At first, it had been so subtle and gradual that they hadn't noticed. But now, there was no longer any reflection or brightness. Their skin no longer glowed. It was flat and dull in appearance. They tired more easily and experienced far more pain than they ever had before sinning. Their sleep was less peaceful.

Everything about their life broke Eve's heart, crushing her with grief.

* * * *

Today they faced yet another laborious challenge with the weeds. Grasping her unkempt hair, Eve twined it into a knot at the base of her neck, yanking the end tight, hoping to keep it from falling into her face. Beside her, Adam appeared grim and determined. They knelt, each using a rock to hack and gouge at some particularly troublesome thistles. The roots burrowed deep into the soil and were nearly impossible to remove.

Accidentally, Adam swung his rock down onto his opposite hand, smashing one of his fingers. He cried out and stopped to examine it. With him, she peered at the bloody injury, her heart saddened, wishing she could alleviate his agony. There was nothing either could do, so he kept working. The finger continued to bleed. He told her it throbbed painfully. This made his work even more punishing.

After their backbreaking and painful labor, he harnessed himself to the plow. She positioned herself behind him, ready to guide it, but the plow kept hitting rocks and buried roots. She couldn't keep hold of it. Repeatedly it bounced up out of the soil, striking the backs of Adam's legs, bruising them, and cutting the skin on his calves.

Blood trickled down the backs of his legs.

Tears coursed slowly down Eve's dusty cheeks.

"Can't you hold onto it?" he demanded, his voice rising. Turning, he eyed her sternly as he bent to rub his bleeding calves.

"Adam, I'm trying! It keeps slipping out of my hands."

"Hold on tighter!" He sounded annoyed.

She tried, but this recurred numerous times. When the plow

smacked the backs of his legs yet again, he seemed to have reached his limit. He yanked himself out of the harness, hurled the plow to the dust, and stalked off across the field without a word.

As he stormed off into the distance, walking hard and fast, Eve watched him. Across the field, she heard his frustration burst out in a loud roaring yell, his fists clenched at his sides. Bellowing, he bent to the earth. When he had finished venting his rage, he dropped to the ground, sitting with his back toward her. He remained there a long time.

Heart sore, Eve left the plow where he had thrown it and walked down to the river to weave more cords. They went through these rather quickly. She had found ways to make them even stronger, but they needed to find something more durable. Fixing her mind on this, her thoughts wended through all the possible solutions. By the time she heard Adam's footsteps approaching, she had accomplished much. A large pile of cords gave testimony.

He dropped down beside her. Draping his folded arms across his knees, he looked toward the river. Shamefaced at his tantrum, he glanced at her sheepishly.

Offering him a sympathetic smile, she patted his shoulder. Lifting his damaged hand to her lips, she lightly kissed the wound. Then she looked back down at her work. No words were necessary. As she wove more grass cords, they sat companionably in silence, side by side.

"Let's get in the water," she eventually suggested, looking up from her braiding. "It's been a hard day. It will feel good to cool off in the river."

Adam untied his sheepskin garment, let it fall to the ground, and walked into the water. When it reached his waist, he sank down, immersing himself completely. Resurfacing, he ran his hands through his hair, smoothing it away from his face. Then he stood facing the river's other side. When he did this, she knew he longed to be there, where the unattainable Garden beckoned.

She liked looking at him in the water. Standing with his back toward her, his strong shoulders glistened with droplets, and his upper body narrowed from broad shoulders to slim hips. With his black hair wet and dripping, he was so beautiful, even though his skin lacked the soft luminosity.

Eve laid down her weaving, removed her sheepskin garment, and joined him. Coming up behind him, she wrapped her arms around his waist. Pressing her cheek against his body, she inhaled the scent of his skin and kissed his back.

"I wish I were with you, over there," he said quietly, eyeing the river's far side.

"I know. Me, too."

"Sometimes I don't think I can bear this. I get so angry. I can't make the plow, the ground, or the weeds cooperate. I can't accomplish anything. I get mad at God, because it's so difficult."

Eve said nothing. She knew all too well what he meant. She squeezed him tightly.

"I need the comfort of your body," he said.

Turning, he picked her up and carried her back to their shelter, starting his desperate kisses before they even arrived. His lovemaking was different when it was fueled by frustration and sadness than when it was drawn from tenderness and affection. But, it bound them more tightly together in both instances. It reminded them that they were one.

When he had spent himself, he lay collapsed upon her, silent and heavy. Crooning comfort to him, she caressed his back and stroked her fingers through his hair. He remained, seeming to need her solace. Soon he roused, softly nuzzling her cheek and whispering endearments.

Later they rose to go outside. Eve stopped, horrified.

Blood besmeared the long river grass strewn on their shelter's floor.

"Adam! Blood! One of us is bleeding."

Turning in haste, he knelt down to inspect it. Examining his body, he discovered blood on his thighs and drew her attention to it, but it didn't appear to be flowing from him. With grave concern, he stared at her.

"It isn't coming from me, but I have some *on* me. Are you bleeding?"

"I don't think so." She checked herself. "I didn't injure myself in any way."

Both startled when they discovered blood issuing from between her legs.

What does this mean?

The color drained from Adam's face. "You're dying! What will I do without you?"

Remembering the ram, its blood spurting out to soak the grass, Eve stared back at Adam. She wasn't bleeding heavily like the ram, but the blood seeped from inside her. She was going to die! Attempting to banish the horror, she clapped her hands over her face. Her breaths came heavy and shaking. She was terrified. She didn't want to turn to dust.

Overwhelmed with grief, Eve contemplated leaving Adam. *Why? Why am I dying now?*

She hadn't yet produced a child to crush the serpent's head.

It then occurred to her that, because of this fact, she couldn't be dying. It couldn't be so. God had promised. She grasped Adam's shoulders and shook him roughly.

"Adam, I can't die yet. God said one of our offspring would crush the serpent's head. I have borne no children."

She watched this truth spread across his face. He breathed a sigh of relief.

"Is this my fault? Did I hurt you?"

"No, I feel fine. I'm not in pain. I'm just bleeding. I don't understand this either."

"What should we do?"

"I don't know. I can't think of a remedy, because I don't understand. But we need something to soak up this blood, and we need more clean grass for our bedding. Can you get it?"

"Absolutely!" He jumped up, seeming eager to take action.

Making certain there was no wound, Eve examined herself thoroughly. What did it mean? Was something wrong? She felt discomfort in her lower back now. Would it stop soon? If the bleeding continued, how could she rise to work with Adam? This was new and unexpected, and she didn't know what to do.

Adam was gone a while, so she lay back onto their bedding. Frustrated, she heaved a sigh—another new thing. New experiences used to be delightful, holding the joy of discovery, the two of them laughing side by side, nearly bursting with happiness and the pleasure of the Creator's nearness. Now, new things were usually painful or difficult, frustrating or annoying. Overwhelmed by her lack of understanding, she cried. Her tears ran down her cheekbones and into her ears.

Adam crawled back in through the branches. When he saw her crying, he dropped everything and gathered her into his arms.

"Are you all right? Did you find an injury? Are you in pain?"

Fear flashed in his eyes again. She pressed her face against his chest and let loose her tears, sobbing against him. When she calmed herself she spoke. "Every new thing is difficult. Life is so hard! What are we going to do? What's wrong with me? My back hurts now."

"I'm perplexed. This is unexpected, and it frightens me. I hurt you. I know I did." He held up his hand when she started to object. "You're in pain, Eve. It's my fault. But I don't know what I did, and I don't know how to help you. I can't fix this."

She knew he didn't want to hear her objections. He still held his hand toward her with a faraway look in his eye, as if trying to sort through all the possibilities. Then he sighed, making a small grimace of dissatisfaction. Obviously, he couldn't reach any conclusions either.

"Let me show you what I brought," he said.

Some of the tall river grass had brown, tubular bulges at the top of their stems. Earlier, they had discovered these brown bulges were full of soft, downy seeds. He had brought this fluffy seed material to absorb the blood, as well as long grass to replace the soiled bedding.

Eve rose, and Adam gathered the bloody grass, replacing it with the clean. She positioned the downy seeds under her and sat down. There was no other way to keep these in position.

"Now what?" she asked.

"I guess we'll keep getting more seedpods until you quit bleeding, but I can't believe I didn't hurt you." His voice rose with a tone of desperation. Horrified, he stared at her. "What if you keep bleeding?"

"Adam, I feel fine. Really. Stop blaming yourself. You didn't hurt me. I have to stop bleeding, since we know I'm not going to die."

"But—" He started to speak, but she talked over him.

"Listen. Let's think about this." She needed to calm him. "Might this have something to do with bearing children, since it's coming from that part of me? The ram died when it bled; we bleed when we hurt ourselves. Bleeding means death or injury. Maybe something is wrong inside me where I'll bear children."

"I don't know. It's possible. But what could be wrong?"

"I'm not sure. I don't understand what's happening to me, and I have no control over it. But when we made love, we didn't do anything we haven't done before. You didn't hurt me." She fixed her eyes on him. He didn't seem convinced, but said nothing. "Let's just see what happens. That's all we can do."

That was the only solution she could see. They only knew she was bleeding and would have to sit on these seedpods until the bleeding stopped, unless they could be positioned properly for her to move about. This was inconvenient, unknown, and frightening.

* * * *

The sun had set while they had completed this cleaning and preparation. Along the far side of the sky, the moon and stars appeared. At the same time, they both became aware of the falling darkness. They hadn't eaten. Adam leapt up.

"I'll grab some fruit, fill the water basket, and gather more fluffy seeds. I'll hurry."

Ducking out of the shelter, he departed. Listening to his feet pounding away into the distance, Eve fell back onto the grass, turning her mind away from the frustrating new mystery. Between the branches, she studied the ever-darkening sky. Peering at the moon as it rose, she realized it again looked as it had on their first night together, slightly diminished from its full round form.

Every night they had observed the changes in the moon. It rose later each evening, sometimes long after sunset. They never saw it on some nights, unless they awakened in the night. Then, the following day, they detected the moon's feathery outlined silhouette, pale and white, as it traveled across the arc of the daytime sky.

The night God removed them from Eden the moon had disappeared completely.

The next night—their first night sleeping alone outside the Garden—had been black, lit only by the stars and the faint glow of the cherubim far down the river. It was frightening, but this had seemed fitting. They had wondered if they'd ever again have their nighttime illumination. They had liked the friendly moon. They would miss it.

But then, gradually, the moon had returned, sliver by sliver, until completely full once more. Now it had again begun to wane. In the Garden on their first night the moon had looked exactly like this. Did the phases of the moon occur repeatedly? If so, they had lived through an entire cycle. It was now the shape it had been at their beginning.

Adam returned with the provisions for the evening and settled down beside her. While they ate, she expounded on her lunar observations. Parting the branches, he gazed at the nighttime orb. She watched him, his face contemplative, his analytical mind ruminating on the facts she had presented. Letting the branches fall, he turned toward her.

"Remember?" He pulled her down beside him. "The Creator said the sun and the moon were given to separate the day from the night and to mark seasons, days, and years."

"I remember."

"If this cycle of the moon is repetitive, we can measure time by the changes in the moon. Did you count the days since it last looked like this?"

"I lost count when we left the Garden," she admitted.

"So did I."

"The moon was completely full the past two nights."

Adam peered between the branches. "This shows us something about the earth, the moon, and the Creator, but I can't figure it out. It may also have something to do with marking seasons and years. God used those words, but I'm not sure what they mean."

"We'll have to watch the night sky. Maybe we'll learn."

"Yes. First, let's determine how many days make an entire cycle—from full moon to full moon. If we make a mark in the dirt for each day, we won't forget. Maybe later we can discern why it rises later each night, even coming up during the day."

Adam grabbed a small stick and etched three marks near the tree trunk, one for each of the two previous days and one for today. Then he reclined beside Eve. As they gazed at the moon through the branches, he twined the fingers of his uninjured hand through hers.

"Remember that first night?" he said softly.

"You were so startled to see me." Eve smiled in the darkness. "And you were in pain from the wound God had made when He created me."

"I had named the animals all day, looking for your face, but not finding you. There was no one of my kind, no mate for me. I fell asleep feeling so lonely. When I woke up and you were there, I was so glad to see your face. I didn't care about the pain in my side. It was nothing. I was overwhelmed by your beauty!"

"And I yours. As I sat behind you, watching you sleep, I admired your form and wondered what you were. You attracted me, but I didn't even know who I was at that moment."

"When I realized the Creator had made you for me, I was filled with gratitude. I still am."

As they talked quietly, they rolled to face one another. Eve kissed Adam softly. Then she raised his injured hand, pressing it to her lips. He scooted closer, his warm mouth caressing her forehead. His breath blew hot on her face, his eyes glimmering at her.

"That night," he said, "when I wrapped my arms around you, I felt so happy I could barely contain it. I was so glad to have you. I still am."

"I felt such peace lying in your arms. I still do."

He kissed her again. "It's good not to be alone," he whispered.

"Yes, it is."

Growing drowsy, they gazed into one another's eyes.

Silver in the moonlight, they slept.

CHAPTER TWENTY-FOUR

EVE SAT IN the shelter on the fluffy seeds, accomplishing hardly anything. She tried weaving grass to hold the seedpods against her body so she could rise and work. But the grass scratched as it dried, and the fluffy seeds wouldn't remain in place. So she simply sat and endured it.

Each day Adam went out to work in the sun—alone. He had to push or pull the plow without her help, which wearied him more than usual. His smashed finger made it difficult to grasp the plow or the rock. In addition, he now had to labor alone. Even from the shelter, she heard and felt how challenging this was for him.

She could only sit in the shelter and weave grass. A large pile of woven grass cords testified to how she passed each day. She also worked on something to shield Adam's face from the sun, but she couldn't get it right. Frustrated, she frequently hurled it across the shelter.

Eve didn't like to be alone. Her thoughts usually wandered back to that awful day. The fact that God had left them, and offered no solace, devastated her. And now, the bleeding made her wonder how she could bear a child to crush the serpent's head. She was failing in her duty to bear children.

But this was entirely out of her control.

She didn't want to think about this either.

To guard her thoughts from wandering in these depressing and bewildering directions, she took every precaution. Seeking relief, she mused over Adam—the sound of his voice, his face when he smiled, his intense dark eyes, the way the blackness of his growing beard framed his mouth, the echoing sound of his laughter, the strength of his body, their times of intimacy, their conversations. She longed for him.

She was always relieved to hear him coming and to see his face.

Throughout each day, he returned to the shelter frequently, bringing her water, fruit, and more seedpods, and then hauling out the soiled ones to bury them. The number she needed gradually lessened every day, which alleviated their fear and worry.

"Oh, Adam! I'm so lonely without you," Eve exclaimed each time he appeared.

Flashing his beautiful white teeth, he smiled broadly before bending to kiss her.

Each time he departed, she worked, anticipating his return, hoping it would be soon. Straining her ears, she listened to him laboring out in the field. Sometimes, she discerned sounds of struggle or frustration. Then, she felt guilty that she wasn't beside him, helping him. But what could she do? She had to sit here, bleeding and waiting.

Evening finally arrived, but this evening Adam stayed out later than usual. Such interminable waiting. At last she heard his approach. With full arms, he stooped under the branches, hauling in more fresh grass and seedpods, along with fruit and water.

"Adam! The bleeding has stopped!"

He grinned at her, and she at him.

"Thanks be to God!" he said.

Taken aback, she pondered his response while he placed the soiled seeds outside. Yes, God be thanked. Since He had promised they would bear children, and this involved that part of her body, thanking Him was appropriate. But could He hear their thanks?

God seemed nowhere near.

Onto the floor of their shelter, Eve layered the new grass. In companionable silence, they then ate and drank, smiling often at each other as darkness fell. When they finished eating, Adam scratched the day's mark into the dirt, and they settled onto their newly laid bedding, still green and cool against their skin. Smiling down at Eve, he lay with his elbow crooked, his head resting in his palm. With his other hand he smoothed her hair back from her face.

"I've missed you so much." He grinned, his teeth flashing pale in the fading light. "I've even missed arguing with you."

"I don't know if I've missed *that*." She smiled at his joke.

Chuckling, he kissed her.

"I can't wait to get into the sun," she said. "I've listened to you out there each day, knowing your work was harder. I felt so bad because I couldn't help you."

"It wasn't your fault."

"I wonder whether this will happen again."

"Perhaps it's related to childbearing, like you said." He shrugged.

"I don't know. Only time will tell."

"I'll be glad to have you back by my side! Your absence makes your nearness so much more precious." He leaned in to kiss her forehead. "I don't feel I've accomplished much these five days. But, Eve! Everything is growing so well now! The plants and grass are this high." He held his hand to the appropriate height. "I mostly kept the weeds out of the new growth."

Silently, they regarded each other. There was something else he wanted to say. His eyes glimmered with it in the faint moonlight. He seemed overcome by some strong emotion, relieved over something with which he had been struggling. She awaited his confession.

Finally, he spoke. "While I was out there alone today I talked to Yahweh. Now I feel as though He's close to me again."

"Really?" Incredulous, she sat up. "What happened? Tell me!"

"Every day while I worked by myself, I reviewed what happened on that day in Eden. I felt such guilt and shame over my words and actions that betrayed both you and God. I've been so grieved."

Adam's voice cracked, and he swallowed hard. Tears brimmed in Eve's eyes.

How differently he handled memories of that day! She avoided them completely, whereas he had been out in the field deliberating over his actions. Something about this struck at her, making her feel guilty. She withdrew from it.

"With you in here, I was lonely every day," he continued quietly, "and I missed God's fellowship so badly. I yearned for Him. So, I cried out to Him, and He felt near again."

"Did He seem angry?" Eve leaned toward him, trying to see his eyes clearly in the darkness. She wanted to observe his face as he answered.

"No. He never seemed angry, not even when He made us leave the Garden, and not now. I didn't think I'd ever know He was with me again. I thought He'd stayed in the Garden, and that all we could do now was long for His fellowship."

Here was something to consider. Adam was right. The Creator had never been angry with them—firm, but not angry.

"What did you say to Him?" She desperately needed to know. Was it possible for her to be restored as well, even after what she'd done?

"I confessed how wrong I was to disobey Him in the Garden. I was angry that He had allowed it to happen. I begged Him to forgive me. My disobedience showed I didn't love Him or trust Him as I should have. I admitted this to Him. I also confessed the many mistakes I've made since that first sin, all the ways I've hurt you, all the angry words I've spoken, all the times my temper has won. I begged His forgiveness for everything. I told Him that I knew I had fallen far from Him and that I couldn't do anything to get back to Him, since I'm now broken. I thanked Him for not striking us dead, as we deserved—"

His voice broke again, and he paused to regain his composure. She waited. After a moment, he looked back up at her, his eyes glistening in the darkness.

"Then I thanked Him for the promise that you'll bear children and that one of them will crush the serpent's head. I told Him I trust His promise. I know He's trustworthy, and I believe He'll keep His word. I thanked Him for you and the blessing you are in my life. I told Him how grateful I am for the gifts He's given us here, which are keeping us alive."

Adam had thanked God for her—even though she had tempted him to eat the fruit and everything had been ruined. Relief and joy washed through her, flooding her heart.

"What happened?" Eve whispered.

"I felt peace and His nearness. My heart filled up with His love. He didn't speak, but I now know He's here with me. I've been restored to Him. I feel clean."

Speechless, Eve sank back onto the bedding, staring through the branches at the stars and the dark night sky. She needed to think. The retelling of his confession made her happy. Maybe she could talk to the Creator God. She hadn't thought communing with Him was an option anymore. She was embarrassed that it hadn't occurred to her, as it had Adam.

But something in her still shied away from it. She remembered the holiness of God's character. *Yahweh*, she whispered silently to herself, unable even to speak His name because of her guilt. There was a barrier between them. To her, He felt absent. It would be difficult to speak when He felt so far away.

She didn't know whether she could even attempt it.

She was still too ashamed.

CHAPTER TWENTY-FIVE

THE NEXT MORNING Adam threw wide his arms and legs, stretching energetically. Today, Eve would be back by his side. He was as giddy as when the Creator gave her to him. Simply looking at her made him happy.

Grinning, he leapt up, turning to beam at her. "A wonderful morning!"

Shyly, she smiled up at him, a quizzical scrunch to her brow.

His enthusiasm encompassed him. His heart pounded with anticipation; not only had he missed Eve's company and conversation, but he needed her body and their shared oneness. He had felt disconnected these past five days. Working without her companionship had produced acute loneliness, even though he had renewed his fellowship with Yahweh.

He yearned for connection with Eve again. He needed her.

But, as he wrapped himself in his garment, a thought occurred: could they join their bodies again if making love had injured her? This troubled him. Maybe they shouldn't. Would she die if she bled again? Had he been the cause of it?

In spite of her insistence that he hadn't hurt her, he was certain she was wrong. Though she seemed to be healed now, her back pain had indicated an injury. But their intimacy had never hurt her before. Adam didn't know what to do, so he ignored the thought and pushed through the branches, turning to gaze upon her.

As Eve stepped into the morning light, she looked radiant—so glad to be outside the shelter. *So lovely!* They smiled broadly at each other.

"You're gorgeous!" He grabbed both her hands. "I'm so glad you're mine!"

"I feel the same about you."

Bursting with happiness, he ran, practically dragging her down to the river.

"Adam, there's no rush."

He glanced back and met her questioning look. "I'm happy to have you with me!"

"And I'm happy to leave the shelter." She laughed.

At the water's edge, she stepped gracefully in to bathe. He sat on the bank to watch, astounded by her beauty. She seemed delighted to be immersed and lingered there. They ate on the bank as her body dried. Then Adam wrapped Eve in her sheepskin garment, holding her against his body and kissing her forehead. It was wonderful to have her outside again.

Eager to show her the changes that had occurred, he seized her hand and hurried her all around. He wanted her to see how tall the grass and green plants had grown, how many weeds he had removed, what plants were now flowering, how much he had plowed.

He wanted to be near her.

She smiled widely at everything and praised all his efforts. This gave him a sense of satisfaction, an inner happiness. He described how difficult this or that project had been without her help and told her how much he appreciated her. This seemed to give her the same inner satisfaction; she smiled demurely.

In every way it was a glorious day, because of the joy they experienced in each other's company. She seemed as elated with him as he was with her! As they worked together, each smiled at the other often. Neither became discouraged or said anything hurtful. They didn't lose their tempers. Therefore, no apologies needed to be made. Throughout the day Adam hummed the melodic tune he had created in Eden. He added words:

My darling is like a fragrant flower,
A fruitful vine, a luscious fruit.
She is mine, and I am hers.
I will climb the tree and delight in her fruit.
I love her with all my heart.
She walks with grace. She steps forth in beauty.
The work of her hands brings blessing.
I will cherish her all my life.

He hadn't sung like this since they left the Garden. What a consolation it was to have her near him once more! As their eyes met, she laughed joyfully, blushing at his song's words.

When the day came to a close, Adam felt content. He hadn't thought he'd ever feel this way again. Yet their God had given them happiness even here, outside the Garden! Silently, Adam thanked Yahweh, cherishing His nearness.

He felt God's joy within him. This made him even happier.

Hand in hand with Eve, he gazed into her eyes. They sparkled back at him. They stooped to enter their shelter, and he scraped the mark into the dirt floor—number nine since the full moon. He lay down on the clean grass, curled around Eve, embracing her before him.

Hooking his chin on her shoulder, he whispered into her ear, "I cherish you." Brushing his lips softly upon her cheek, he bestowed a kiss.

"And I you." Eve turned, meeting his lips with hers.

"It would be impossible to live this life without you."

She murmured a soft sigh of agreement.

Adam nuzzled her ear and then lay considering the day. He had decided it wouldn't be wise to make love again—at least not yet—if ever. He didn't know. He didn't want to lose her. He couldn't believe he hadn't injured her, and he didn't want to hurt her again. What if his desire for her clouded his judgment? He tried to think about it dispassionately.

As he lay meditating, she also seemed to be deep in thought.

She kissed his arm, where it wrapped around her body. He kissed her head in answer, but they both continued their silence. Neither of them shared their thoughts. Adam wanted to figure this out before he confided in her. He didn't want her to try to persuade him one way or the other. He needed to solve this himself. Gradually, he felt her relax.

Her breathing slowed, so he whispered, "It's good not to be alone." As she drifted off to sleep, he wanted her to have the reassurance of his love.

"Yes," she said simply. Softly, she stroked his arm.

All night long he tossed and turned, twisting against her then turning away. The grass mat rustled each time he shifted, though he tried to move quietly, to no avail. She awakened several times and murmured to him. He reassured her, and she fell asleep again.

He dropped off to sleep and dreamt of holding her close. Then he jolted awake and pondered the implications if they lay together and she was injured. Her bleeding had stopped this time, but what if she bled again and didn't stop? What if she died, like the ram?

In anguish, Adam flipped over and slept again. He couldn't tell when he was awake or asleep, because he often dreamt he was awake when he wasn't. Additionally, he felt uneasy and guilty for some reason. He wasn't sure why.

It was a miserable night.

Weary the next morning, he sat up and rubbed the back of his neck. He had slept awkwardly with all the tossing. Still in conflict, he looked down at Eve. With patient eyes, she studied him then rolled away to crawl through the pine tree's branches. Clearly his turmoil showed on his face this morning. He liked that she could discern when he wasn't ready to talk.

Together, they completed their labors, but all day he preoccupied himself with his considerations. He didn't sing, and she didn't speak. Silently, he argued with himself. He grew more tense and anxious. As he considered losing her, she grew doubly precious.

What if the very thing that drew them so close took her from him? What if his desire for her ultimately killed her?

She would turn to dust. He would be completely alone.

If that happened, he wouldn't be able to live with himself.

Around and around he went, growing more confused and frustrated.

As he withdrew further inside his head, he noticed her

watching him with concern. She was trying to discern his deliberations, and he wasn't letting her be a part of them. Something stubborn and inflexible rose up within him. He wanted to make this decision alone.

But because the Creator felt far away again, he felt agitated.

That night, without exchanging more than the simplest conversation, they crawled back into their shelter and went through the same motions as the night before. Though he held her in his arms, the silence between them enlarged as did his sense of guilt, but he still had no idea why.

The same disturbed sleep was repeated. His tossing and turning kept waking her, and she then turned a few times as well. Finally, Adam could bear it no longer.

He awakened her and pulled her to himself, kissing her passionately. Eagerly returning his kisses, she seemed relieved that he had reached for her and threw her arms about him. It was such a pleasure to have their bodies joined again. Their lovemaking was enthusiastic, and both were overcome with their ardor for the other.

When they were satisfied, he rolled over into the soft, green grass, enjoying its coolness against his back. Eve's head rested on his outstretched arm.

Looking up, his eyes met the sinister stare of the serpent.

It glared down at them from the branch above. Fear gripped him! How had it gotten here? From its concealed location in the branches, the horrid creature's tongue flicked at him. But this wasn't the pine tree. He looked more closely and spotted large dark-green leaves with crimson fruit hidden among them. Tiny sparkles from the noonday sun glimmered off the shiny fruit. He and Eve lay in the thick grass under The Tree. It was midday.

The serpent hissed maliciously, leaning to stare at him.

Tearing his eyes from it, Adam glanced at Eve. She was stock-still and not breathing, her eyes staring back at him, glazed and lifeless, her body completely limp. Panicked, he turned toward her, and her head lolled across his arm, her mouth falling open. She lay in a pool of crimson blood spreading out from her lower body, clearly the result of their lovemaking.

She's dead!

Adam screamed.

Echoing in his ears, his shrieking awakened him. He jerked upright in a cold sweat. It was dark. Through the branches he detected the dim crescent moon. No luxuriant green grass cooled his back, merely the rustle of their dried-grass bedding.

Disturbed by his movement and the muffled screaming, Eve muttered in her sleep, turning to readjust her sleeping position. With trepidation, Adam peered up into the pine tree's branches, expecting to meet the serpent's evil eyes.

Nothing but blackness. All was quiet. Insects chirped.

They weren't in the Garden. It had been a horrible dream, a nightmare.

Terror washed over him. He couldn't make love to her again! If he did, he would kill her. He would have to take every precaution. He was determined. He couldn't lose her.

Once, he had failed to protect her and it had cost them everything. He must protect her from his desire. He couldn't take the risk of hurting her again. If he accidentally killed her, he might as well die, too. He didn't want to live alone, without her near him.

His decision made, he groaned inwardly. How could he resist her?

He'd have to avoid touching her or looking at her. Maybe that would help. He fell back onto the grass mat bedding and lay sleepless for the rest of the night.

All of this troubled him.

After an interminable night, the sun finally rose.

Adam carried out his plan. He hadn't touched Eve since the nightmare. He rolled off the mat, bent under the branches, and walked to the river. Behind him, he heard her emerge. As he washed his face and drank, her footsteps slowly approached.

"Here's some fruit," she said, nudging it against his arm.

Quickly he glanced and grasped the peach. "Thank you." He turned away.

They ate in silence. When he had finished, he rose, climbed the hill toward the field, and started weeding. Eventually she followed him. Neither spoke.

As they worked he didn't allow himself to speak or to gaze upon her. Looking at her or hearing the soft lilt of her voice tugged at his heart too much. But resisting her made him uneasy.

He couldn't resist momentary peeks.

With pale face and trembling lower lip, she worked, her expression as fearful as after they had fallen. He was hurting her. He didn't want that! He recalled their confrontation by the river on their first day outside the Garden. They had both walked off in opposite directions, thinking the other was lost.

But the terror of the nightmare crushed him with its cold certainty.

The stifling sense of guilt troubled him. He felt agitated and confused. His throat ached with it. There seemed to be no answer to this dilemma. He was at the end of himself and didn't know what to do. Without a word, he left, striding across the field and over the hill. Sitting down with his knees drawn to his chest, he silently cried out to God:

What do I do?

But God was distant and silent.

Adam heard Eve walking toward him. *Oh no!* Could he talk about this without hurting her or allowing her to sway him? He sighed. He would try.

"Adam, what's wrong?" she asked.

"I don't know if I can tell you. I have a decision to make, but I don't want you to sway me."

"What decision?" She sounded offended. "Why would I sway you?"

Adam exhaled slowly and pondered how to frame his considerations. While he gathered his thoughts, she waited, settling down beside him on the ground.

"I don't want you to die," he said.

"I *will* die someday, and so will you."

"But I don't want to be the cause of your death."

"How would you cause my death?"

Defensive and knotted up inside, Adam was pulled in one direction by desire, and in another direction by reason. But his reason was all confounded, and the nightmare only confused the matter.

Was his reasoning even logical? That was the question. And why did Yahweh feel so distant again? His absence perplexed Adam. Why was He gone? Could Adam talk this over with Eve or with God? Would Eve be reasonable, or would she try to sway him toward desire? Or was his decision reasonable at all? Could he say more to her?

What should I do?

"I can't talk about this." Adam rose and walked down the hill to the river.

He would stay close where she could see him. Then she wouldn't fear he was abandoning her. But he couldn't discuss this yet.

His stomach clenched. His mind knotted. His body sweated. Eve sat back on the hill where he had left her.

Darting periodic glances at her, he dissected his quandary. While he paced down by the river, she sat up on the hill. Now the sun sank. Adam stared at Eve. She met his eyes. He walked toward their shelter. She stayed where she was. He went inside, waiting for her.

The crescent moon had risen, and the stars blanketed the sky before she crawled onto the grass mat, but he was still awake. Without speaking, she turned her back and curled into herself, as far away from him as she could lie and still be within the shelter.

They didn't touch. Stiffly, they lay in the dark.

This wasn't good! There was a barrier between them. Neither of them slept for a great while. Awkwardly they lay, breathing fast. How could this be resolved?

Finally, Eve slept, inhaling and exhaling softly. But Adam spent another restless night of tossing and turning. His thoughts wouldn't allow him any rest, and he felt terrified to sleep and dream again. When the sun rose, he sat up, prepared to face another day of turmoil.

Eve rolled over and pinned him with a stare, her face hard, her eyes cold. "Why don't you want me anymore? Did my bleeding ruin your desire for my body?"

She thinks that? How could that be? The dilemma was exactly the opposite!

"No! I want you more than ever! How can you say that?"

She produced her evidence. "You've withdrawn from me. You don't look at me or touch me. We haven't made love since before I bled."

"I'm afraid I'll hurt you, and you'll die." He had to make her listen to reason. "I don't think we can ever join our bodies again, and it's tearing me up inside."

She considered his words, but said nothing, her expression still distant. Clearly, she had felt rejected. He had tried so hard to avoid this! How frustrating! When he had walked away, he had stayed where she could see him. He had been kind. He hadn't lost his temper. But, he couldn't let himself look at her or touch her, or he knew he wouldn't be able to resist her.

How could he make this decision not to make love to her again but still convince her of his love? He needed to explain himself. He had learned this lesson earlier.

"We made love, and you began to bleed. I know you said I didn't hurt you, but I don't see how that can be true. If I hurt you again and you start to bleed but don't stop this time, I'll lose you. I had a horrible dream about it. You'll die like the ram. I can't bear that! I have to resist you. If I look at you or touch you, I can't resist you."

"Adam, I told you I wasn't hurt by you," she said quietly.

"I know you said that, but that can't be true, given the timing." He had her there. He watched her turn his words over in her mind, pondering the implications.

"So, because I bled after we made love, you're afraid it will happen again, maybe not stopping this time. You think it will take my life, just as the ram died."

"Yes."

"Because you're afraid of this outcome, you're avoiding me so you're not tempted to lie with me again. This is why you're pulling away."

"Yes."

"Adam, do you think the Creator sees us?"

"Yes," he said hesitantly. He wondered where she's going with this.

"Do you think He knows what we're going to do, even before we do it?"

"Yes." Adam remembered His words. *When you eat of the fruit you will die. When . . .*

"God said one of our offspring will crush the serpent's head. He said I'd bear more than one child. He knows this will happen. How can we have children if you won't touch me?"

She was right. She had been completely rational and absolutely correct. He was stunned by the simplicity of it. Why hadn't he talked to her earlier? If God had a plan for their offspring—indeed, He had said they'd have more than one child—He must mean for their bodies to be united. Eve wouldn't die but would instead bear children, more than one.

Why didn't I think of this? Why didn't I remember?

She had reminded him of this when she had first started to bleed, but in his frenzy of worry and fear, he had forgotten. There was nothing to fear. She wouldn't die. As the knots in Adam's mind untwisted, he studied her with admiration. With kind patience, her luminous eyes regarded him; her lips gently curved upward.

He was the one who had been irrational. She had unwound his confusion. But, once again, he had hurt her by withdrawing. He had so much to learn about his broken and fallen nature. It was a constant challenge to listen to her, learn, and then love more thoroughly. A stubborn resistance within now kept him from obeying these simple instructions from the Creator.

If only he weren't so stubborn, she could have easily reminded him of the Creator's promise. So quickly he had forgotten! How could he grow if he always lost this battle?

Disappointment with himself washed through his chest, bringing tears to his eyes. Hers teared up in response. God had said Eve would be the mother of all the living. Adam had given her a name that meant *life*. Her name was supposed to remind him of God's promise.

Her very name was a reminder. And yet, he hadn't recalled it.

Now he understood why God had felt far away. Yahweh hadn't gone anywhere; Adam had left God again. He had forgotten God's words. He had thought and acted as if those words had never been spoken, as if the promise had never been given. He had forgotten that God watched him and hovered near. He hadn't cried out to God at the beginning of his confusion. He had ignored God's quiet, convicting urging within. That was precisely why he had felt so guilty.

Adam hung his head and squeezed his eyes shut, saddened by his broken state and grieved over his actions. He used to bask in the continual awareness of Yahweh's presence, but now he had to be reminded of his God and needed to train himself to recall His words. Because of his sinful nature, this would be the continuing need of his life.

Quietly, he asked Yahweh to forgive him. Then he looked up at his wife.

"Eve, forgive me for pulling away from you. I tried to figure it out alone. I'm sorry. If I'd talked to you sooner, you could have reminded me of God's promise."

She sighed and then laughed softly. "You've been in turmoil all these days about *this*? I couldn't figure you out. I thought you were angry or didn't want me anymore."

"No! I want you more than ever. I was overcome by my love and need for you. Remember my singing? I was so excited to show you everything. Didn't you notice?"

"Yes." She smiled, caressing his beard. "That's why I assumed you were rejecting my body. You didn't reach for me. It never occurred to me that you were thinking this."

Hmm. They seemed to think so differently now.

"I love you so much." He took her into his arms.

Holding her against his chest, he tipped her head back. First gazing into her face, taking in her beauty, her full lips, her shining eyes, he then kissed her tenderly.

She looked up at him with certitude, all doubt about his love vanished, and all coldness and anxiety removed from her face. Relief and joy washed over him.

They could be united again. There was no need to resist her—so, he didn't.

CHAPTER TWENTY-SIX

EVEN THOUGH THEY lay together regularly, the bleeding didn't recur. Eve's body felt fine. Maybe it had been a one-time oddity, or perhaps she had been hurt in some way and hadn't been aware of it. Neither of them had any idea why she had bled.

In the weeks since she had bled, their stamina had increased. They seemed to have adapted to their hard labor. Eve felt relieved. Those first days had been so difficult! She had been afraid they would always feel like that.

Now that they no longer fell asleep the instant they rolled exhausted onto their grass bedding, they reviewed the Creator's words each night as they had in the Garden.

Adam confided the details of the frightening nightmare. The dream was horrifying, and she now understood why he had felt terrified to lie with her. For nights afterward, he had difficulty sleeping, afraid he'd dream of it again. Each night he inspected the tree branches above their heads, making certain the serpent wasn't hiding there.

As night after night passed and no nightmare recurred, he slept better.

She was glad to see his mind at ease. The union of their bodies bound them even more securely. They had the indentation and scar in Adam's side, showing she was made from his body, but making love seemed to meld their very deepest selves. This seemed even more necessary than in the Garden, because now their sinful natures divided them, pulling them apart every day.

As they watched the moon move through its phases and the stars rotate around the invisible axis each night, they tallied their marks at the tree's base. While the moon followed the same path each night, the stars all shifted slightly as they revolved, as if the alignment of the axis wasn't stationary. Every evening, they studied the heavens, discussing what God had said.

They noticed that the outlined shapes of animals, such as the bear Adam had first noted in the Garden, gradually rotated and skewed to slightly different locations. These all moved in unison, distorting as they traveled through the blackened canopy.

The swath of tightly clustered stars spread across the heaven's middle like an untidy waistband slowly arcing through the night sky, shifting a little each evening.

Just as they didn't comprehend why the moon passed through phases—diminishing sliver by sliver and then enlarging again in the night sky, they didn't know why God had created the stars to rotate through the sky like this. All was mysterious.

Yahweh had told them in the Garden that He had placed the sun and the moon in the sky to help them mark seasons, days, and years, so they figured they or their offspring would grow to understand. The heavens seemed a complicated conundrum to puzzle out.

On day fifteen the moon vanished completely again. With an absent moon, the night pressed upon them, as if the black could be touched. The stars appeared even more vivid. In the distance, the glow from the two shining cherubim could be detected, the visible reminder that they could never return to their former life. The dark had felt bleak when they began their life out here.

Eve clung to Adam more tightly on these black nights. The glow of the cherubim was a painful reminder of her actions. In the darkness, her heart lay heavy.

They recorded the marks for twenty-eight days. They now knew those were the days required for the moon's entire cycle. Adam named the twenty-eight day cycle a *month*.

As they etched the mark for the twenty-eighth day into the dirt, it had been two entire cycles of the moon, two months, since the Creator had made the earth. Rather than continuing to mark each day, they now merely keep track of full cycles of the moon as a measure of time. They counted the months. As they did, the stars continued to shift in the sky ever so gradually.

Yahweh had formed them and their world in six days and rested on the seventh. Adam labeled each seven-day unit a *week*. Other than their lapse immediately after they had been cast out of the Garden, they now kept the Creator's holy rest day each week.

On each holy rest day, Adam went off by himself to talk with the Creator, but Eve was still too embarrassed and ashamed to speak to Yahweh. She acknowledged the day by resting and reviewing the Creator's words spoken in the Garden.

Between the holy days, they waged their ongoing battle with the thorns and thistles—their lifelong struggle. Daily they took the sharp rocks into their hands, walking carefully among their tender, young plants, and they hacked out the weeds that had sprung up among their crops.

And through the work of their hands, the Creator again provided them with food. Adam's cheeks and the hollows at the base of his neck were filling in again. The seeds God had scattered on the ground here produced interesting and delicious green plants to eat. In addition to the fruit trees scattered along the river, there were now legumes, grains, and root crops growing. Some they ate now. Some they watched for signs of ripeness, so they could sample them.

They also worked to expand the area where their food grew. The Creator had promised they would have children, therefore, they would need more food and more cleared land on which to grow it. There would be more of them to feed.

They didn't know when this would happen, but they wanted to be prepared.

Beyond their cultivated area, the ground lay hard, and the thorns and thistles enlarged and strengthened. The work grew more strenuous and grueling outside the boundaries they had already claimed. They had many days of wrestling with the plow, Adam's legs cut up and scraped as his plow bounced up out of the earth, Eve struggling to keep it in the ground, and them exchanging hasty, hot words when the difficulty overwhelmed them.

They argued, but they inevitably reconciled. Adam walked off over the hill to talk to God—he seemed to need this to keep his temper in check. This happened frequently. Eve watched him go, and then turned back to her work. When he returned, he always apologized.

One time, Adam had dealt with his frustration by jumping into the river. They had quarreled. Once more, he had thrown down the plow and had stalked away from her and the unyielding earth. After he had reached the field's far end, he had turned to look at the Tigris.

Suddenly, he had sprinted toward it. As he ran, he had stripped off the ram's skin. Naked, he had hurled himself off the bank, sailing through the air out into the deeper water. Eve had watched from the field as he had tossed the water over his head again and again.

Then, he had turned and faced Eden on the river's far side.

For a long while, he had stood completely still, his shoulders and wet hair glistening in the sun and then gradually drying as he contemplated the other side. Slowly, his tense shoulders had relaxed. When he had finally turned to wade back toward the river's edge, he had looked peaceful. As he had climbed out of the water, he had searched for her, walking toward her once he had spotted her sitting on the riverbank.

"I'm so sorry I do that to you," he said, before he had even reached her. "I don't treat you like the valuable helper you are. You must feel worthless when I get so angry at you and at the work we're doing together."

She had only shrugged. His words had hit the mark.

"I know you do. I can see it on your face. Then I feel terrible. It's like something stabs me in the heart when I hurt you. I feel so guilty, but I keep doing it. I'm really sorry."

Silently, she had looked at him, nodding. Her eyes had smarted as they teared up. He had squatted down by her, gently caressing her cheek.

"Please forgive me. I'm trying to listen, learn, and love. I really am."

"I know you are. I can tell. Of course, I forgive you. You forgive me often enough."

"Thank you." He had looked down, embarrassed that he had lost his temper again.

"What happened to you in the water?" she had asked.

He had looked up at her. "What do you mean?"

"You went in so angry, and you came out so peaceful."

"I talked with Yahweh."

"What did you say to Him?" she had asked.

"I told Him I was sorry for my fit of temper and for hurting you again. I explained how difficult and frustrating it is for me to fight these weeds. Then I yielded to Him and thanked Him for the work and for the patience it's teaching me, and I asked for His help."

"Then He gave you peace?"

"Yes," he had said simply, gazing at her gently.

But, in spite of this recollection, Eve couldn't bring herself to talk to God.

CHAPTER TWENTY-SEVEN

IN THE WARM sunlight, Eve stretched out on her stomach, enjoying their day of rest. Their work produced such weariness. There was no longer any time or strength for play. It had been two cycles of the moon—two months, since they had begun counting. Maybe in time, they would grow strong enough to enjoy play after their work.

With his arm thrown over his face, Adam lay beside her, the inner part of his elbow shielding his eyes. His short black beard framed his nose and his mouth. Since his breathing came slow and heavy and he looked completely relaxed, Adam clearly slept. Studying him for a moment, Eve then returned to her musing.

Because God's words held so much mystery, she considered them often.

God had said: "I will greatly multiply your pains in childbearing, making it more difficult. It will be hard work for you. With pain you will give birth to children. Yet, you will yearn for your husband, desiring him, and he will govern and rule over you."

She yearned for Adam. She desired him. They lay together frequently. But when would the children arrive? How? How would it hurt to bear them? Where would it hurt?

In Eden she would have borne children with relative ease. However, now her task would be more difficult, requiring more effort. Though she would have experienced some pain in the Garden, now the pain would increase. Of course. Pain seemed part of life outside the Garden with their now-selfish sinful natures. The pain multiplied—emotional pain, pain in their relationship, bleeding, wounds, pain in their work....

All because of me. Was this longing and waiting part of the pain?

Eve sighed. They now had conflict over even their coming together, their decisions, and their emotional reactions. Adam ruled over her, sometimes stating decrees without any discussion, other times losing his temper and hurting her feelings. Now she resisted him or argued with him, rather than cooperating and helping. At times she usurped his decisions, as she had on that awful day.

This seemed to be the new state of normalcy outside the Garden.

Eve had hoped to have children by now, so one could crush the serpent's head. But she had borne none, and she didn't know how to bring that about. What else did she need to do? She seemed to have failed in this, too. Was there hope?

Lying on her stomach hurt her breasts, so Eve rolled onto her back. This had begun a few days earlier. She hadn't revealed this to Adam. He worried about everything concerning her. He would blame himself, so she kept this to herself.

Recently, she had also felt oddly hollow inside, as if she needed more food, yet the food didn't taste right. She felt slightly nauseated as she had the day they ate the forbidden fruit. Adam's stomach spilled onto the ground several times that day. It felt as if this could happen to her, but everything stayed down.

The nausea was simply another difficulty outside the Garden, and she would deal with it. Complaining to Adam wouldn't make her feel well or help her cope. When she had grumbled about the bleeding, moping her time away as she had sat in the shelter, it had only made the time more wearisome and the waiting more difficult. She would keep this to herself.

They enjoyed the holy day of rest immensely. They spent much time reclining by the river or wrapped in one another's arms. Eve especially felt in need of rest today. She was more tired than usual, though she had done nothing out of the ordinary this past week—merely the usual fight with the weeds and trying to ease Adam's burden in some way.

His arms and legs had grown large and powerful from pulling the plow and from the backbreaking task of hacking out the weeds. From working alongside him, her arms had increased in strength, but she felt so weary.

* * * *

The next morning they awakened when the sun first shone through the shelter's branches. Eve had slept with her arm twined around Adam's waist, embracing him from behind, rather than he embracing her. As she kissed him between the shoulder blades, her stomach seized.

Twisting away, she hoisted herself to the grass mat's edge, hurriedly shoving her head under the branches so the contents of her stomach didn't spill onto their bedding. She barely made it. There wasn't much in her stomach, and she had to heave and cough to get it out. Adam had done this on the disastrous day.

Uttering soothing sounds, he now held back her hair as he gently rubbed her back. Onto the hillside's dirt, she heaved out the bitter-tasting stomach liquid. Adam continued to soothe her, now on his knees hovering over her. When nothing else seemed to be coming up, she rolled against his knees and looked up at him.

"Are you all right?" he asked tenderly. "All done?"

She moaned.

He peeked into the water basket. "There's a little water that hasn't seeped out. Would you like to wash out your mouth? I remember what that tastes like."

She nodded. The acidic flavor left in her mouth was unlike anything she had ever tasted—pungent and harsh. He lifted her head and tipped the basket to her lips. The strong scent of the aromatic tree sap that sealed the basket assaulted her senses, squeezing her stomach again.

The smell had never bothered her before. In fact, it had a pleasant scent. But now, it made her queasy for some unknown reason. Strange. Nevertheless, she sucked in a dribble, swished it around, and spit it under the branches. Adam watched her anxiously as she sat up.

"I didn't feel well yesterday," she said, "and I guess I'm not better. But I'm going out with you. I need to put something back into my stomach."

Acquiescing to her plan, Adam gripped her hand, and they exited. As usual, they sat by the river eating together. The food soothed her stomach, but she still felt exhausted, almost as if she hadn't experienced a good night's sleep.

Adam examined her anxiously, so she pretended to feel fine, so he wouldn't worry.

As they worked, her limbs felt as if they were weighted down, and she had no energy. But she pressed on with the weeding. About mid-morning her stomach again twisted, and she threw up her stomach contents into the field.

What was wrong with her?

Adam extricated himself from the cords binding him to the plow. He picked her up and carried her down to the river. Scooping out fresh water to rinse her mouth, he held her head.

"Do you want to rest here? Or do you prefer to rest in the shelter?"

"I don't want to rest anywhere," she stated stubbornly. "I want to be with you."

"Eve, you don't feel well. I've been watching you all morning. You're listless. And now, your stomach's upset again. Please, lie here by the river where you can watch me work, and I'll come back to you often."

Now she acquiesced. Frequently he stopped working to peer down at her, waving when he was assured that she was fine. He appeared disquieted about this change in her health.

What was wrong with her? This was baffling.

They had both been healthy, other than her bleeding. The bleeding had been two entire cycles of the moon ago, and she had felt fine until the last few days. Now she had no vigor. She felt flattened. Eve nibbled on the fruit Adam had left beside her. Having a small amount of food in her stomach lessened the nausea.

When the sun reached its blazing zenith, Adam brought some of her favorite legumes and green plants. Her stomach rumbled with hunger. Maybe she was recovering. With serious eyes, he studied her. Her enthusiastic response to the food seemed to relieve him.

Drinking plenty of water from the river, they ate and talked. It pained her to lie here not helping him, so she rose when he prepared to return to work.

"Stay here if you still feel sick," he instructed.

"I feel better. I want to help you."

Though she was still tired, she didn't feel nauseated any longer. She wanted to work beside him. The rest of the day, she labored alongside Adam, but she sensed his eyes on her frequently, gauging her health and her energy levels.

The sun was still far above the horizon when Adam turned to her. "Let's stop for the day."

"What? This is early for us."

"We've worked enough for one day."

Without further discussion, he stepped out of the woven cords and headed down to the river. She suspected this was because of her. He knew she wouldn't stop until he did.

She followed him. At the riverside, Adam stripped.

"Let's bathe," he called over his shoulder.

He waded in and began scrubbing the dust from his body. She smiled. He knew she liked to wash off the dirt and sweat before they slept. As she removed her garment and joined him, she admired his strong shoulders.

"I'm glad you're mine." She smiled at him.

He grinned back. "I feel the same. What would I do without you! I'm going to run upriver to get some more fruit. I'll return quickly."

Hoisting himself out, he ran naked up the river. She finished bathing and sat on the bank to dry. When he returned, he clothed himself as she dressed. Eve inspected what he had brought. Again, he had gathered green plants she preferred and now her favorite fruits. As if measuring her every mood and desire, he seemed especially solicitous.

How well he knows me!

He had obviously realized she was hiding that she didn't feel well so that she could work with him. She had loathed the days she had spent away from him while she was bleeding. Love for him warmed her heart.

At sunset Adam fixed his eyes on hers. "Let's go to the shelter."

Before she could object, he took her hand and led her there. She followed.

Usually, they waited until the stars had formed their canopy, watching each star peek out and the moon trek across the night sky. This was different. She knew then that he'd been watching her. He'd seen she was tired, and had made these suggestions in an attempt to take care of her.

How I love him!

Eve drew Adam to herself. Welcoming him to caress her, she kissed him warmly.

When the nausea awakened Eve the next morning, she barely recalled making love and had no recollection of falling asleep. Pulling herself to the edge, she emptied the minimal contents of her stomach under the pine tree's branches. Adam's face appeared more concerned, and he behaved even more solicitously. The events of the previous day were repeated.

Day after day, she worsened. Adam grew anxious, and Eve knew he feared losing her again. Often she observed him with a faraway look in his eye, deliberating over his apprehensions. When she caught his eye, he tried to hide his fears, adopting a brave and cheerful expression.

"I won't die, Adam," she said each time. "I have borne you no children yet."

Briefly appearing relieved, he nodded his agreement and went back to work.

Other than that, what could she tell him? She didn't know what was happening.

The exhaustion worsened, her breasts continued to hurt, and her body altered. Her waist thickened. Her breasts enlarged. Each night she fell asleep almost as soon as they lay down, sometimes immediately after making love, often before Adam could even embrace her.

* * * *

Four months had passed since they had begun the record. They lay on the riverbank, a favorite activity on the holy day of rest. When he wasn't working, Adam now kept at least one hand on her, as if to reassure himself of her presence. He still worried. He didn't speak of it, as if he were afraid to broach the subject for fear of its implications.

But Eve saw it eating away at him. This was what he mulled over as he struggled alone with the plow. On the days the nausea and exhaustion were particularly bad, she watched him from the riverbank. He stopped often on those days, peering down at her before returning to work. Frequently, he walked over the hill, and, faintly in the distance, she heard him speaking to God.

Now he slept beside her in the grass. As usual, he lay on his back, his arm thrown across his face blocking the sun. But even in his sleep, his other hand held hers.

Eve cradled her free arm under her head. She gazed down at her abdomen. Bulging above the front bone of her pelvis, a hard and round lump arose. What was that? It hadn't been there the preceding week, when she had last studied her changing body.

Moving aside the ram's skin, she examined this protrusion. The bright light of the sun beamed down, and something within the bump stirred about, causing rippling and heaving under her skin. Busy and vibrant, it moved, jostling from side to side. Barely breathing, Eve held perfectly still, faintly sensing its nudgings inside of her. And suddenly, she understood.

She was bearing a child! God's promise to them was coming to pass.

I'm with child!

That was why her body altered day by day, why she was nauseated and tired. Inside her body, God created a living being like them. This being wasn't made from dirt like Adam. She herself had been made from Adam's body, and this child was wrought from the love between them.

Instantly, her capacity to love doubled. Overpowered by love for this coming child, she adored him, just as she did his father. Both of them were absolutely essential. Tears ran down her face. All this love burst the resistance inside her.

God had begun the process of bringing His retribution upon the serpent.

There had never been anything she could do to guarantee that a child would grow within her. No special effort had gained

God's favor, thus causing a child to grow. She and Adam had merely done what they had always done, uniting their bodies because they loved each other.

God had proclaimed the promise, and He would bring it to pass.

He obviously still loves me! He hasn't rejected me!

Eve could again speak to Him.

"Creator God," she whispered silently, so as not to wake Adam, "thank You for this evidence of Your love. Thank You for this child and for keeping Your promise. I thought I had to earn Your favor to atone for what I did in the Garden. But now I see that Your favor is a gift You freely give. But I don't deserve it. I ruined everything. I'm grieved. Yes, I was deceived, but I was still wrong to eat the fruit. I disobeyed You. I blame myself. I'm so sorry. Please forgive me. Every day I need You. I keep sinning. I need Your help. I long for You. Forgive me for taking so long. I've missed Your fellowship, and I want it back."

And, immediately her heart filled with God's presence.

Yahweh was here with her. He had always loved her. He had never left.

Tenderly and patiently, He had been waiting for her to return to Him. Once more, she felt His peace and love. She had missed Him so much! She lay still, relishing their communion and unity. Into her mind came the Creation Song that Yahweh had sung over them.

The magnificent story begins—the story of My love!
All praise to the glorious Father for His perfect plan!
All praise to the comforting Spirit for His presence!
We are One, and you are Ours! Ours!
You are Ours forever and evermore!
I love you with an everlasting love!
I have created you for wondrous things!

Clearly, he had planned for them to be His forever and evermore. There was no obstacle that God Himself couldn't overcome, including their sin. Softly and reverently, she uttered His holy name, "Yahweh, my God, I adore You."

She needed to tell Adam. With the hand linked with his, she nudged. He jerked.

"Adam, wake up! I have something to show you."

At once, he awakened. Rolling onto his side and propping himself on his elbow, he frowned down at her with worried, sleepy eyes. "Yes?"

"Put your hand here."

She grabbed his hand, placing it on her stomach's bulge. The child inside struggled about.

Quickly, Adam withdrew his hand, shocked, his face alert and concerned. Carefully, he lifted the skin garment to examine her. Then his fear-filled eyes stared into hers.

"What *is* that?" he asked.

"It's our child!"

Astonished, Adam gaped at her and then again inspected the moving bulge.

"My fatigue and nausea, the changes in my body, were all to prepare me to bear a child. Look at it moving! I can feel it inside of me as well."

Tenderly, he caressed the mound of her lower abdomen, engrossed by what he felt. At first, a look of relief spread across his face. But then it dawned on him what this meant. Eyes shining and face glowing, he wrapped her in his strong arms.

"Eve, I'm so relieved. I was so worried. But, you're fine. We're having a child!"

"There's more," she told him gladly. "I spoke to our God, and it was as you said. I feel the comfort of His presence again. You're right. He didn't stay in the Garden. I know now that He sees us here and still loves us. I've been restored to Him."

Overcome with happiness, Adam beamed at her. There on the bank of the river, they laughed and hugged and rejoiced together.

"I've been asking God to heal your heart," he said, "and He has!"

Then he flashed a big smile and pulled her up tightly against his chest. Throwing back his head, he shouted with joy.

WaaaaaHooooo!

His rejoicing yell carried across the fields and the nearby river. She laughed as happiness bubbled up within her.

"Yahweh, our God, thank You for this evidence of Your love!" Adam shouted. "You keep Your promises. We trust in You!"

Eve's heart filled with gratitude. She agreed.

* * * *

Satan shrieked with rage, a blazing inferno of wrath rocketing through the atmosphere.

He had lost them, *both* of them. Though he had whispered bitter thoughts into the woman's heart, trying to persuade her that God did not love her and that He was unjust, yet her heart had been softened by the Spirit's whispering. Though Satan had tried to harden her against the man, the Spirit had worked, too, and Adam had become more tender and gentle with the woman again. The man's love had won her back.

Satan couldn't keep a hold on the man *or* the woman.

How had God the Spirit done that? The Spirit's words had only maddened Satan. Yet, the Spirit had lured and drawn the two humans toward repentance and desiring God.

This was why God had spared them, why their bodies hadn't died when they had eaten the fruit, why He had been wooing them: Yahweh had wanted to draw them back to Himself!

Satan screamed again. He had been thoroughly thwarted.

All had gone according to God's design.

And now, the Spirit was present *within* them again, as He had been before they had eaten the forbidden fruit, beckoning and urging them ever closer to Himself. Even after He had won them, He washed them with love, mercy, and compassion.

And they responded.

They seemed to have some sort of need that only Yahweh could satisfy, as if their souls were designed for God to pervade and to fill. And they yearned for Him, desiring more and more of Him, so that He did.

Even after He had drawn them to Himself, though their sinfulness reared its selfish head frequently, they grew frantic to return to Him. Ever since the man was restored, each time he had sinned and had pulled away from God, he had been desperate to turn back to Him. Though he often couldn't tell what was wrong immediately, he quickly discerned his error and returned to God.

Why? Because, the Spirit was there working the whole time. And now, He had drawn back the woman, and she, too, would surely continue to crave unity with God.

Of course.

Yahweh could do whatever He wanted. Of course, He would have created the humans like this because of His fervent love and attachment to them. He desired to win humanity back to Himself, and He would continue when more humans were born in the future.

It was a certainty. The Lord God was a lover.

The fervor of Yahweh's love for the two humans nauseated Satan. This had to have been God's plan from the beginning, from even before He had created them. Their satisfaction in Him was now even greater than it had been before they fell. Then, they hadn't known what they possessed in Him. Now they had experienced His lack, and so were even more thrilled to have Him.

How Satan hated Him!

And, to make matters worse, there was now the coming child. That explained the sound of the tiny beating heart. From within the woman, Satan had heard the faint sound and had observed her symptoms suspiciously. The beginning of the fulfillment of the promise to crush his head had come. The woman was now with child.

Was this one the head crusher? Would this first child be the one who destroyed him?

Just in case, he would give this one special attention. But he had no way of knowing. It could be any of them. He was sure there would be many. In spite of Satan's best efforts, the man and the woman still joined their bodies frequently—even after they fought. In fact, spurring them toward conflict seemed to be counterproductive. They especially seemed to need each other afterward, as if this physical act bound them back together somehow.

Satan didn't understand it. God used even this. Of course. God had created it this way.

Thwarted and infuriated, Satan bellowed across the heavens, calling to the other fallen ones, commanding them to come. They had to plan some sort of action.

But they were constrained by God's will and the sovereign plan He had laid down. They could not override the work of the Spirit. Clearly. In addition, Gabriel, Michael, and a host of celestial angels remained ensconced in a shielding barrier around the two and the coming child.

Clenching his ashy spirit fists, Satan's scream of frustrated rage echoed through the heavens. He would continue to watch. Surely he and the other fallen angels could discern something that would harm these ones whom God loved so much.

But what could they do?

CHAPTER TWENTY-EIGHT

EVE AWAKENED THE next morning filled with happiness! She opened her eyes to find Adam gazing back, smiling widely. Then, as usual, she moved to the shelter's edge to empty her stomach onto the ground. As she coughed up the small amount of bitter liquid, Adam held her hair and gently rubbed her back.

Still, she felt happy. The thrill of the coming child buffered all unpleasantness. Rolling back into the shelter against Adam's knees, she looked up into his eyes. His expression of concern gave way to a smile when he saw her grinning.

"We're going to have a child!" She beamed. "Knowing makes this so much easier to bear."

"Well, it definitely spares me the worry and anxiety I've been feeling."

Laughing softly, he smoothed her hair and handed her the water basket for the obligatory mouth rinse. They wrapped themselves in their sheepskin garments and stepped out into the morning sun, moving to relieve themselves away from their shelter.

Adam stopped and looked about, appraising their living area. He had a sense of purpose about his bearing. His demeanor had been the same in the Garden when he had discerned that they needed to turn the soil, so the grass could grow. Clearly, he planned some improvements.

Eve reached under the branches, pulling out the basket of fruit and the basket of green plants recently gathered. Settling onto the ground facing one another, they ate. Adam continued to survey the area as if with new eyes—he studied everything carefully.

They didn't speak; Adam looked deep in contemplation. Waiting, Eve ate and watched him, glad to get some food into her stomach. Finally, he spoke: "We need to prepare our living area and determine how we'll care for the child. And, I have to figure out how to work the field without your assistance."

"Why wouldn't I be able to help you?"

"We don't know how much time you'll need for the child's daily care. I doubt you'll be able to help me as much . . . *and*, one day we'll have more children, so we need to prepare. You'll help me by caring for our children."

"But," she said, "I have no idea what will be required."

"Neither do I. How can we know what your days will be like after you give birth? We may need to change the way we do things."

"But how will we know? What will we need to change?"

"I don't know. But we need to prepare." He looked at her, both of them mystified.

"I wish we had the other creatures near us." Those beautiful, blissful days drifted through Eve's mind. "Surely some animals in the Garden have borne young by now. If we were there, we'd be able to watch them with their offspring. I miss their presence."

"So do I. It was helpful to observe them. Their behavior showed that our physical union was Yahweh's plan, because they did the same thing. Remember?" He caressed her cheek.

She looked up into his eyes. "Of course. Apart from our joy in Yahweh, lying together is one of God's greatest gifts. It binds us together and reminds us that we're one."

"And now, God is using our act of love to create a child within you." He leaned in to kiss her. "So we need to prepare."

"Do you think the Creator will speak to us and tell us what to expect?"

Adam pondered this silently. When his mind went through this type of mental deliberation, Eve always enjoyed watching his face as he sifted through his thoughts.

"I don't think He will," he finally said. "He's left many things for us to discern. He told me that He would give me a helper. But He didn't tell me how or what to expect. We figured out how to interact through our urges and responses to one another. He told us to be fruitful and multiply, but let us discern how that would happen." He grinned. Leaning in, he gave her another quick kiss. "Maybe He'll give more instructions later. But for now, I think He wants us to ask for wisdom and then trust the instincts He's given us. What do you think?"

"Sometimes I don't trust my instincts. They can be flawed. My own urges led me to walk near The Tree, in spite of what you said."

He nodded. "We have much to learn."

"We need to learn to rely on Yahweh, I think."

"Yes, that's certain."

"And, we'll have to discern which feelings and urges to follow. We were naïve in the Garden, even though all our motives were pure. We didn't understand how our actions affected each other. But now we're fallen, and our natures are broken. Our instincts can lead us to yell at one another, or to be angry or selfish. Learning to know whether to follow our instincts or to rely on God might be the hardest work of our lives."

"Hmm. You're right," he said. "You've given me much to think about."

They finished eating. A preoccupied look on his face, Adam helped her up, his thoughts already turning inward. They walked toward the river.

"We're going to make mistakes," Eve said quietly.

"That's another thing that's certain." He looked back at her ruefully.

This saddened Eve. She didn't want to make any mistakes in bearing or raising their child, or the other children who would follow. But she would. They both would. They were flawed.

They knelt down to drink from the river, both absorbed with their own thoughts. The enormity of this overwhelming task pressed upon Eve. How could they do this? They had already destroyed everything by not obeying God's one direct prohibition, and they hadn't even had sinful natures then.

Silently, they both turned toward the field, beginning the daily fight with the weeds. They picked their way carefully through their growing food, looking for weeds encroaching into their already claimed area. They worked without speaking.

Eve's thoughts turned inward, toward Yahweh.

My God, we're flawed! We couldn't even obey You before we became selfish and sinful! How will we care for this child?

It was a blessing to talk to God now, to have the barrier between them removed. She no longer feared examining her actions from that awful day or her many mistakes since then. As she thought about that fateful day, she actually felt reassured of God's love. His love for them far exceeded their love for Him. His love had existed from before He had created them.

There was a larger narrative here than Eve could comprehend, a love that covered even the fatal aspect of their humanity. This part was both a gift and a curse—their ability to reason and to decide, the curiosity, questioning, and doubting that had produced this inevitable outcome.

But God had created them this way. Because this was how He had made them, surely His love would cover the mistakes they would make in the future as well.

Future mistakes would happen. It was certain.

Eve recalled the triumphant echo of God's voice as He announced that one of their offspring would crush the serpent's head. Clearly, this had already been God's plan. God had already been prepared to redeem their error, even before they had made it. They knew only a small portion of the loving labor the Creator would do on their behalf.

Something about the coming child helped her comprehend the vastness of God's love—this love that was immeasurable, that even covered sin and planned ahead for love to conquer it. Motherhood would teach her even more about this unconditional, sacrificial love.

Her body sickened and tired as the child was woven inside her. But, since she had felt him growing and moving faintly within, she couldn't comprehend anything the child could possibly do to quench her love for him. Yet, in her human frailty, even her mother-love was small in comparison to the love of God.

Eve had to tell this to Adam. Where was he?

"Adam," she called, searching the field.

He was nowhere to be found. This meant he had gone over the hilltop to talk to God. He did this when he was overwhelmed. Should she encroach on his time alone? The thoughts she had been meditating on might encourage and help him. Yes. She went to find him.

Eve crossed the field and the weeds beyond, and then walked down the slight decline into the woods. Stretched out facedown in the dust, there was Adam, talking quietly to God. She backed away. This was sacred and private. It didn't seem she should interrupt.

But he had heard her. He looked up.

"Eve, are you all right?" Tears streamed down his face.

"Yes," she said quietly. "I'm sorry. I thought of something that encouraged me and I wanted to tell you, but we can talk later." She turned to walk away.

"Stay." Wiping his eyes, he shoved himself into a sitting position. Then he patted the ground beside him. "Come. Sit by me. Tell me."

It felt good to sit beside him; she was already fatigued. This part of the morning was usually when she felt sick and nauseated. She wished she'd brought some fruit to nibble.

"Go ahead." He gave her an encouraging smile.

As she related all she had been contemplating about God's love, Adam listened thoughtfully. Each time she paused to gather her thoughts, he urged her to continue. Tilting his head as she spoke, he nodded throughout, his eyes gleaming as she unfolded her thoughts.

When she had completed, he sat quietly, momentarily lost in his thoughts.

"The Creator has shown you something important." He looked up at her. "I was begging Him for help, discouraged because we're going to continue to make mistakes. But, your thoughts help me glimpse more of God's love. It's larger than we understood before."

"Yes." She nodded.

"Think about what life was like in the Garden. Before we ate the fruit, all we knew was God's goodness."

"We didn't even know evil existed," she said. "We didn't know what it was."

"You're right. But then, we disobeyed God. What did we get from our fatal pursuit of the knowledge of good and evil—our flawed attempt to be like God?"

"Pain, wounds, anger, bitterness, frustration, fighting, hatred, sin, certain death."

He nodded as she recounted this litany of heartache. "Now we make mistakes every day, because we've become sinners. But you've added a new perspective. Our brokenness and His love in spite of it teach us about something we didn't know before: His mercy—His forgiving and restoring lovingkindness."

Desperate to extract every lesson from the tragedy, she leaned toward him. "Explain."

"God used our sin to give us even more knowledge of His goodness. The fact that He loves us in spite of our disobedience shows us His mercy more clearly. There's now a contrast. We can see how beautiful His love really is because we now know we don't deserve it."

Eve nodded. "His love was beautiful in the Garden, but we didn't know what a gift we had. We didn't know what it was like without Him. His love was simply a certainty of life."

"Yes. But now, His love is revealed to be even more beautiful, because we know how bleak life is when we're separated from Him."

"It was unbearable not to have His fellowship. I yearned for Him the entire time, but I was afraid to talk to Him. I didn't think He loved me anymore. But that was a lie, like the lie the serpent told me."

Adam bent to kiss her forehead. "Exactly the opposite was true. He wanted to show us the beauty of His mercy. Seeing this causes us to praise Him even more. He Himself is all we ever needed. We didn't need to seek knowledge from some tree. We had Him. And now, He's reassuring us of His love and making us more aware of it as we prepare for the child."

"In spite of all the mistakes we're sure to make, He'll help us and love us, just as He has loved us in spite of our mistakes in the past. He's merciful and good."

"Yes. You've given me hope, Eve. Thank you for telling me."

Oh no! My stomach...

Quickly, she leapt up, leaned around the tree, and vomited onto the ground. Adam stepped up behind her. Chuckling softly, he grasped her hair as usual. Gently, he stroked her back until she was done emptying her stomach.

When she could speak, she choked out, "I'm sorry. The timing." If she didn't feel so horrible, she would laugh with him, but she shook and felt weak and empty now.

"This is all outside our control," he said tenderly, picking her up. "It's appropriate that the evidence of the coming child would interrupt right then." He laughed softly.

Eve twined her arms around his neck and allowed him to carry her down to the river. He gave her a drink to wash out her mouth. Then he cupped cool water in his hands and soothed her dusty face. It felt restorative to be cared for at that moment, as if Adam personified God's love through his gentle service. He carried her to the shady trees and sat with her on his lap.

"Thank you, Adam. I love you so much."

"As I love you." He kissed her head. "Do you want to sit here while I return to work? Or do you need me to stay and finish our conversation?"

"Please stay with me." So, he did.

"How did you realize this truth about God's love?" he said.

"Since I realized our child was inside me, I've loved this new human passionately. In spite of the nausea and changes within my body, I'd do anything for him, even though my human love is broken. I know the Creator loves us more than that, because He already had His plan in place."

Adam nodded. Then they stared into each other's eyes, flabbergasted. God's ways were wondrous, impossible to comprehend. Who knew what He had planned for them?

* * * *

As the weeks went by, they talked of these things every day.

They hoped the serpent's head would be crushed soon. They couldn't comprehend God's love or why He would be merciful after they had disobeyed Him. They puzzled over what little they could discern about the child. They knew that, though they were flawed, God would help them. He would love them in spite of their mistakes, which would be plentiful.

If they had failed in the Garden, before their natures had changed, they would surely err now. But now, they knew God's plans covered their faults, blunders, and willful disobedience. He would teach them even more about Himself as they learned to rely on Him.

Confident of His help, they tried to imagine how their lives would be changed by the child's arrival. They didn't know how much time and care the newborn would require, but they knew that after him there would be more children. Therefore, they worked on several other things.

They needed a place to store food and seeds for planting. These crowded their sleeping space. With a child coming and then more children, they would need more room. Also, they needed to discern how Adam could turn the soil alone, without Eve guiding the plow.

Additionally, God seemed to be preparing Eve's breasts to nourish the newborn. They would determine this when the infant was born, but they didn't think he would eat as they did.

And finally, though her abdomen continued to grow larger, they knew the child would be small. It was certain he wouldn't spring forth from Eve's body the same size as they. The feeding and care of the newborn, while they had a few clues, would be determined when they saw him.

All of these realizations required preparation. They both began to implement their ideas: Adam began enlarging the shelter and trying different methods of turning the soil, while Eve observed her changing body for clues and planned more efficient ways to store their food.

Most of their experiences were mystifying. They were constantly learning.

* * * *

It had now been six months since Eve had bled. She didn't know whether they would ever understand why. The bleeding seemed to be related to the child, because it involved the same part of her body. She hadn't bled again, and now the offspring was coming. Whether she was wrong or right about the bleeding, they had started counting then.

They kept track of the months. A record would help them know what to expect for the next time. They had no idea how long she would carry the child in her body. They always referred to the coming child as a male. Though they weren't sure why, they felt he would be a man-child. They hoped their firstborn child would crush the serpent's head. They longed for it to happen soon.

This evening, Adam lay behind Eve in the darkness. They had reviewed Yahweh's words and now snuggled together, awaiting sleep. Her strength had returned, and she no longer fell asleep the instant her head touched the grass matting. They often had time to talk together as they settled down.

Hoping to feel the movement of the growing child, Adam lightly stroked her abdomen. Sometimes the infant moved around more when she lay down; other times he seemed to sleep, lying still within her. As Adam waited, he pressed his face into her hair and kissed her head, whispering endearments into her ear.

"Eve, you're so precious to me."

She nestled closer to him, turning to kiss his face. His beard tickled her cheek.

"I'm grateful the Creator made you for me," he whispered.

Whenever he said this, it caused her heart to swell with love. They had been restored to one another. Stroking his beard, Eve caressed his cheek.

"I love you so much."

"And I love you."

"Are you entirely comfortable?" he asked.

"Lying in your arms makes me happy."

The child jumped within her. Her husband became completely still, as if listening to the movement of the child through the palm of his hand. The infant kicked and bumped, twisting around as through seeking his own comfortable position.

Adam smiled. Eve heard and felt the movement of his face and beard as his lips pulled back from his teeth. She smiled with him. The fact that he delighted in the coming child caused her love for him to grow, her passion for both Adam and their child overwhelming her. Eventually, the child lay still; he had probably settled back to sleep.

Pulling her close to his body, Adam kissed Eve's head again.

"Thank you, Yahweh, our God, for giving us this child," he whispered. "Please use him to crush the serpent's head."

She agreed. It was such a blessing to have the barrier removed between them and their God, to again be aware of His nearness. Knowing He heard them, they often spoke to Yahweh together. As she silently considered Him, she became filled with gratitude.

"What does that feel like inside you?" Adam said.

"It's hard to explain. It feels somewhat like the rumbling that happens in your stomach after you eat a meal, but much more magnified. Feel with your hand. You can tell where his little head is and the little bottom."

Adam poked around her belly, moving his hand as she guided. She hoped he could discern the infant's shape. There was a larger bump at each end of what seemed to be the child's torso.

"Maybe it's easier for me because I also feel his movements inside me," she said.

Gently, he pressed his hand into the places where she directed. The infant kicked his hand. Adam chuckled softly.

"It's hard for me to imagine. He seems to be proportioned differently than we are. If this lump here is his head," Adam said, feeling the particularly large bump in her lower abdomen, "then his head will be much bigger than ours by comparison. Maybe he'll have to grow before he can walk and move about. How could he carry such a big head on such a little body?"

The way he said this made Eve laugh. She couldn't imagine what that would look like.

He laughed with her.

"He'll be beautiful in every way." She patted Adam's cheek. "Just like his handsome father, though his head may be bigger."

Adam's shoulders shook with laughter.

"I'm sure he'll be proportioned in ways we don't understand, but which are necessary. The Creator designed you perfectly, and He made you differently than me. You're certainly not shaped like I am—especially now." He laughed quietly and then added softly, "And, I'm very grateful for that."

Pulling her body up against his, he lightly caressed her full breasts and the roundness of her spherical abdomen, running his fingertips lightly over her skin as he kissed the back of her neck.

He whispered to her with longing. "Eve, I need you."

All the uncertainties of the coming birth caused her to long for Adam's physical nearness. It was a necessity. She felt vulnerable. She knew God would help them, but she was grateful for Adam's strength and love. This passionate unity seemed especially needed now.

Turning her face to kiss him, Eve answered his need.

CHAPTER TWENTY-NINE

AS THEY PREPARED for the coming child, Eve's insight about God's love enabled Adam to live with less fear. They would make mistakes, but, because God loved them, He would help. He would teach them about Himself, and they would learn more about His mercy. They requested His help to discern what to do, and they worked to get ready.

Neither had any idea when the infant would be born. How long did it take for a child to grow inside his mother? Everything seemed outside their control, superintended by the Creator to prepare them for the child's birth.

Ever since they had left the Garden, helpful changes had occurred. Some birds had found their way outside the Garden of Eden, and they often detected many varieties. Sometimes they awakened to the joyful sound of birds singing, as they had in the Garden.

They had still seen no animals that moved along the ground. However, they had seen fish in the river. These were creatures they hadn't seen in their two weeks in the Garden. It made them feel less alone on the earth. The presence of these creatures nearby gladdened their hearts.

They had observed some baby birds hatching from their eggs. Having first seen eggs in the Garden, they now knew what these were. When the small birds hatched, Eve had wondered if she would lay an egg that she would then sit upon. But Adam didn't think so. She had been formed in a different way—no wings or feathers.

The parental birds flew back and forth, feeding their small voracious offspring, which had seemed to be comprised entirely of wide-open mouths when they first hatched. The newly hatched birds had been unseeing and helpless, needing much care. Keeping the parental birds in constant motion, the tiny, naked birds had always been hungry.

And then, once they had grown feathers, the young birds had to be taught everything—how to fly and how to eat on their own outside the nest. They followed their parents everywhere, squawking to be fed, even though they were now the same size as the parental birds.

Like the baby birds, Adam and Eve now knew their child would probably be totally dependent upon them when he was born. He might be continually hungry and in need of constant care. Their lives would be much like those parental birds. Watching the birds provoked many serious conversations. They prepared more purposefully.

Everything would change.

Adam had learned that plowing was more effective when the edges of the rocks were honed. While chiseling the plow's edges into sharpness, he made an additional discovery. One day he struck a rock over and over, attempting to sharpen it. Nearby lay some fluffy grass seeds. A spark ignited them. Quickly, they burned up, turning into blackened ash.

Fascinated, he gaped at the seeds' incineration. Eve was nearby. They talked about it for many days, trying to discern a use for what he labeled *fire*. Its blaze had been somewhat similar to the flaming sword held by the cherubim, though much diminished in brilliance.

Fire might be helpful in the dark. Eve wondered whether they could use it to prepare foods in different ways, heating them and mixing various ones together. So they decided to see whether they could make another fire. Both were excited to experiment.

First, they searched for material that looked as if it would burn, and they gathered these. Then he tried again to create a spark, hoping and praying for a repetition of the flame.

It took a great while to start the fire. Finally, the dried grass ignited.

He threw his head back and laughed for joy. Eve grinned at him.

Once it was started, they fed bits and pieces into the fire. Learning what burned best, they added dried leaves, small twigs, and the fluffy seeds. Green vegetation merely smoked, nearly snuffing the fire. Days passed and they played with this every day. Eventually, they discovered how well wood burned when added in increasing thicknesses.

When they could keep a fire going, they tried heating vegetables on flat rocks placed right within the edge of the flames. They knew there was much more for them to learn about fire, and they constantly experimented with it.

After much effort, Adam felt pleased with the condition of their fields. Many different types of food now grew, all in various stages of ripeness. When they had eaten all the green plants, vegetables, grains, legumes, roots, and seeds from one area, he turned the soil again. Keeping their favorites, he put aside some of the seeds to replant.

Since it took him so long to clear the weeds from a new area and to turn in the good seeds the Creator had sown, the timing worked well. Just as they finished the food from one area, another area ripened. God took care of them. Eve's cheeks were full and rosy. They had enough. When they had first left Eden, he had panicked. Now he felt grateful to Yahweh for His provision.

Because the fruit trees lay scattered far along the river, they walked quite a distance to retrieve their favorite fruits. Eve had discovered she could dry the fruit in the sun. They stored it in baskets in their shelter. These baskets crowded their sleeping area.

To clear space, Adam used a flat, sharp rock to dig into the hill beside the pine tree. This made a cool storage area for dried fruits, legumes, roots, grains, and seeds. He continued enlarging and deepening the cave. Nearby, close to the river, they planted seeds from their favorite fruit trees, anticipating future growth and yield. He called this their *orchard*.

To prepare for the coming child and the others who would follow, Adam began a more solid shelter of stones. He built beside the small storage cave. After his initial trials, he now used mud from the river between the stones, giving each layer time to dry before adding the next. This would take him a while to finish. He could only work on it when he wasn't in the field.

All of these things made him feel that they were better equipped for the unknown events that would accompany the birth. He believed they had anticipated some of the possibilities and had prepared for ways their lives might change.

Yahweh would help them discern the rest when the time came.

* * * *

Eight months had passed since Eve's bleeding. It surprised Adam how long this was taking. The birds' eggs had hatched quickly, in a matter of weeks. But they had no idea how long they would have to wait for their child. Every day, it seemed Eve's belly grew larger.

It was a miracle! A new life grew within her!

As the Creator had made him from the dust and Eve from his side, He now formed another living being inside her body. They didn't know what to expect. They simply knew that the child would come when God had ordained, and that Eve would experience hard work and pain. This was the first child ever born, so they could only surmise.

Each night they sat together discussing it. Adam enjoyed sitting against a tree with Eve between his legs, leaning back upon him. As she reclined against his chest, he wrapped his arms about her expanding waist. Under his hands, he felt the child move. The infant felt vigorous and strong. As he grew, they bound the ram's skin more loosely about Eve's abdomen. Under the garment, her belly felt round and full, smooth and fertile.

Now she walked differently, as if her bones had loosened and disjointed within her hips. She had a more difficult time getting up and down. The burden of the child pressed against her ribs, creating discomfort whenever she drew a deep breath.

Adam now insisted that she spend the hottest part of each day sitting or lying in the shade. There she wove the grass cords and the basket she created to hold the child. When the sun blazed at its hottest, she grew weary.

* * * *

As the sun moved toward the horizon, Adam glimpsed Eve sitting by the river. In the fields above their shelter, he worked with the plow freeing more earth from the constant incursion of the thorns and thistles. They had made some improvements to the plow. Though it was heavier, he could handle it because he had grown in strength.

Adam stopped working to watch Eve. She was weaving the infant's basket.

After seeing the size of the baby birds compared to the parents, they both thought they would need to carry their child about with them. When they felt Eve's belly, the proportions of the child seemed small. They didn't know how big the infant would be.

Adam watched as Eve encompassed her round belly with her hands and then transferred that measurement to her weaving. The basket had to be long enough, with room for the infant to grow. It had to shade the child from the hot sun and be easy to carry. Eve intended to line the inside with the downy seeds.

Pausing in her work, she straightened, stretching her back. Glancing up, she spied him gazing down at her. She waved, and he returned her wave. He missed talking to her throughout this part of the day, but she needed to rest. It was difficult for her to keep cool in the heat now, as if the child added warmth to her body.

Eve struggled to rise to her feet, supporting the small of her back with both hands. When upright, she stretched, as if her back pained her. Then she waddled toward their shelter. He smiled. Her gait now reminded him of the ducks he had named on the first day. Love for her overwhelmed him as he watched her carrying their child within her body—his seed and hers woven together by God.

From the shelter, Eve removed a basket. She returned to the fire-pit and added wood, making the flames leap higher. Then she positioned food on the rocks beside the fire. Before long the smell of the fire and the cooking food wafted up the hill. Adam's stomach twisted with hunger. He dropped the plow and ran down from the field.

Laughing as he dashed past Eve, he stripped off his ram's skin and leapt into the Tigris. It was exhilarating—so good to cool down! Quickly, he washed off the dirt and salty substance left by his sweat. Climbing back out, he flopped down onto the grass to dry.

Back by the fire, Eve laughed softly, clearly amused by his antics.

Adam felt happy. When they had left the Garden, he had thought they'd never be happy again. Their God was so kind to them! Even though they had disobeyed Him and continued to sin, Yahweh had given them joy. He was merciful.

When dry, Adam rewrapped the ram's skin and climbed the hill to be near Eve. She had gathered some of his favorite fresh herbs and green plants to serve with the dried fruit. The onions and legumes smelled delicious cooking together. The hot food had been pushed away from the fire so it could cool.

Bending in over Eve's large belly, Adam twined his arms around her, kissing her cheek. She clasped his neck, drawing his face down so she could kiss his mouth.

"I miss you when you're up there on the hill and I'm down here by myself," she said.

"I know." He pressed his forehead to hers. "I miss you, too. Do you see how often I stop working simply to look at you? Seeing you down here, large with our child, makes me happy."

He smiled at her, and she smiled back.

"The food's done," she said. "Sit, and let's eat."

The food was as delicious as it smelled. Adam had a voracious appetite, but she had prepared exactly the right amount. When they finished, the fire had died down. He picked up the flat, thin rock on which she had cooked and carried it down to the river.

On the riverbank, he scrubbed it with sand, and the water washed the remains away. Then he brought it back, used it to bank the fire, and placed it by the glowing embers at the fire's edge.

One by one, the stars appeared. The moon shone down upon them. The fire shrank to small glowing coals. Adam encased Eve in his arms, cradling both her and the child within. She lay back against him, resting her head on his shoulder and snuggling against his neck.

"Adam," she said quietly, "I'm afraid to give birth."

"Why? God has made your body to do this."

"Look how large the child grows. It will be difficult to get him out. I'm afraid of the pain."

Yes, that was something to fear. Adam's heart seized within him, and he clutched her more tightly as he stared into the dying embers. Neither of them knew what birthing entailed. They only knew that, compared to what her pain would have been in the Garden, it would now be many times more difficult.

If everything else they had experienced was any measure, it would be very painful. When Adam imagined seeing her suffer, his chest ached. How could he possibly help?

She looked up at him, awaiting his response.

"Just thinking of you in pain, and how I'll feel as I watch, fills me with fear."

"Me, too. I'm frightened."

"But, Eve, I know the Creator will help us. He wants this child to be born. He promised one of our children will crush the serpent's head."

"Yes, He'll help me endure it," she said quietly. "But, it will still hurt."

"I'm afraid it will." Placing his cheek against hers, he pulled her even closer. "I'm sorry."

Eve simply sighed. Nothing more needed be said. Heavily, she leaned against him, and he knew she was weary. When she yawned widely, his suspicions were confirmed.

"Let's go to sleep," he said. "You can barely stay awake."

She nodded drowsily. Even though she was heavy with child, Adam could still easily lift her. Rising, he scooped her into his arms and carried her to the shelter. Wrapping her arms about his neck, she nestled her face against him.

To thicken their mat of bedding, he had layered copious amounts of grass, attempting to ease her body, so she would be more comfortable. Gently, he lowered her onto this abundant bedding and settled down behind her. She was asleep before his head touched the mat.

He whispered, "It's good not to be alone," into her sleeping ear and then lay in the darkness, holding her and considering the unknown future.

How would he know how to help her?

How would they know what to do?

Would her pain be unbearable?

What would it be like to have a child?

With a stab Adam realized he would no longer have Eve all to himself. He would have to share her with someone else—his child. But still, her attention would be divided. He felt ashamed for feeling his own child was a rival, but he was afraid of how their lives would change.

Eve and he only had each other. They had no other dividing affection. He would miss the intimacy of being the only two people. Would the little interloper feel like one of them, or would he feel like someone they didn't know? Another human on the earth would seem strange. So many unknowns—Adam felt uneasy and out of control.

Since leaving the Garden, he had come to feel a rhythm and sense of predictability.

For one thing, he had learned much about his relationship with the Creator. When he remembered God's words and trusted His promise, God felt near. But when he forgot God's words, resisted the inner urging of God's voice, or squelched his conscience—the sense of right and wrong within him—God felt far away.

Yahweh never left him. That had become increasingly apparent.

But Adam's sinfulness hardened his heart and caused God to feel distant. He still couldn't adapt to this alien sensation. But he was learning to heed God's quiet urging within his heart, to meditate on His words, and to remember His promise. He loved God and cherished His nearness. Adam despaired over the loneliness and isolation he felt whenever he pulled away from Him.

In addition to God's quiet exhorting, he also had the relationship lessons learned in the Garden. These guided his behavior toward Eve, so he could continue growing to know her. Listening, learning, and loving were so difficult now. If they hadn't had the experience in the Garden, they wouldn't know how to treat each other. They would more often go astray.

What would their poor children do without this guide?

They wouldn't have this reference for their behavior. Adam was saddened as he considered this. What would the world be like with more sinners in it? As difficult as it was for two sinners to get along, the thought of more was worrisome.

At least there was comfort that their life outside the Garden grew more predictable. They repeated the same work. They knew each other's moods. They knew how to plant the food, harvest it, and store it. They were learning new methods for plowing, for attacking the weeds, and for making their lives more bearable. They knew each other's bodies, though Eve's now changed every day. It was often a mystery to him—a portent of things to come.

Adam twisted onto his back and stared at the stars. As his warmth moved away from Eve, she shifted. He placed a reassuring hand on her back, and she relaxed again. Adam looked back up at the stars. They revolved back toward where they had been in the Garden. There was an order to the Creator's world that he could barely comprehend.

While the moon and the stars varied in the night sky, each morning Yahweh never failed to beckon the sun over the horizon. Every day, the blazing sun rose and journeyed across the bowl of cerulean sky. It never varied. God ordered their world. Surely He had control over the birthing of the coming child. Silently, Adam cried out.

Creator God, Yahweh, help me! I'm afraid of this change. I don't know what I can do for Eve. Please, help her to endure the pain. Help me to be strong for her. Give me wisdom.

As he gazed at the stars, God's peace gradually filled him. God would surely help them with the birth of this child—which He had planned—and with the adjustments afterward. Their God was entirely in control of all these events. When he was afraid, he would ask Yahweh what to do, and God would help him.

Adam rolled back against Eve. In her sleep, she snuggled in, curving to fit his body. Embracing her rounded abdomen that held the precious gift, he curled about her. Then he buried his face in her hair, breathing in her fragrance and relaxing.

Adam slept.

CHAPTER THIRTY

TEN FULL CYCLES of the moon had passed since Eve had bled. Her abdomen bulged enormously. She could barely walk. Her bones all seemed loose. She voided many times during the day and night. She couldn't breathe when she lay down.

Surely, Adam thought, *it is time for the birth of our child.*

Over the past few days, her lower back had pained her off and on, knotting and cramping by the end of each day. Her abdomen tightened and relaxed at regular intervals, rising up within her where the child grew. She assumed this would bring the birth, so she tried to cooperate with her body's efforts. Concerned, he watched her suffer.

As they lay down to sleep, Adam felt dismayed. *Surely not another day of this.*

How can she endure it?

Her face was drawn, and dark circles purpled the skin beneath her eyes. She barely slept, having to creep out of the shelter many times to relieve herself. She tried not to awaken him, but she did. Each time, he drew her into his arms, kissed her head, and then lay worrying about her as she settled back to sleep. Moaning and shifting even in her slumber, she seemed unable to find any position of comfort.

The full moon shone brightly halfway through its journey across the night sky and the sun was far from rising when Adam felt Eve jolt awake, tensing her entire body. She held her breath and gritted her teeth, seeming to have been startled. Soon, she relaxed and breathed again.

"What's wrong, my love?" Adam murmured sleepily.

"I dreamt of a terrible pain where the child will emerge. I awakened to find it wasn't a dream. It scares me. I don't know whether it will happen again."

Murmuring sympathetically, he kissed her head, embracing her more tightly. Since she drifted off, so did he, only to be awakened by another jolt. Apparently, another of these pains had seized her. Adam wondered if their child would be born this night.

As she tensed and held her breath again, he gently stroked her abdomen, considering how he could help. Then he remembered: *When Eve was made from my side and when I am hurt in the field, if I hold my breath the pain worsens.*

Adam whispered. "Eve, try not to fight it. Tensing and holding your breath makes it hurt more. You have to let the child come out." He cradled her in his arms, pulling her securely against his chest. "I'll support your back. Breathe with me and relax your body. You would have thought of this if the pain hadn't startled you awake."

He trusted her instincts. God had created her to bear children. As the next pain occurred, she lay with her body heavy against his, relaxed and breathing slowly.

"That was much better," she said when it ended.

"Don't be afraid. The Creator made your body to do this. I'll hold you all night, if you want." He kissed her head, and she nestled in more closely.

"Yes, do." She nuzzled his cheek.

Through the rest of the night, they lay cradled together.

Between each pain, if they didn't drop off to sleep, Adam whispered to her, affirming his love, praising her strength, and reminding her to trust God. Softly, she thanked him, responding to his reassurances. Often she drifted off to sleep.

Because he embraced her, Adam could easily detect if she

resisted the work within her body. Throughout the night, she rarely tensed. But when she did, he breathed slowly and deeply with her, helping her surrender to the labor within.

As the moon moved through the darkened sky, one pain followed another more closely. More frequently, she needed his support.

"Feeling your chest rise and fall helps me."

Another pain cut off her comments. Her body performed the work the Creator had designed for birthing the child. When the pain ended, he asked if she wanted to change position. The sun now peeked over the horizon. It was obvious that today's work was the birth of their child.

"Let's sit up," she said. "Can you sit behind me? I'll lean against you."

Adam nodded and helped her up. Now that it was daylight, he assessed her state.

She appeared weary, though they had spent much of the night sleeping between the pains. Her eyes looked as if her focus had shifted internally, her face as if she were intent on the sensations within her body. A thought occurred to him.

"While we're moving, I'll run for water, and I'll grab some fruit. I'll return quickly."

Without wasting time dressing, Adam scooped up the water basket, ducked under the branches, and raced naked down the hill, pausing to void on the way. Then, hurriedly, he filled the basket. Behind him in the shelter, he heard Eve's moans growing louder.

"*Adammmmmmmmmmmm! Husbannnnnddddd!*"

Obviously, he was more essential to the process than he had thought.

He tore back up the hill and stooped to enter. Moaning in pain, Eve crouched on her hands and knees, a panicky expression on her face.

"Dearest love," he crooned, kneeling before her. "Look into my face. I'm back."

With glazed eyes, she focused inwardly. He didn't know if she even perceived him. It was difficult to watch her suffer.

When the pain ended, she slumped forward against his shoulder.

"Oh, Adam." She exhaled his name like a sigh, sounding exhausted.

"Eve, you haven't voided. Let's get you outside. It may help with the pain."

Without speaking, she allowed him to lift and guide her outside, where he helped her to squat to relieve herself. As she attempted to rise, another pain gripped her.

"*Husbannndddd!*" she moaned.

Crouching down before her, he supported her body. When that pain ended, he scooped her up and carried her in. Positioning her on his lap, Adam sat against the tree trunk. She leaned back against him, and he enveloped her in his arms.

Whispering that he loved her, he smoothed her hair back and gently caressed her head. Her lips were dry and cracked; he was glad he'd gone for water. Lifting the water basket to her lips, he offered a drink. She sipped.

Now that they had stopped moving around, she seemed less frightened. She relaxed completely against his body. But the change of position had apparently sped up the process. The pains now came one on top of another, each causing her abdomen to rise up, hard and straining.

During each, she laced her fingers through his and pressed back hard against his chest, moaning as she rolled her head from side to side. Her breathing seemed to catch, and her body shook at each peak of discomfort. When each pain ended, she collapsed against him, falling immediately to sleep, only to awaken with the next pain.

This pattern repeated. Totally engrossed in her labor now, she didn't converse. As she sagged against him yet again, he relaxed, leaning against the tree trunk. Through the branches he saw that the sun was now halfway up the morning sky.

Twisting her head, she looked at him, whispering through parched lips, "If only I hadn't eaten the fruit. I'm so sorry I tempted you. Please forgive me." Then her eyes lost focus, and she moaned, "*Help meeeeeeeeeee!*"

He was stricken. Why did she feel she had to apologize at this moment? He was the one responsible for the extreme pain she now experienced. His mind flashed back to his moment of decision, recalling her confused face as she had offered him the bitten fruit. He hadn't comprehended the pain and hardship that would follow his bite.

Adam pressed his cheek against hers. Against her soft skin, he whispered, "I grieve that I didn't pull you away. I didn't protect you. This is my fault." His voice cracked. He swallowed hard. He must encourage her. "Be strong. Ask Yahweh to help you. I love you so much."

When the pain ended, he raised the water basket to her dry lips, and she sipped. With gratitude in her eyes, she fixed them upon him, and then instantly fell asleep.

Emotionally drained, Adam collapsed against the tree trunk. *Yahweh! My God! Help her!*

With the next pain, her abdomen rose up more prominently. Grabbing behind her knees, Eve leaned forward and bore down, letting out a guttural cry.

"Ahhhhhhhhhhhhhhhhhh!"

Bearing down and crying out several more times, she groaned loudly with the effort. When the pain ended, she lay back. The bulge in her abdomen had moved lower.

"Something's changed." Her voice was hoarse. "I have new strength. I need to push against the pain. I think the child will be born soon."

"At last!" Relief washed over him.

Adam swept her hair off her sweaty, flushed face. Then he dipped his fingers into the water basket to cool her forehead.

"You're strong, Eve. You can do this! God will help you."

Hoping his words had encouraged her, he kissed her cheek. She dozed again.

During the next pain, she bore down, uttering loud exclamations, sometimes yelling, and then leaning back upon him when it ended. She repeated this with each new pain. Outside, the sun climbed to its zenith. Inside, his wife worked hard to birth their child.

Between each struggle, Adam praised her efforts, telling her how much he loved her, smoothing her hair back from her hot face, and offering her drinks.

He leaned around her abdomen, trying to detect any sign of the infant—nothing yet that he could see from behind her. Then, screaming with her effort, she bore down with the most strength she had yet used. Fluid burst forth from her, and the top of the child's head appeared.

It was covered with thick, black, wet hair.

Another period of rest was followed by more effort, and the entire head of the child slid into view. The head turned toward Eve's leg, revealing the tiny face, scrunched and grimacing. Then the entire small body slid out of Eve onto the now-soaked grass of their bedding.

They both gasped and leaned forward to gaze upon him.

So little! A small man-child—a baby—lay gasping and sputtering from the fluid that had come out with him. Such tiny hands and feet! His fingers spread wide, stretching outward, slender and delicate with miniscule nails. Delighted, Adam studied all of the infant's intricacy. He turned toward Eve, and she met his eyes. Together, they laughed for joy. The baby was exactly like them—with a proportionally larger head as he had anticipated, but oh, so small.

Eve scooped him onto her abdomen. The newborn's tiny head bobbed up and down against her skin, his little mouth searching for something he couldn't find. Persistent and frenzied, he pursued each part of her flesh that touched his open mouth. She wiped the fluid and blood from his little face; then she guided his small searching mouth to her breast.

His mouth latched hold, as if he had found what he needed.

How did she know to do that? She knew exactly what to do.

A river of love washed through Adam. He marveled at his beautiful and strong wife, now the mother of his child. He had named her well: *Eve*, the mother of all the living. He was staggered by respect and admiration.

As the infant suckled at her breast, he studied their adoring faces with serious dark eyes. Together they bent low, examining him just as closely. Their bodies moved as one to bring their faces near to his. They gazed into his infant eyes, all of them becoming silently acquainted.

This was no little intruder as Adam had feared, but one of them—part of Eve and part of him. As he stared into the infant's eyes, he was overcome with love. This powerful flood of love transformed him into a new kind of man—a father. This was his son. He longed to protect him from the hard world. He would fight to protect him from all harm.

Watching the little mouth tugging at Eve's breast and observing her absorption with their baby, Adam brimmed with joy and satisfaction. As if sensing his joy, she gazed into his eyes. Her eyes glowed with the same love that Adam felt for the two of them.

"Yahweh has given us our little man," she whispered, tears of joy on her cheeks. "Our God *will* redeem. He's the one who was, who is, and who will always be. He's the giver of life, and I'm truly grateful." Through her tears, she gazed back down at their son.

"As am I! Thank you, God! And, Eve," Adam spoke gently. She raised her wet eyes to his. "I love you. Thank you for bearing our son. His name is *Cain*. Your name means life. You're the mother of all the living. His name means he was brought forth from you. He is ours."

Bending down, he gently pressed his lips to their new son's head. "Perhaps you will crush the serpent's head, my little son."

Encasing his family in his arms, Adam's gratitude overflowed.

"Yahweh, our God, bring redemption. And, if not Cain, if You use another of our offspring, even far in the future, we know You will bring it to pass as You promised. Thank You that You always keep Your promises. Please crush the serpent's head soon. Bring Your justice. Bring an end to the reign of sin and death. Heal us, and heal Your earth."

Adam knew their God would make it so.

The Beginning

AUTHOR NOTE:

THE OLD TESTAMENT was written mostly in Hebrew. Because it was inspired by the Holy Spirit, Genesis contains the factual and infallible account of what happened in the early history of mankind. But because these events are humanity's common history, accounts of creation, of the Biblical worldwide flood, and of the events immediately afterward were recorded in all the histories of ancient peoples all over the earth. Of course, these legendary, non-Biblical accounts vary widely in their accuracy. And, because they are not Scripture, all contain varying degrees of mythology in the details. The names of the first people also vary according to the languages in which each of these ancient accounts was recorded.

Therefore, it was difficult for me to decide which names to use for my characters, since pre-Flood people were ancient Sumerians, not Hebrews. Adam and Eve were not Jews. Adam and Eve are the ancestors of *all* people—Gentiles *and* Jews. The Jewish people are descended from Abraham, who came out of the Sumerian city of Ur. Abraham, the father of the Jewish people, was but one descendant of Adam and Eve's son Seth—though one very significant descendant.

Through Abraham's lineage came Jesus Christ—God born as a man, God the Son, the one who crushed the serpent's head. With His sacrifice on the cross, He destroyed the power of sin and death. In order to more clearly portray God's eternal plan for Christ to lay down His life in order to bring all believers—Jews *and* Gentiles—back into God's family as they were in Eden *(Ephesians 1-3; Titus 1:1-3; Col. 1:15-20; Heb. 1:1-4; John 1:1-*

18; 1 Peter 1:19-21), I considered using the pre-Akkadian names from the genealogy of the oldest secular record, the Sumerian king list. I wanted to show the Gentile status of the people who lived during this portion of history *(Genesis 1-11),* before one branch of the family tree became the Jewish people and before the law was given.

But, for the sake of clarity and accuracy, I decided to stick with the familiar and certain Biblical names. The names of the first man and the first woman are significant and their meanings are captured very beautifully and precisely for us by Moses in the Hebrew language. So, while mostly using the Hebrew names for our first ancestors in my fictional retelling of these foundational events, I have chosen to use the name *Eve,* rather than *Havah,* as the name Adam gave his wife after the Fall. *Eve* or *Eva* is the English translation of *Heua* or *Eua,* which is the Greek transliteration of the Hebrew proper name *Havah* recorded in *Genesis 3:20. Eve,* a Gentile name, was used intentionally. I also intentionally use the English (Gentile) *Cain,* not the Hebrew *Qayin,* or the Greek (also Gentile) *Kain,* in the last chapter.

Quite possibly, Cain was Alulim, the first of a line of eight (or ten, depending on the source) kings from the Sumerian king list who ruled in a walled city in the days before "the Flood swept over" the land, as recorded in that history and in *Genesis 4:17-18.*

But that's the subject of the sequel, *Refuge.*

Refuge is available at:
Amazon: http://amzn.to/1kRTU3p
Barnes & Noble: http://bit.ly/1ijIQEH
Apple iBook: http://apple.co/1Gx9VWl
ChristianBook.com: http://bit.ly/1kRVuCw

FALLEN STUDY GUIDE

This novel presents many foundational truths regarding salvation and redemption. To begin, let's examine some of the passages listed in the Author Notes on the preceding pages.

God's foreknowledge and planning for our salvation before He even began creation are detailed in Ephesians 1:3-11. We also see God's plan for the future, to bring all things again under the authority of Christ as they were in Eden.

Draw a box around what happened before creation. Underline the parts of this passage that show God's advance planning for our salvation. Circle the parts that detail His plans for the future. Some of these will overlap. Afterward, write down your thoughts.

Ephesians 1:3-11 (NLT): "All praise to God, the Father of our Lord Jesus Christ, who has blessed us with every spiritual blessing in the heavenly realms because we are united with Christ. Even before he made the world, God loved us and chose us in Christ to be holy and without fault in his eyes. God decided in advance to adopt us into his own family by bringing us to himself through Jesus Christ. This is what he wanted to do, and it gave him great pleasure. So we praise God for the glorious grace he has poured out on us who belong to his dear Son. He is so rich in kindness and grace that he purchased our freedom with the blood of his Son and forgave our sins. He has showered his kindness on us, along with all wisdom and understanding. God has now revealed to us his mysterious plan regarding Christ, a plan to fulfill his own good pleasure. And this is the plan: At the right time he will bring everything together under the authority of Christ—everything in heaven and on earth. Furthermore, because we are united with Christ, we have received an inheritance from God, for he chose us in advance, and he makes everything work out according to his plan."

The work of Jesus Christ as Creator, Sustainer, and Savior are detailed in these passages. Have you considered before the active role Christ played from before time as well in the present?

In each following passage answer the question or complete the instructions:

- What was Christ's role in creation? What did He do?
- Underline portions that show Christ's nature as fully God.
- Circle the parts that show Jesus Christ's current role. What does He do now?

Hebrews 1:1-4 (NIV): "In the past God spoke to our ancestors through the prophets at many times and in various ways, but in these last days he has spoken to us by his Son, whom he appointed heir of all things, and through whom also he made the universe. The Son is the radiance of God's glory and the exact representation of his being, sustaining all things by his powerful word. After he had provided purification for sins, he sat down at the right hand of the Majesty in heaven. So he became as much superior to the angels as the name he He has inherited is superior to theirs."

John 1:1-5, 9-14, 15-18 (NIV): "In the beginning was the Word, and the Word was with God, and the Word was God. He was with God in the beginning. Through him all things were made; without him nothing was made that has been made. In him was life, and that life was the light of all mankind. The light shines in the darkness, and the darkness has not overcome it. The true light that gives light to everyone was coming into the world. He was in the world, and though the world was made through him, the world did not recognize him. He came to that which was his own, but his own did not receive him. Yet to all who did receive him, to those who believed in his name, he gave the right to become children of God—children born not of natural descent, nor of human decision or a husband's will, but born of God. The Word became flesh and made his dwelling among us. We have seen his glory, the glory of the one and only Son, who came from the Father, full of grace and truth. Out of his fullness we have all received grace in place of grace already given. For the law was given through Moses; grace and truth came through Jesus Christ. No one has ever seen God, but the one and only Son, who is himself God and is in closest relationship with the Father, has made him known."

Colossians 1:15-20 (NIV): "The Son is the image of the invisible God, the firstborn over all creation. For in him all things were created: things in heaven and on earth, visible and invisible, whether thrones or powers or rulers or authorities; all things have been created through him and for him. He is before all things, and in him all things hold together. And he is the head of the body, the church; he is the beginning and the firstborn from among the dead, so that in everything he might have the supremacy. For God was pleased to have all his fullness dwell in him, and through him to reconcile to himself all things, whether things on earth or things in heaven, by making peace through his blood, shed on the cross."

Who was to blame for what happened in Eden?

- In the story, we see Satan's role as tempter and destroyer, and we see Adam and Eve's actions. Throughout history, women have often been blamed for the fall of humankind. Yet, Biblically, what does God say in this passage?
- Underline what Adam did. For what is he held responsible?
- Circle what Jesus Christ did—notice His role of redemption as fully God and fully man.
- Draw a box around the word "God." What all does God do *through* Christ?

Romans 5:6-19 (NLT): "When we were utterly helpless, Christ came at just the right time and died for us sinners. Now, most people would not be willing to die for an upright person, though someone might perhaps be willing to die for a person who is especially good. But God showed his great love for us by sending Christ to die for us while we were still sinners. And since we have been made right in God's sight by the blood of Christ, he will certainly save us from God's condemnation. For since our friendship with God was restored by the death of his Son while we were still his enemies, we will certainly be saved through the life of his Son. So now we can rejoice in our wonderful new relationship with God because our Lord Jesus Christ has made us friends of God. When Adam sinned, sin entered the world. Adam's sin brought death, so death spread to everyone, for everyone sinned. Yes, people sinned even before the law was given. But it was not counted as sin because there was not yet any law to break. Still, everyone died—from the time of Adam to the time of Moses—even those who did not disobey an explicit commandment of God, as Adam did. Now Adam is a symbol, a representation of Christ, who was yet to come. But there is a great difference between Adam's sin and God's gracious gift. For the sin of this one man, Adam, brought death to many. But even greater is God's wonderful grace and his gift of forgiveness to many through this other man, Jesus Christ. And the result of God's gracious gift is very different from the result of that one man's sin. For Adam's sin led to condemnation, but God's free gift leads to our being made right with God, even though we are guilty of many sins. For the sin of this one man, Adam, caused death to rule over many. But even greater is God's wonderful grace and his gift of righteousness, for all who receive it will live in triumph over sin and death through this one man, Jesus Christ. Yes, Adam's one sin brings condemnation for everyone, but Christ's one act of righteousness brings a right relationship with God and new life for everyone. Because one person disobeyed God, many became sinners. But because one other person obeyed God, many will be made righteous."

In this story we saw Adam and Eve turn toward God to become reconciled to Him again. Their faith was in God and in

His promise to send One who would crush Satan's head. The way to God has not changed. We believe that God fulfilled His promise when he sent Jesus Christ to atone for our sins and to defeat sin, death, and Satan.

What are the common threads in these passages? How are we made right with God?

1 John 4:14-15 (NLT): "Furthermore, we have seen with our own eyes and now testify that the Father sent his Son to be the Savior of the world. All who declare that Jesus is the Son of God have God living in them, and they live in God."

John 3:16-18 (NLT): "For this is how God loved the world: He gave his one and only Son, so that everyone who believes in him will not perish but have eternal life. God sent his Son into the world not to judge the world, but to save the world through him. There is no judgment against anyone who believes in him. But anyone who does not believe in him has already been judged for not believing in God's one and only Son."

1 John 5:1a, 4-5 (NLT): "Everyone who believes that Jesus is the Christ (this means: Messiah, Anointed One) has become a child of God. For every child of God defeats this evil world, and we achieve this victory through our faith. And who can win this battle against the world? Only those who believe that Jesus is the Son of God."

Romans 4:1b-5 (NLT): "What did Abraham discover about being made right with God? If his good deeds had made him acceptable to God, he would have had something to boast about. But that was not God's way. For the Scriptures tell us, 'Abraham believed God, and God counted him as righteous because of his faith' (quoting Genesis 15:6). When people work, their wages are not a gift, but something they have earned. But people are counted as righteous, not because of their work, but because of their faith in God who forgives sinners."

Job 19:25-27 (NLT): "But as for me, I know that my Redeemer lives, and he will stand upon the earth at last. And after my body has decayed, yet in my body I will see God! I will see him for myself. Yes, I will see him with my own eyes. I am overwhelmed at the thought!"

1 Corinthians 15:20-26 (NLT): "Christ has been raised from the dead. He is the first of a great harvest of all who have died. So you see, just as death came into the world through a man, now the resurrection from the dead has begun through another man. Just as everyone dies because we all belong to Adam, everyone who belongs to Christ will be given new life. But there is an order to this resurrection: Christ was raised as the first of the harvest; then all who belong to Christ will be raised when he comes back. After that the end will come, when he will turn the Kingdom over to God the Father, having destroyed every ruler and authority and power. For Christ must reign until he humbles all his enemies beneath his feet. And the last enemy to be destroyed is death."

More on Marriage and on Lucifer/Satan is contained in the Study Guide of *Refuge*, the sequel to this novel. For more information see: http://melindainman.com/about-refuge/ or purchase *Refuge* at one of the links previously given.

Fallen is a fictional account based on these Scriptures:

- Genesis 1:1 – 4:1; 4:26b-5:2
- Zephaniah 3:17; Isaiah 62:3-5; Jeremiah 32:41; John 17:1-5
- Job 1 and 2; 40:15 – 41:34
- Proverbs 8:23-31
- Ecclesiastes 3:11
- Isaiah 14:12-15; 40:28-31
- Ezekiel 28:12-19
- Matthew 25:31-46
- Mark 10:6-9
- Luke 3:37;10:18-20
- John 1:1-18; 10:14-18, 25-30; 12:27-32; 14:6,7, 29-31; 15:16; 17:1-26
- Romans 5 and 8
- 1 Corinthians 6:12-16
- Ephesians 1:3 – 3:21; 5:22-33
- Colossians 1:15-23
- Titus 1:1-3
- Heb. 4:12-14
- 1 Peter 1:10-12, 20; 3:1-9

These sources were also consulted:

Angels: Elect & Evil, by C. Fred Dickason, Moody Press, Chicago, IL, 1975, 1995.

Biblical Demonology, by Merrill F. Unger, Kregel Publications, Grand Rapids, MI, 1994.

The Expositor's Bible Commentary: Twelve-Volume Interactive CD-ROM, Frank E. Gaebelein, Editor, Zondervan, Grand Rapids, MI, 2006.

Genesis: A Commentary, by Bruce K. Waltke with Cathi J. Fredricks, Zondervan, Grand Rapids, MI, 2001.

The History of the Ancient World, by Susan Wise Bauer, W. W. Norton & Company, Inc., New York, NY, 2007. Pertinent ancient sources mentioned were consulted.

Jesus Feminist, by Sarah Bessey, Howard Books, New York, NY, 2013.

The New International Commentary on the Old Testament (NICOT), The Book of Genesis, Chapters 1 – 17, Victor P. Hamilton, Editor, William B. Eerdmans Publishing Company, Grand Rapids, MI, 1990.

Recovering Biblical Manhood & Womanhood, A Response to Evangelical Feminism, John Piper and Wayne Grudem, Editors, Crossway Books, Wheaton, IL, 1991.

The Serpent of Paradise, by Erwin W. Lutzer, Moody Publishers, Chicago, IL, 1996.

ACKNOWLEDGMENTS

Special thanks to Joe Coccaro, my editor on both *Fallen* and *Refuge*. Joe's keen eye and ability to move a story along with perfect pacing enable me to present my novels exactly as I imagined them. I'm grateful for his editorial skills, and I hope to work with him on every novel I write.

Special thanks to John Koehler, my publisher on my first novel and my provider of editorial, publishing, and design services for this second novel. Savvy, innovative, prompt, and full of wit—it's been a blessing to work with him on both projects. I hope to continue our partnership.

Special thanks to these generous donors who also backed *Fallen* through my Kickstarter campaign. Without their encouragement and support, we wouldn't be where we are today:

Colby Brown
Katrina Worrell
Rita Rackmil
Teresa Manial Bratton
Lynda Rice
Lindsey Grace Hayes
Patti Chesney
Cindy Belville
Dawn Kinzer
Leann Strain Woleslagel
Kim Fisch
Liz Pothen
Mary Miller
Susan Sell
Maja Knighton
Paula Smith
Deb Wages
Chris Jackson
Melanie Johnson
Renee Garofoli Lauth
Amy Ekblad

Debi Schuhow
Kristi Hanby
Laura Drumb
Jacqueline Garrett
Abraham Varghese
Terri Hetfield
Patricia Durgin
Ellen Evans
Allison Plom
Karina Herring
David Brown
Barbara Best
Sara Hyde
Brenda Morningstar
Heath & Seth Robinson
Robin Hakanson-Grunder
Kevin & Natalie Daughtry
Kelli Flanagan
Valerie Taccolini
Les & Rita Jackson

CPSIA information can be obtained
at www.ICGtesting.com
Printed in the USA
LVHW08s2358060818
586216LV00002B/192/P